Jayes Jamestown 1627

The Jamestown Series

Kelli Rea Klampe

Copyright © 2015 by Cavaliers Publishing

All rights reserved. The events, characters, and entities depicted in this book are fictional. Any resemblance or similarity to any actual events, entities, or persons, whether living or dead, is entirely coincidental. No part of this publication may be reproduced, distributed, or transmitted in any form or by any means, including photocopying, recording, or other electronic or mechanical methods, without the prior written permission of the publisher, except in the case of brief quotations embodied in critical reviews and certain other noncommercial uses permitted by copyright law. All inquiries should be submitted to Cavalierspublishing.com

ISBN-13: 978-1-946292-00-1 Cavaliers Publishing

Second Edition, 2017
Printed in USA

Dedication

This book is dedicated to the wonderful people in my life who helped make it possible. My amazing family who has always stood by me and gave me encouragement to reach for my dreams.

To all of the Brain Aneurysm Survivors, we can do anything with support from one another. Thank you for the encouragement and support which made me 'believe' anything was possible. You are all a part of my family.

I also would like to dedicate this book to the hundreds of thousands of 'indentured servants', adventurers, and convicts whose freedom and lives were stolen and sent to America. Those who were taken from their homeland, their family and all they had ever known, their freedom stripped from them, and shipped off to an unknown land they called the new world. For all of those souls who suffered and died building Jamestown and farming the fields of tobacco, the export which allowed America to be. For all of the Irish, Scottish, and English slaves whose blood, sweat and tears made it possible for those of us today to live in the 'land of the free,' I dedicate this story to your memory. This story belongs to each and every one of them, whose voices and have been filtered throughout our history. I truly hope that by finally giving them a voice through Jayes, our ancestors are remembered so the truth of their lives are exposed and finally brought to light.

Virginia, 1681

As Jayes tied the strings around the several bundles of collected papers she felt a tear form and slowly fall from the corner of her eye, and run down her cheek. So much of her life, and her past had been recorded onto these pages. They held within them all the pain, all her fear and above all the many tears of her life. All these emotions and events now being tied up and put away forever. Her simple words, her life preserved forever in these papers.

Jayes prayed that someday, future generations would read these words. They would learn how they came to be here in America. They would learn their roots had been planted firmly in Ireland and only stolen away to America. Perhaps someday, they would even seek out their family in Ireland.

Jayes noticed a red stain on the corner of one of the sheets of paper. Her mind raced back to the many, many times she had written with bloody fingers.

At one time in her life she was certain she would be forgotten. As she placed the bundles of papers in the corner of the attic, she knew someday, through her words, she would be remembered, not forgotten.

Virginia, 2015

Kayla had spent days cleaning out her Great Grandmothers house. The Virginia heat this time of year was unbearable, she could not imagine how people lived here. Earlier she had attempted to climb the small ladder which led into the attic, the heat had taken her breath away.

She set up a small fan and had spent the afternoon loading the U-Haul she had rented. She was almost done now, the house was nearly emptied and cleaned, ready for the new owners. Kayla would begin the 2500-mile trip back to Idaho tomorrow.

She was excited about the antiques and family treasures she had acquired from the house. Among her new treasures were a chest and hutch which had probably been in her family for generations. They would now someday be passed down to her children and grandchildren.

The lengthy drive was most definitely going to be worth preserving these heirlooms in the family. Her mother had no intentions of saving anything other than the photographs. She had instructed Kayla to merely 'clean it out, give it away. I don't care!'

As Kayla climbed into the attic she was grateful the heat had subsided. Turning on the camping lantern, the room was instantly brought from darkness and bathed in the glow of a soft light. She was delighted to find the attic was almost bare. A rocking chair and a couple wooden boxes and then her job here was done. The attic was the last to be cleared, and there was little to do. She smiled and reached for one of the crates. As she lifted it the bottom gave way and out tumbled rolls of papers. *Old newspapers?* she thought. She gathered up the documents and one by one dropped them gently to the floor below the ladder.

After she climbed down she realized the papers were actually pages from an ancient manuscript, each tied carefully with a bright red ribbon. They were obviously very old, brittle and yellowed through time, totaling five bundles. She took them into the kitchen and turned on the light. On the outside of the rolls they were dated separately: 1630, 1640, 1650, 1660, and 1670.

Kayla was both shocked and elated with her discovery! How often did one get to hold history in their hands? The excitement she was feeling could not be explained.

Kayla uncorked a bottle of wine, taking it with her into the living room where she made herself comfortable on her blow up mattress. She untied the ribbon to the pages which were marked 1630. As she did so, she noticed a stain on the first sheet of parchment, she wondered if it could be blood. She laid back on the pillow and began to read… Moments later, Kayla found herself in Sixteen Twenty-Seven Ireland…

ONE
Dublin, Ireland – July 3, 1627

Jayes was violently shoved into the makeshift courtroom to stand before one of the English judges sent by King Charles. She had no idea of the fate which lay before her on this day, forever changing her life within the hour. How could she have? She had merely borrowed a bucket of milk from Mrs. McDougal, a bucket which Mrs. McDougal had been happy to loan her. Surely this was a mistake – what else was she to think? It was a misunderstanding, she had done nothing wrong. She certainly was not a thief!

Mrs. McDougal would quickly clear everything up and then these men, these awful men, who had roughly handled her and abused her would beg for forgiveness, of this she was certain. Unfortunately, she had never been more wrong of anything in her life. This is a future she could have never foreseen coming, one which would shape not only her life, but every generation after her.

The small room was crowded, overly crowded. The temperature was so hot it was almost unbearable. The men inside were rowdy and loud. It was complete havoc. Her guard had given her another shove forward. Jayes lost her slipper and quickly stopped, instantly trying to retrieve it. The tall man gave her another quick push as she turned. Jayes lost her balance and toppled backwards unable to catch her fall with her bound hands. The room erupted into a loud roar of laughter. The judge began to pound his gavel onto the wooden table.

"Here-here!" he shouted into the unruly crowd. The room slowly began to settle down. All eyes were on Jayes.

"Jayes Mackey," the judge said looking at her. He was seated near the middle of the room upon a box which had been covered with mismatched pillows for comfort. A small table had been placed in front of him, scattered with papers and a small glass jar, which housed three quills, and one jar for ink. He held the feather near his face, stroking his cheek, as he looked at her over his reading spectacles.

"You are accused of thievery. It was reported to this court that you 'stole a bucket of milk from the McDougal Farm.' Do you admit to us this day of your guilt?"

"Nay, nay tis not true. I took the milk aye, Mrs. McDougal told me I could. Ya see our cow is sick and…" Jayes was interrupted by the Judge.

"Mrs. McDougal!" He bellowed into the crowd. "Where are you, come forward!"

The crowd parted and Mrs. McDougal appeared beside her husband. Jayes looked at her, at first was relieved to see her. Why wasn't she looking at her and giving her assurance? Why hadn't she spoken up before? Why was her husband with her? He was a mean and horrible man Jayes thought as she shivered.

"Nay," Mrs. McDougal whispered but Jayes heard it. Her heart skipped a beat. She stood and stared in disbelief. Finally, Emma McDougal looked towards her. She apologized with her eyes silently to Jayes. That was when Jayes noticed the fresh bruises on Emma's face and the tears in her eyes.

"Speak up woman!" the judge shouted once again.

Emma's husband raised his hand and shoved her closer to the middle of the room.

"Nay!" Emma McDougal yelled.

Her husband looked at Jayes with an evil smile.

She suddenly realized what was happening to her, paralyzing her with fear and helplessness. She could feel her heart as it began beating hard in her chest, pounding so hard she could see her chest moving.

The room began to spin. In the faint distance she could hear the roar of the crowd, the cheering. It was like a loud drumming in her head. Suddenly the voice of the judge came out loud and clear.

"Jayes Mackey, you have been found guilty in the eyes of this court, by the rights given to me by His Majesty..." Jayes felt her knees buckle when she heard the word guilty. "You are to be sent to the Virginia Colony...," Jayes only heard the judge say 'Virginia Colony.' Everything went black and she passed out for the first time in her life.

Jayes awoke and felt her cheek pressed against cold stone, she had no idea how she had gotten here. She could feel bugs crawling all over her body and she slowly opened her eyes to strange surroundings.

She reached up and slapped the side of her neck where she had just been bitten.

Surveying the room, it was obvious she was in a jail cell. It was damp, dark, and very crowded. Jayes heard crying, and she saw a very cute, little blonde girl. She was younger, seventeen maybe, Jayes guessed. She was huddled in the corner of the room with her knees bent and her head buried between them. Jayes slid herself closer to the young girl, wanting to console her, to distract her from her own thoughts.

"Are you okay?" she asked her.

JAYES – 1627

The girl looked up at her, her pale skin stained with bright red splotches, her face wet from tears.

"No, I don't want to be here! I need to get out of here! I don't belong here. I hate Ireland, I hate the Irish. Nothing good has happened here! Nothing!"

Jayes could not agree with her in any way, she looked at the girl with confusion. Their plight was caused by the Englishmen, not the Irish, and Ireland had nothing to do with it at all. Did this girl not realize that?

"You're not Irish?" Jayes asked her, she did not know what to say to the girl with the odd accent.

"No. I am from England, your mother-country, my mum brought me here. We came to bring my da's body back here to this awful place. This is where he had wished to be buried, to his homeland, near his family. Although, I cannot imagine what he loved about this horrible place, I swear to God, I will never understand why!" She cried, wiping the tears from her cheeks. "On the way here, my mother got sick, so very sick and sudden, and then she just died. She did not feel well and then she was gone. I was all alone. My da's family did not want me here. They just kept saying I was only another mouth to feed." She started sobbing more deeply and gasping for air. "They turned me out!" She cried heartily. "I had nowhere to go."

"How did you get here though?" Jayes could not help but ask.

"I was looking for a ship, a ship which would sail to England. My mum's family would take care of me, and my passage." She nodded her head to Jayes to assure her that was true. "They just took me! They threw me into this place!" She looked around fearfully.

Jayes wrapped her arms around her trying to console the poor girl.

"You know where they're sending us don't you?" she accused suddenly. "They are sending us to those heathen islands!"

Jayes just looked at her. Surely she was wrong about that. They could not do such a thing, could they?

She looked at the tiny slit of light in the stone wall. 'Virginia Britannia, the New World'. She had heard stories of the New World, stories about the slaves who were sent there. Stories about the ships and of pirates who stole children and brought them there to work the fields, to build the buildings and houses for the English; brought them there to die. It was rumored that King James and his Son Charles, who now followed in his father's footsteps, was so stingy with his monies, he supplied the labor to the colony although he cared very little for Virginia.

When James had been king, he needed money to give Irish castles to his vast number of lovers and supporters, he imprisoned children and good Irish citizens. He transported them to work as slaves and to labor in the fields of America so he could profit from the tobacco; tobacco, a heathen weed which he so adamantly hated. England wanted to conquer the resources which were sitting and waiting to be taken in the New World. She had not really believed all the stories. None of them really made sense to her. Now she had reason to doubt them as rumors. Was it true? Was that why she was here?

Jayes knew in her heart they had not been rumors, they were stories of the truth, stories which were now far too real. She was living proof they were real. Jayes was beginning to understand, the world was not the carefree one of her village. People were not always loving, and caring, they did not always look out for one another. The world of her youth was slowly disappearing before her eyes. She was beginning to realize the villains her mother had protected her from, telling her of them only in nighttime bed stories, were not fictional villains, they were real.

"This will not happen to me," she told herself quietly. "Something or someone is going to walk in this room and rescue me. They will realize they have made a mistake and I do not belong here. My family will plea to the courts for my release. Mrs. McDougal will come forward and admit her husband had forced her to lie. Somehow, some way this nightmare will end and I will go home."

She assured herself of this over and over again in her head. She could envision the scenes playing out in different ways, and they always ended the same. She was walking into her home, all of her family and friends would be cheering and happy because she was returned to them safe and sound. The entire village would be celebrating her return.

As she stroked the little blonde girl's hair she thought she would rescue her, too. She would never allow such a sweet innocent orphan to be sold as a slave. It was not her fault she was stuck here in Ireland all alone and afraid in a strange land.

The damnable English doing this to one of their own! Instead of helping her find her way home they tossed her in here and thought to profit off of her misfortune. Selling her as a slave proved the English had no heart, they were only thinking of making a profit off of others, selling them as though they were theirs to sell.

A familiar voice was calling her name; it was faint but Jayes heard it. She immediately began to scramble towards the window.

"Mum! Mum! I'm in here! Here!" She saw her parents running towards her with the English soldiers close behind. They had made the two day journey quickly. They must have come straight away after realizing she was gone.

"Jayes!" her mum wailed as she reached the window. She slipped her fingers inside and Jayes took ahold of her mother's hand kissing it as they both sobbed.

"I am innocent, I am! I swear to you, I did not steal anything. Mrs. McDougal loaned me the milk!"

"I know Jacey girl, I know," her mum consoled her daughter although her face remained tormented.

"Get me out of here please!" she begged looking over to her da'.

He lowered his head, he could not look at her. His body was wracking with sobs.

"Da'? You are going to get me out of here, right? We are going home? Surely you are not going to let them send me away across the sea!"

Her da' remained silent with tears falling down his cheeks. He raised his sorrowful eyes to meet hers. "I am sorry, Jacey child. We have tried, there is naught we can do. We honestly tried."

Her eyes widened when she understood what he had just said. She began to shake her head. "No! No! There has to be something! You need to try harder! Talk to Mrs. McDougal! Make her speak the truth to the judge!"

Her mother began crying harder as she gripped Jayes' fingers. She wanted to tell Jayes something, but the English soldiers began pulling her mother back. She held onto Jayes until the soldier yanked her backwards forcing her to release her daughter. Both women screamed "*NO!*" in unison.

Jayes watched in horror as her parents were ripped away from the window. She pulled her hand slowly back staring at her fingers as if they were something she had never seen before. She lifted them towards her face and smelled them for any scent which remained of her mother. She gently touched them to her cheek, wondering if this was the last time she would ever feel her mother's touch.

Suddenly she felt a sharp pain on her backside, instantly dropping her to her knees. She turned as one of the jailers was about to strike her again with a whip. With her arm raised in protective defense, she cried out in pain as the stinging lash of the whip flashed through her arm.

"Enough from you little girl! You will behave in here or get more of this!" he yelled as he turned to leave, shutting the door loudly behind him. The sound of the lock sliding into place was the most awful sound Jayes had ever heard. Jayes knew it was the sound of her fate being sealed.

For the second time she felt utterly hopeless. She rolled herself up into a ball on the floor, her heart so heavy she could barely breathe. She just cried endlessly and prayed for hope. There had to be a way for her to find hope because she could never survive without it.

Late that night the door opened once again and an endless trail of new prisoners filed into the room. One after another they piled in until there was no room left to stand, yet they kept coming, stepping on prisoners sleeping on the cold floor.

"Ouch!" the blonde girl yelled out in pain, she was being trampled by people scrambling to find a place in the room.

Jayes moved forward and slapped the man who was shoving her new friend. She grabbed ahold of the girl and they made their way to the far corner where she stood guard.

"Thank you for helping me. I'm Guinever." She smiled sweetly.

"You're welcome. I'm Jayes, you can call me Jacey, my family calls me Jacey, even though I've kinda' outgrown the name," she said thinking she had hated the nickname before, and yet she prayed she would hear her mum calling it one more time. "We have to stay together now don't we?"

"Yes, I suppose we do and I would like it." Guinever grimaced.

Jayes did not take offense, she knew it was the circumstances which brought on her frown.

"You can call me Gin," she said it as if it were an afterthought.

The door was once again opened long before the sun rose. Even though it was dark, she was able to see the figures of English foot soldiers as they entered the room. They began stomping and kicking the prisoners out of their way as they began to form lines along every wall and corner of the room.

One soldier began yelling and then they all began hitting the prisoners with the butts of their guns – "get up" - "get out" they shouted. Prisoners scrambled for the door, falling and tripping over one another in the process while trying to avoid being hit or kicked.

Jayes watched fearfully as they reached the main room of the prison house. It was there where each prisoner was stopped and their hands were roughly placed into a pre-formed circle on an unending rope. Jayes had Gin in front of her so she could keep an eye on her and offer protection, determined to try and keep her safe if she could.

When it was her turn she put her hands out and the ropes instantly tightened against her wrists in an unforgiving hold. She was then tugged forward with a jerk.

Jayes saw the ship shortly after they exited the jail, not realizing they had been so close to the docks. She could smell the salty air in the cool morning breeze which had been absent in the stuffy jail cell. She frantically searched for her parents, her baby sister, and her brother. They were not there; the streets were all but emptied save for a few beggars sleeping on the cobblestone in front of the ancient stone buildings which lined the streets near the wharf.

Jayes watched as a couple of the guards went and grabbed them. They were quickly tied to the chain rope, unaware of what was happening to them in their sleepy condition.

She began to shake uncontrollably, realizing she wasn't going to have the chance to say goodbye, the thought hitting her like a bolt of lightning suddenly appearing from out of the sky.

Jayes made it across the plank which led up to the ship in a daze. Everything appeared hazy. The moment her feet hit the deck of the ship she panicked, she knew her fate was truly being sealed, and escape became impossible. This nightmare was real.

Someone in front of her fell. The rope which was tied to her hands pulled her forward violently. Jayes flew through the air, fell hard onto the deck, her head hit the planks just as she felt another crushing blow to the back of her head. She turned and realized the man behind her had fallen too, slamming his head against hers. She could feel the blood starting to slowly drip down the back of her neck. She looked up in a daze, took a deep breath knowing this could be the last time she ever breathed the fresh, cool, Irish air. She looked into the distance toward her home. It was the last thing she remembered.

Jayes woke up lying against the wooden planks of the ship. With the rocking motion and the sounds of water splashing up against her wooden bed, she realized they were at sea. Suddenly the ship shifted sideways and her head slammed against the wooden wall she was leaning against, causing an even more horrible pain in her head. She could hear the waves violently crashing on the other side.

Gin screamed as the ship lunged sideways.

Jayes found herself flying across the floor, banging against bodies as she tried to protect her head from further assault. She looked up to see a little, red-headed boy, with curly hair and two missing front teeth looking down at her with a shocked expression.

"I saved ya, missy," he said smiling.

"Yes you did," Jayes replied, realizing her mouth was so dry it was difficult to speak. She tried finding her balance and lifting herself off the little boy's lap. "Are you okay? Did I hurt you?"

The woman sitting next to him lifted him quickly onto her lap. "Andy, you okay? Are you hurt?" she asked lovingly with concern.

She was about Jayes' age and there was no doubt she was the child's mother, they had the same red hair and sky blue colored eyes.

"I'm fine Mummy. I saved her!" He beamed up to his mother proudly.

"Yes you did! You're a gentleman savior. I've always known that."

The little boy smiled with pride.

"I'm Kerry. Are ya alright miss?" she asked Jayes.

"Yes, I think I am," she replied even as the ship jolted again.

Andy flew off his mother's lap and hit the wall. He started to cry.

Both women reached for him and he jumped back into his mums comforting arms.

Jayes heard Gin scream from the other side of the small ship. She looked back at Andy's mother who was soothing her child. "Thank you," she said as she made her way back to the other wall to find Gin.

She was crawling over bodies, some obviously dead, others near death and many others injured. Jayes realized then the horrific odor was the smell of death and dying. One man had his arm up, blocking her way. She tried to move it, but it was stiff and unmovable.

Jayes screamed in horror when she discovered the arm was ice cold because the man was dead! She attempted to stand and practically flew towards Gin trying to get away from the horror. Her heart was racing and she was barely able to breathe. Her eyes wide open in terror, Jayes looked around, realizing the still bodies lying everywhere were dead.

She understood this was a death ship. She thought she was going to slowly die like everyone else. There was no air, little water, and even less food provided to them. She looked towards Gin, who seemed to be fading from her vision before everything went black again.

TWO
The Ship of Death... – Mid-August, 1627

The ship's men once again came down into the hold, from the looks on their faces Jayes knew it was not good. With immediate panic, she turned to Gin telling her to hide herself quickly. People started screaming as they were forcibly removed and sent up above.

Jayes could not figure out what they were doing or why. They were grabbing the prisoners by their arms and hair and tossing them from one soldier to another until they disappeared above. One woman began screaming for her husband who had been torn away from her. One of the soldiers hit her hard across the face with the thick stick he was carrying in his hand.

Jayes was suddenly yanked upward by her hair making her cry out in pain. Every muscle in her body ached with the slightest of movements. She could barely stand, her body was so stiff, and her legs were weak and unable to fully support her weight. Jayes frantically looked towards Gin, grateful she had not yet been spotted. In front of her the little red-headed Andy was yanked up, his mother reached out for him, and she, too, was pulled brutally to her feet. They were pushed towards the ladder in front of Jayes.

As she reached the top of the wooden ladder, she felt as

though her body was going to collapse. Again she was pulled and dragged forward by her hair. The sunlight was painful and blinding to her light-deprived eyes, they were unable to adjust to the brightness after weeks of darkness. She was pushed towards the railing of the ship.

Screaming began almost instantly, they were ghastly screams, followed by splashing. She watched through her teary vision a scene she could never have imagined. She quickly closed them again, terrified as she frantically grabbed onto a nearby rope holding on for dear life. She placed her other hand over her ears to try to drown out the horrific sounds around her.

They were tossing prisoners into the ocean! For a moment she thought maybe they were near land? *Yes of course, that had to be it*, she told herself. *Maybe they had reached America and they were supposed to swim to shore.*

She squinted her eyes open again and searched, hoping to see land. This could be her chance to escape! She saw nothing, only ocean as far as the eye could see. Her hopes sank like the people who were being thrown overboard.

They were killing them! Tossing them into the ocean, to their inevitable death. She heard herself scream *NO!* A man approached her, reached for her waist and began lifting her away, up and over the railing.

Jayes held onto the rope now with both hands in a death grip, pleading with the man. "Please, NO please, dear Lord, please do not do this. Please!" She could not help but look down into the water.

From the corner of her eye she saw the little boy being tossed overboard, screaming in fear as he fell. Jayes then watched as his mother Kerry desperately crawled up the gunwale, searching frantically for her son in the water and then jumped to her imminent death behind him. Jayes saw her swim towards Andy, just as a swell reached them and they both instantly disappeared under the roll of the water.

Jayes then heard the most terrifying scream and realized it was her own scream. Another man appeared now and put his hand over her mouth.

"Hold!" he said to the man who had been trying to throw Jayes overboard. "This little vixen has some spirit." An evil smile crossed his lips as he looked her up and down.

Jayes narrowed her eyes at him. She hated these men! He laughed at her in response. Jayes bit down hard on his hand which had been silencing her screams.

He yelled out in pain and released her mouth, raising his hand to slap her but stopped himself.

"Spare me, sir, I beg of you. If you do nothing else good for God today, please do only one and spare me my life!" she pled with desperation.

The man smiled at her, as though he thought he was as mighty as God himself. Jayes was so angered by his grin. She did not realize he alone held the power of life and death at that moment.

No longer could she beg this man for something he had no right to take from her. She yelled at him angrily. She should have been begging for her life rather than cursing him, she told herself. This was her one chance to plead mercy and she was yelling at him! She knew she was losing her mind, but she would not let her last words be kind to her murderer, she told him he was the devils spawn and much more.

To her amazement though he was smiling, he shook his head at her, and grinned, not the evil one, but an amused one. "A little, green-eyed, vixen with spirit," he laughed. "You remind me of Queen Elizabeth, only Irish." He held her red hair in his hands. Both men were laughing now.

JAYES – 1627

Jayes glared with hate at them both.

"Spare her. Take her to my cabin," he instructed. He was still staring at her; he could seem not take his eyes off Jayes.

She shivered as she noticed the grin on his face had changed, it was much different than before, which scared her even more.

He turned and walked away as Jayes sat there in amazement realizing her life had been spared!

Was this a trick to make her let go of the rope? She did not trust this man who still held her by the waist, trying desperately to pull her away from the safety of the rope she held onto.

"Let go missy, I'm not tossin ya. The Capt'n gonna do that himself." He laughed.

"Do you promise yer not gonna throw me into the water?" she asked, searching his face for honesty.

"I promise, now will ya let go of da damned rope? For a slip of a girl ya weigh like bricks."

"That's rude!" Jayes accused as she let go of the rope and slapped him.

The Captain turned around and laughed again. "Such spirit you have! I wish I would have found you weeks ago green eyes. You're going to make this trip so much more enjoyable."

Jayes glared at him and was once again aware of the many screams and splashes as people were still being tossed into the water. There were least a hundred who had been brought on deck, half of them still screaming and pleading for their lives. She looked into the water to search for Andy, knowing as she did she would never see his little face again. Her heart broke for him and the many others still in the water struggling to survive. A stabbing feeling pierced her heart because she knew that none would.

Jayes was once again dragged by her hair into a small and

nearly empty cabin. She knew this must be the tall, dark, and evil man's room, the one who had spared her life and found her so amusing. There was one chest, a small table, and a bed. Her eyes settled on bread which was sitting on the table. She lurched stiffly towards it and stuffed it into her mouth. She took a large gulp from a decanter and gasped. The golden liquid burnt her throat along with her insides as it went down. Her throat felt as though she had drunk fire. She did not care, she drank more and finished off the bread.

Her eyes then settled on the bed, only then realizing why she was there. She darted towards the door only to realize it had been locked from the outside. There was no escape, she felt herself panic as she remembered that man's words, *'I aint gonna toss ya, the Capt'n gonna do that.'*

She walked back over to the table and finished off the golden liquid fire as her eyes filled with tears. After a few more drinks, she was surprised to find she was actually beginning to relax. Sitting in the corner of the room under the window, she refused to look outside, too afraid of what she might see in the water.

Her lips felt numb, her entire body feeling tingly, not from fear, she actually was not feeling anything. The fear had escaped her somehow for the first time in weeks. She was relaxed. She closed her eyes and stretched out on the floor.

Behind her eyelids she could still see the horrors she had just witnessed. She wished she could erase them from her mind, knowing those pictures would forever haunt her. She felt a tear drop down her cheek as she thought of sweet little Andy and his brave mother. She said a silent prayer for their souls and for the souls of all the others who died and were dying in the Atlantic Ocean just then.

Jayes fell asleep praying.

It was not long after she heard the lock click in the door. She was startled awake, trembling with fear as he entered the room. She watched him walk towards the empty bed. She knew the moment he realized she was not there, he swung around scanning the room. He spotted her in the corner, smiled and walked towards her.

Jayes could feel the pounding of her heart with every step closer he took.

"You cannot hide from me my little, green-eyed vixen." He pulled her up by her arms. With Jayes' toes barely touching the ground, his arms wrapped around her, crushing her against his large frame.

She watched in horror as his lips descended toward hers. She turned her head to escape his advances and clamped her lips tightly together.

He laughed and dropped her to the ground.

She nearly fell before her weakened body managed to gain its balance.

The Captain walked over to the table and realized the golden liquid was gone. He laughed again and went to the leather trunk against the wall to retrieve a full bottle. He poured two glasses and handed her one.

"Drink this, it will benefit us both."

Shivers of fear traveled down her spine as he looked her over.

"You are very lovely for an Irish girl. I don't want you to resist me, I prefer willingness."

Jayes glared at him, she was scared of him, terrified even, but she would not give herself to him willingly and she was not afraid to tell him. "I beg your pardon, sir, but I will not go to you willingly. I do not belong to you."

He laughed.

This man irritated her and she gave him a hateful glare.

"You are wrong green-eyes. *You do* belong to me, and the sooner you realize that, the better off you will be." He poured himself another glass and walked towards her. He put his arms around her and smelt her hair.

He smelled her hair! No one had ever *smelled her hair!* Was this man out of his mind?

"You need a bath. I will have one brought in for you."

He turned and left the room, leaving Jayes standing there in complete disbelief.

Not long after, a few sailors came into the room carrying a brass tub. Several others followed carrying buckets full of steaming water. One by one they poured the buckets into the tub until it was full.

"I apologize, it is salt water, but it will get the stink off you which is all that matters," the captain said as he entered the room behind the last man bearing a bucket. "We cannot spare the fresh water for bathing."

The men left the room and he closed and locked the door behind them. Turning towards her he smiled the evil grin of his. "Well, get in while it is hot. I am a patient man, but I am a man."

Jayes was not really certain what he meant by that, but she had an idea. He wanted her to take off what little clothes she had on in front of him. She remained frozen in place and refused to move, knowing she just simply would not do as he had ordered.

Impatiently he lunged towards her and turned her around with one jerking motion. He began to untie the ribbon on the back of her gown.

She lurched forward, trying to get away from him, but he caught her shoulder and let out a warning growl. Jayes could feel the tears of fear well up in her eyes as she wished for the ability to disappear, wanting to be anywhere but here right now.

He turned her around to face him, the evil grin on his face was replaced with a look of hunger. In one quick downward motion he removed the gown from her shoulders, letting it fall in a heap at her feet as he began to unlace her petticoat, his eyes lingering on her bared breasts.

Jayes raised her hands protectively over her chest and he slapped them away, warning her with his eyes.

The thin petticoat fell to the ground leaving her standing naked. Her heart was no longer beating fast, her breathing slowed, she felt as though she could not breathe through her paralyzing fear.

"Into the tub green-eyes," he whispered in a lusty voice.

Jayes nearly ran into the water seeking it for cover. Standing naked in front of him had been unbearable, never before had she been so vulnerable.

He walked towards the tub grabbing a white cloth on his way which he dipped into the water. He began to rub her back with it, as she shivered violently causing him to laugh.

"Your body responds to my touch. I like that."

Jayes was silent. She tried to hide herself in the water, knowing it was pointless. His hand reached over her shoulder and he began to wash her breasts. She tried to slip deeper down into the water but he prevented her by holding onto her arm tightly.

She could feel his breath on the back of her neck. Suddenly she felt his hand on the top of her head and found herself pushed down into the water. She immediately lifted herself up gasping for air and spitting out the salty water.

Quickly she realized she was sitting up in the tub and fully exposed to his avid stares, she slipped back down straightway.

"No, you need to soap, you still reek of stink." He laughed at her embarrassment even as he soaped up the rag and, to her horror, forced her to stand up before him as he began to wash every inch of her body.

Jayes stood shivering helplessly, feeling exposed and violated. When his hands lingered between her legs with the soapy cloth her horror intensified when she felt an odd feeling. Silently tears of fear and frustration fell down her cheeks.

His hands gently pushed her down into the water which had already cooled a bit before he began to soothingly wash her hair.

"Rinse well," he instructed.

Jayes obeyed. When she was done he was kneeling next to her with a glass of the wonderful golden liquid. Jayes took it and finished the contents in one gulp, feeling the burn as it made its way down.

He stood, picked up a towel, and held it out for her with a short command, "Out."

Reluctant to leave the relative privacy of the tub, although the water was pretty cool now, Jayes hesitated. He gave her a warning look and she stood. He wrapped the towel around her.

She quickly covered herself up tightly, not waiting to dry her dripping hair. She began to shiver again, this time from cold.

"Dry!" he ordered her. "I don't want you catching yourself a fever."

Again Jayes obeyed, trying to ignore him as she removed the towel from her body and dried her hair. She knew his eyes were on her; she could feel them burning into her skin. She turned around to discover he was naked himself and watching her intently, every movement she made causing the look in his eyes to burn even hotter.

Frozen with fear, she was not certain what was to come, but she knew what he meant to do. She wanted to scream, yet she remained silent, wanted to run, but she knew there was no point. She could only stand there as he began to close the distance between them, knowing it was only a matter of seconds before he would touch her without any way of stopping him.

He was staring into her eyes as he approached, removing the towel covering her nakedness, dropping it carelessly onto the floor. He bent over and smelled her hair, nibbled at her ear and began suckling her neck. "Much better," he mumbled.

Lifting her into his arms, his hot flesh searing her frozen skin, he strode to the bed, lying her down gently as he covered her body with his. His mouth devouring her with his desire. His hand reached behind her head and took a handful of her hair and began to lightly bite her neck.

Jayes struggled against him and he yanked her head backwards so violently she was afraid her neck would break. He bit down hard causing her to scream; she stopped struggling while his chuckles vibrated against her throat.

His other hand reached between her legs. She could feel the pain as he grabbed hold of the inner part of her thigh and squeezed tightly as he grunted. His hand moving upwards, Jayes closed her eyes tightly and cried out in both fear and pain.

He kicked her legs apart with his foot while his fingers continued stroking her. Jayes let out another cry. She felt him positioning himself above her before she experienced a sharp, burning between her legs as she screamed in pain.

Three

The next morning Jayes lay naked in the bed as the captain closed the door behind him. She immediately started crying. The feeling from the liquor had now worn off and she was horrified at what she had allowed to happen to her last night. Her body was bruised and painfully tender, her legs and the bed were covered in her blood.

She took the shirt which was lying on the bed, the one he so carelessly discarded last night, and attempted to erase the evidence of what had been done to her. She noticed horrible discolorations on both of her arms and wrists and just began sobbing harder.

She jumped off the bed in an attempt to separate herself from the place of nightmares she could never have dreamt. Every nightmare she had ever had and then some had all played out in this bed.

Part of her thought she would have been better off in the water with the others, yet she kept telling herself she should be grateful she had survived. She did not feel thankful she had escaped that fate, at least not so much right now. What was yet to come? How many more nights like that would she have to endure? Could every day for the rest of her life be like a living hell? Would she have been better off sinking into the depths of the cold Atlantic sea?

How could she thank God for sparing her when the cost of living was so high? Especially now, when she was merely living in hell here on earth.

'*God forgive me. I do not mean to doubt you. Nor do I doubt your love for me. I am your child, your servant. I love you and believe in you. I believe you have a greater plan for me."*

Even as she said the words, there was a stabbing pain in her heart knowing she was so full of doubt. She felt as though she were losing faith. She hoped beyond hope that God was not listening to her since she knew her momentary thoughts were a sin.

September 20, 1627

Jayes never returned to the hold with the other prisoners. Instead, she remained in the cabin of the captain whose name she now knew was James. She had quickly learned not to resist him, he had been honest when he had told her that. He was never violent with her when she was fully cooperative. It seemed her sole purpose at this point was to submit to his sexual desires for the remainder of the trip.

There were times when his reactions were a little rough, even then he was giving in his passion. Jayes even found herself enjoying it at times even though she resisted those feelings.

She had to admit, he had not really treated her badly in anyway. He had clothed her, fed her and even gave her a new pair of slippers. She had never recovered hers from the day they had been lost in the courtroom.

He delighted in trying to make her smile, and as much as

Jayes wanted to, she did not hate him. She did not know why she didn't. He was not responsible for putting her on this ship, and he had spared her from certain death in the ocean.

Jayes worried everyday about Gin, although she would never ask James about her. She did not want to draw his attention to her. She worried and prayed for her instead.

Tonight as she sat at the table staring out the small window at the moonlight on the ocean waters, it was an unusually hot night. James must have mistaken her misery from the heat to that of his company. He stood watching her and frowned.

"You should be grateful my little, green eyed, slave," he said as he shoved the cold pork into his mouth.

"Why is that my lord?" she asked in surprise.

"Our cargo is ill. Half of them have already died. You my dear are safe here with me, for that alone you should be grateful. You have good food, good drink and good company too," he stated in a matter of fact manner. "This is turning out to be a very bad shipment. This illness is going to greatly affect my prices of course."

"It is too bad you lost part of your 'shipment' into the sea. I am sure that will affect your price as well *Captain*," she said with contempt. "You make them sound as though they are cattle. They were people, they *are* people, and you seem to forget that," she stated with a disapproving glare.

He laughed. "Aye, I regret throwing them to sea now! Had I known the future I would have spared them. I do not have a magical glass to see the future though my little vixen, besides, had it not been for that day, I would not have had your pleasures."

He irritated her, he still could not admit his *cargo* was made of living souls. He had a quick reply to everything, seeming to have a cavalier attitude. Even her rude remarks did not seem to affect him. He would easily brush her off with a smile.

He poured them some wine. "I must say, if they were cattle green eyes- they would be worth so much more than mere Irish servants. Most servants do not last as long as the cattle in the New World."

"Servants? So now they are servants and not prisoners or slaves?" She asked.

"It is the same, but in America they call them servants. If you were in the Indies, you could possibly be called a slave, more likely you would just be a servant, simply because you are a female and most females are spared the fields."

She was not going to argue with him, or try to make him realize how barbaric he was. This was not a battle she could win, not with such a stubborn and cold hearted man. How could he be so kind and gentle at times and yet so heartless at others?

She also did not know if her fate would be the same as those below had she not been chosen that fateful day. He had saved her from drowning and saved her from illness. Could he possibly spare her from slavery?

"When will we arrive?" She asked.

"Soon. We have been at sea nearly eleven weeks now," he said. "That storm set us off course. There is nigh no wind in our sails even now." He seemed disappointed. Perhaps this was not the subject to bring up, his mood seemed to instantly sour.

"A week? Two?" she asked, curiosity getting the better of her. His answer was a frown. "How many times have you sailed to America? How do you even know where you are going or how near to this new world we actually are?" She asked him.

Jayes was very anxious for the answers. James was happy that she was open to having a conversation, they had been making slow progress where communication was concerned.

He merely laughed at her in reply. He stood up wiping his

hands with the napkin. "A week maybe," he answered. "It is nothing that you need to worry your pretty little head over green eyes. You will be on the ship for several days even after we arrive in Jamestown. There are arrangements and business matters that need to be taken care of before we unload the cargo." He walked towards her and gently lifted her from her seat smiling. Jayes had learned what that smile meant.

He wiped her fingers one by one with his mouth, and then the corners of her lips with his tongue. "As for the sailing of the ship, you would not understand. You need to let me worry about that. I promise I will get us there safely." He smiled and started undressing her. "I have captained this ship to America many times before and I do know where I am going my little, green eyed vixen."

His eyes twinkled as he started walking Jayes backwards. "I can steer her in the dark just as easily as I can steer you into our bed." He had that look again.

The next morning Jayes was awakened by James re-entering the room. She heard the lock click and watched him put the key in his pocket.

He turned towards her and sat down on the bed. "You're awake. I am sorry if I woke green eyes, I tried to be quiet. I had to go out on deck and release a crow this morning. I had to make sure that we're traveling in the right direction." James started to remove his shirt.

"Are we?" she asked, "Traveling in the right direction?" Jayes was confused. What did a crow have to do with that? She quickly spoke her mind. "Why a crow? Does a crow have a better sense of direction than you do?"

James burst into laughter. "Well," he said unable to contain his amusement in her question. "I suppose the truthful answer to that would be yes."

Jayes could not hide her alarm, which apparently amused James even more. He crawled into the bed next to her, taking her into his arms.

"Do not worry little one." He spoke to her as though he was trying to sooth a scared child. "It is a common practice. We are not lost," he assured her. "A crow will always fly towards land. He is sort of the sailor's guide. We always keep them onboard."

Jayes was surprised. "Really? Who would have known?" she asked in wonder.

James laughed again pulling her in closer. "That is why I am the Captain, green eyes. I know all the secrets. Have you not yet realized you're in good hands?" He kissed the top of her head.

"James, can I ask you a question without causing you anger?" She had her head snuggled into the crook of his arm. She could not see his face. He answered yes without hesitation.

Jayes decided to ask although she was still a bit hesitant. "You do not really seem to be a monster, so why did you have all those people thrown into the Ocean to die a horrible death?"

She felt him instantly tense up. She was already emotional just thinking about what she had witnessed that dreadful day. She would never forget the horrible screams. She would never forget Andy's mother jumping to her death, wanting to die with her son.

James sucked in his breath, he held it long before he slowly exhaled. "Jayes, I am not a monster." He paused several moments before finishing. "You will never understand. This is a job, an order that I have no choice but to follow. I am doing the Kings service; I cannot disobey my King. My job is to deliver this cargo. Whole freight, live cargo it doesn't matter, to me it is all the same. It is just cargo I am transporting to Jamestown. I did not charge you or any of these people with a crime. I did not sentence anyone to this ship, or cause you to be here. I am not responsible for putting you here. You're a prisoner of England, I am only doing the King's business."

"What does that have to do with murdering all those people?" She asked angrily. "Would your King not be upset that you killed his prisoners? Murdered them in cold blood? That is a much worse crime than anything any of these people are charged with! Most have been spirited away. Sold against their will. Victims of false charges made against them to collect a price for your Kings freight!" She sat up. She had to see his face, she wanted to see remorse or denial. "I can tell you this! I certainly did not sign up to serve your King! He does not serve Ireland, I will not serve him!"

He was angry now. He slammed his fist into the bed. He grabbed her shoulder and forced her to lay back down. He was so angry she could see the veins in his forehead throbbing as he looked down at her. "Jayes! I am ordered to deliver this cargo to the planters of Virginia. I had no choice. The success of Virginia, its very existence is dependent on its tobacco. To grow tobacco, you must labor, to labor you must have servants. If I had not sacrificed a few, everyone on this ship would be dead right now," he began raising his voice, she had really piqued his temper this time.

"We have had nearly no water left for weeks now. I am not the kind of Captain that starves his passengers and lets them die a slow death. I give them bread and water daily. I travel in the winter to avoid mass death and illness on the ship caused by high temperatures. I do all I can to give them a chance to adjust to the new world climates rather than die the first month by keeping them as strong and healthy as I can. Do you not understand? We would *all* be dead right now had I not done what I did. Call it murder if you must, but I spared many more lives than I sacrificed." James looked hurt and angry, it was a new look, one she had not seen.

"James, you're not telling me why. Let me understand," Jayes pleaded with him. She really did not like being the cause of him being so upset, yet she also could not understand how this man could do what he had done. She wanted to understand, she *needed* to understand.

"Water!" He shouted so loudly the entire ship probably heard him. "We did not have enough water! Do you understand now?" He jumped out of bed and started to put his breeches on. "*Now* you know why I *murdered* all those people!" He grabbed his shirt and turned to leave.

"James, you promised...." The door slammed behind him. "...not to get angry," Jayes finished her sentence to an empty room. She waited for the lock to click, and it never did. She sat staring at the unlocked door for what seemed like eternity.

A little voice whispered inside her head- '*Run Jayes Run*'.

She jumped out the of bed and nearly into her clothes. She ran towards the door but then stopped short. In slow motion she put her hand on the knob and turned it slowly. It opened. She was careful not to make any noise as she looked. It was silent and James was nowhere in sight.

She climbed the short ladder that led to the main deck. She could smell the ocean breeze and feel the wind on her face with every step closer to the top. When she peeked her head out of the small opening above deck, she could see several men working frantically not too far away. She carefully made her way to the stern of the ship, and hid between two large wooden columns that held the huge sails. She had a wonderful view of the entire ship.

Men were throwing something into the ocean. She moved a little closer to get a better view and stood horrified in absolute shock. Bodies, the deck was littered with the dead bodies, prisoners from below. They were carelessly tossing them into the ocean! Jayes watched as a man picked up another body and tossed over, she had shivers when she heard the familiar splash. She automatically said a silent prayer for their soul, and she continued her prayers with every splash she heard. She counted at least a dozen, who knows how many had been thrown over before she had got there. She was thankful she did not see Gin. She thanked God for her life, for his protection and prayed for Gin's continued safety.

"What are you doing up here! How did you get out of your room?" An angry James nearly ruptured her eardrums shouting. He grabbed her arm and yanked her roughly towards him. "Am I really that horrible of a murderer that you would damn your soul to hell to escape me?" He looked upset. Not in an angry way anymore. He looked really hurt. She realized what he had just said.

"No, I was not going to jump. Truly, it never even crossed my mind."

"Then what are you doing here?

"I don't know," she said knowing that he would not believe her. "I really did not know what I was going to do. I didn't have a plan. I just wanted to get out of that room," she tried to explain, not even knowing the answer herself. "Well, you see, you left the door unlocked. There was this little voice in my head that just said 'run'. So I ran. I had no plan."

James smiled. "I believe you. I think you're crazy but I do believe you. You're an honest person Jayes. I also believe you're innocent."

He managed to shock her. Until suddenly his smile faded

and he looked angry again.

"Do you have any idea what could have happened to you up here?" He snapped.

"No what?" she snapped back defensively. He grabbed her shoulders and spun her around. "Them! All of them! It's all I can do to keep them from going below deck, to keep them from raping the prisoners. If they found you up here, the damage would be done. They would rape you and face the consequences later. Some would even think you came up here to find 'them', that you were asking for it."

Jayes understood exactly what he meant before he had even finished. She had not thought of that, it had not even crossed her mind that there could be any greater danger up here than there was in his room.

"You would protect me; I know you will protect me."

"It would be too late Jayes, do you not understand?" He was still angry. "Yes, I would whip anyone who touched you to near death. The damage to you though, would already be done!"

"Okay, I am sorry. I promise I will never leave the room again without you. I swear to you," she assured him.

"Jayes," He said he seemed to be calmer. "I was not locking you in the room. I did not think you would be so senseless to leave. I was locking them out." He pulled her into his arms and kissed the top of her head. "Please try to keep yourself safe. I have learned to care about you."

Did he really care? Would he keep her safe? Could he, and for how long she asked herself.

That night they ate in silence. She was not really sure exactly what had suddenly changed. Did he regret admitting that he cared about her? There was an unbearable wall that had suddenly appeared between them.

"You are still mad at me. I am really sorry. I really am. I

promise I will not do it again," she blurted out.

"Jayes, you do not belong to me. I cannot protect you," he said angrily. "I am not mad at you."

For some reason Jayes did believe that he was not angry with her. She knew that he had no control over her fate. He had already told her that. She could not understand why he still seemed so upset.

"We are close. It will not be long now. We should see land fall any day," he stated.

Jayes felt her heart skip a beat. An alarming sense of fear overcame her. She had to place her hands flat on the table as if to steady the fear quivering inside her. She could not immediately speak.

"Have you brought prisoners to America before? What happens?" She finally asked.

"I have delivered convicts to Jamestown twice. I do not carry 'illegal' cargo. I am going to have a few discussions after this trip. I have never aligned myself with the kind of captains that spirit away innocents into slavery. I have always transported for private parties, plantation owners, the company and my King. Most everyone to my knowledge was either a convict that was given pardon in exchange of transportation to service or men and women who have contracted services with owners or the company in exchange for passage." James was not the monster she had thought. He was being used just as she was.

"Who is this company?" She asked.

"There is no company anymore, King Charles removed its charter and disassembled the council, and he is in charge now. Virginia is a Royal Colony. It was the Virginia Company, now replaced by King Charles and his royal commission," James said with a mocking voice. "Virginia Company was a venture that created and supplied shares and tracts of land to develop and make Virginia a worthy trade market, a hopeful settlement that could bring new goods and products to England at little expense and great profit. I even invested in the company. I had great hopes along with many others for the New World. There are many men, myself included, that have never traded our morals to fill our pockets."

"What does that mean?" She asked.

"Jayes, there are many men that are ruled by greed. Greed of tobacco, greed of profit. The plantations are somewhat new. There is so much land to be worked, to be developed, to be grown. It takes people." James got up and started pacing the room. It was as if he was trying to figure out in his mind how to tell her the truth of the situation she was in. "Virginia is not an easy life. It is backbreaking work in horrible conditions. Most of the adventurers that originally went to Virginia years ago, they are worn out or they are dead. They have demanded the lands that were promised to them years ago, lands that have been withheld far too long. Most of them are just now starting to develop their own lands. They need servants to help them build plantations, plant and raise the tobacco along with the food needed to survive." He sat down, took a deep breath and continued.

"They are desperate to see the fruits of their years of labor begin to pay off. There are ships that go to unheard of measures to gather up as many people as they can to deliver to these planters, they are so desperate they have forgotten what is right and what is wrong. It's a good profit for the Captains, they do trade morals for land and coin. People are being stolen off the streets in England every day for these purposes. Children and women are kidnapped to be sold into service to work the fields. I do not do that, I do not trade my soul for coin Jayes." James looked at her, she knew he was telling her the truth.

"Years ago, King James had ordered that criminals and vagrants be transported to the colonies, he had his own interests in the fields of Virginia. I transported those that had been legally convicted in the eyes of the court. I transport them still for King Charles, legally. I do not steal women and children. I never have and I never will. If I have been deceived, and you are telling me the truth, I will take care of it," he said.

Jayes wondered if her conviction was legal. She had been convicted, even if she was innocent.

"I was not 'legally' convicted. It was a lie! That man, Mr. McDougal, had tried to rape me. I was going to tell, but I did not have time. I was arrested and taken away before I had the chance. He lied about the milk! He must have beat his wife to lie too! He wanted me gone before I could accuse him. I was just so scared that if I told, it would hurt his wife." She cried, realizing finally what was done had not been a mistake. Why had she not realized it before when she could have spoken up?

"I am sorry. There is nothing I can do right now. I can make sure though that you are treated well until there is something I can do." He just held her. "You have to try and trust me Jayes."

She believed that James would help her if he could. Somehow he had begun to really care about her. She knew there was nothing he could do right now.

"Can you say you threw me overboard? That I am dead? Hide me?" She asked him hopeful.

"Jayes, I cannot do that." His expression was saddened. James was too honest of a man. She knew his answer before he even explained. "We could both end up working the fields. They will search and inspect my ship. I will do what I can, in a legal way. Trust me," he said as he took her hand and led her to the bed.

That night he did not undress her. He just held her in silence. She felt safe in his arms. She did trust him. For some reason she believed that he was a good man.

Four
Near the New World Coast –
October 2, 1627 – Where freedom dies…

Jayes sat in the small room for three days, the anticipation was killing her. She found herself running towards the window every time she felt the slightest turn in the ship. She dreaded the sight of land and was relieved when there was none in sight. She knew her fate, her freedom was to never be hers again, yet her future was unknown.

She was not ready to face it. Yet, there was a part of her that knew land was the only hope for those poor souls stuck down below in the hold of the ship. Those who were lucky enough to make it to land. They desperately needed to breathe fresh air, and she knew it could not come soon enough.

She heard a loud pounding sound coming from the deck directly above her room, boom, boom, coming from the ceiling. It sounded like metal hitting against metal and then a loud scratching across the ceiling. She ran to the door but stopped before she opened it.

Her mind was torn. Should she satisfy her curiosity and see what was going on or should she keep her promise to James and stay in the room? She knew if she did not go it would drive her crazy trying to figure out what those sounds were.

She turned the knob slowly, she would have just a peek she decided, and then she would quickly return to the room.

She quietly made her way up the ladder, and stopped as soon as she had a good view of the men above. They were hammering on what looked like chains, large chains linked together in circles almost as wide as her hand. She watched as they took metal collars and pounded new links into them and then attached them to the long lengths of chain.

Jayes could visualize the ghastly collar being attached to her neck, it all became real. She stared at the horrendous thing, she was petrified. Without realizing that she was still standing on the ladder she instinctively turned to run. She found herself stepping into thin air and falling hard onto the deck below her. Jayes just lay there huddled up in pain.

She was not sure if the tears were from the pain or from the realization of what was going to happen when they reached land. Jayes tried to get up, it took her several attempts to steady herself, and she was unable to put weight on her ankle. Slowly she hobbled back into her room and threw herself onto the bed and began to cry. Jayes buried her head in the pillow and wept uncontrollably, that is how James found her hours later.

"What is wrong? Has someone hurt you?" He demanded. His face was unable to hide his concern as he sat down beside her, rubbing her back.

"Yes, someone has hurt me! Those awful people who put me here," she cried. "I do not belong here! I want to go home. I belong at home with my family- I need them! I hate this ship! I have been kidnapped and you know it! Take me home James! Please take me home!" She begged. "If you care even a tiny bit, please," she cried.

"Jayes, I cannot do that. You know that. I will do what I

can. I promise," he said with genuine remorse. Suddenly, he noticed the swelling and bruises on her ankle and legs. His concern turned quickly to anger.

"What has happened? Do not lie to me Jayes! I demand you tell me the truth, why is your ankle bruised? Did someone do this to you?"

'I tripped. No one has done anything, today." That was all she was willing admit to him, and she was not going to ever tell him she had left the room. "I am sure it is nothing compared to what will come of me in Virginia! I hope I get killed by the Indians! I swear I do! I pray that they will put me out of my misery!" she rolled over and cried into the pillow.

James was silent for a moment. "Do not say that, I do not want anything to happen to you."

"Then take me home!" She screamed into the pillow. He said nothing. After a moment she lifted her head up. "Do the Indians truly kill the white people? Is that really true?" She asked. She really wasn't sure. She had heard some stories, she never believed them though.

James twisted his lips, deciding if he would answer that question. Finally, he said, "Yes, they do. About five years ago they killed hundreds in a surprise attack. The Powhatan chief had died. Relations between the Colonists and the Indians had faltered." He was looking off into the distance as if he was remembering the events that had taken place. Jayes knew of course he had not been there.

"I think that the new Chief, the brother of Powhatan, needed to show his strength. Secretly they planned an attack. It could have been devastating to the existence of the Colony had it not been for an Indian who had converted to Christianity and told us of the impending plans of attack. Even with an advanced warning, about four hundred people were lost or stolen that day. It was a difficult time, many lives were lost," he sighed.

James must have known some of the people who had died she thought. "Hundreds?" she asked, shocked and terrified.

James suddenly got serious. "Jayes, promise me one thing."

"What do you want me to promise?" she asked.

"Stay away from the Indians. If you ever see them, do whatever you can to hide yourself. If you cannot hide, run. Stay away from the savages, they are murderous heathens," he said seriously.

"You're just trying to scare me James. Do you not think that I am not already terrified of this land they call Virginia? This awful place my people go to die?" She pulled her hand back. "You don't have to lie to me, believe me, I'm scared enough already."

"Jayes I'm not trying to scare you. I will never lie to you. I'm trying to help you," he said defensively.

Jayes was finally angry. Mostly with herself. With her confusion about James, was he a good guy? Was he a bad guy? How was it she could not figure that out? It was all too much, she just did not know the answer, she did not know how to feel or think anymore. She seemed to be in a state of confusion, a place she had never traveled to before.

Jayes turned on him. "Help me?" she seethed, gritting her teeth, shaking her head, and glaring at him. "You are trying to help me? Am I really supposed to believe that?" She screamed pointing to the bed.

He did not seem to take offense that she had just accused him of abusing her, maybe he did not consider that a bad thing. Instead, he calmly tried to convince her she was wrong by taking her hand in his and shaking his head no. She slapped it away and gave him a hard shove. He took a step backwards.

"Help me by kidnapping me?" She advanced on him,

pushing him again. He tripped this time and nearly lost his balance.

"Help me by taking me to this Virginia? This New World that is so horrid?" She was screaming at him now, poking his chest as she walked, and making him retreat. "Selling me as a slave? Taking away everything I have ever known, including my family? My freedom? My very life? YOU have no right to ask me to trust you!"

James was now backed up against the wall, a startled expression on his face along with that evil grin of his. She hated that smirk of a grin! She hit him again. "You! You forced me in here. You! You are the man who took my body as if it belonged to you! I'm supposed to believe you're 'helping' me?" Jayes was so angry she could not stop pounding on his chest as he stood there.

"Jayes, I've grown fond of you, you know that. I care about you. I do." James had never seen this side of her, he did not know how to explain his feelings and his duty to her. He took her hands in his to stop the assault to his body, yet he never raised his voice to her.

Jayes was so angry, she knew he was lying. "You Do Not Sell People You Care About." With each word she punched his chest, breaking her hands free from his. "You just don't do that," she cried and then exhausted she fell to the floor at his feet.

James bent over to either pick her up or hold her. "Don't," she cried with her face in her hands. She curled up in a ball on the floor. "Please just leave me alone. You're only making this harder."

Jayes heard him walk towards the door, open it and leave. When she heard the door close, she felt an empty pain move through her chest. She wanted him to hold her.

James did not come back. It had been dark for hours. She sat, listening. She heard nothing but the creaking of the ship and the pounding of the ocean against it.

She decided to go see if there was something wrong. Just a peak she had told herself. That was quickly forgotten the moment she had her head above deck.

She was mesmerized by the beauty. The moon appeared so close, it looked as though it had fallen, landing above the surface of the ocean and one could reach out and touch it. It was as round and perfect as the apple the devil bribed Eve with. The color she imagined would be the same as that glow around an angel. She walked on the deck with her eyes fixed on the sky.

The moon shone so much brighter than she had ever seen it before, it was almost as though it was sitting in a valley of sparkling diamonds. Suddenly Jayes felt herself flying forward. She landed, gently and found herself buried in a pile of thick cloth, discarded sails thankfully had softened her fall.

She almost laughed as she tried to dig herself out. "At least I had a soft and dry landing." She told herself thinking that this was the only luck she had had in weeks. *No, that's not true. I could be dying slowly in the bottom of the ship*, she thought to herself. Instantly she felt guilt. Poor Gin, she should try to help her. What if she is dying?

Jayes heard voices that interrupted her thoughts, men were talking and getting nearer. She sunk back into the canvas and hid herself.

What a wonderful little hiding place she said aloud as she quickly made her way back to her room.

James had never come back to the cabin that night. Jayes waited, crying. Was she wrong? He has shown her kindness, he had taken good care of her, considering. He was only following orders and he had said he was going to help her. She was still so confused, and she did not want James to be the enemy. She liked him. She was surprised to admit that she did like him, had they met in Ireland they would have probably been great friends or maybe even suitors. Jayes fell asleep thinking of James in a different, happy life.

She woke up as soon as she heard the door. James stood above the bed staring down at her. He looked awful.

"I'm sorry," she said.

"You have nothing to be sorry for." He sighed, he sounded beaten. "Jayes, I want to help you. I want to turn this ship around and set course to Ireland. I want to take you home. I do. I can't. Not yet."

Jayes knew at that moment he was telling her the truth. She knew the truth was killing him inside.

"We cannot change what we cannot change," she said, "No matter how much we may want to. We can't. I understand, James."

He knelt beside the bed. "Jayes, I am going to do everything. Anything. Whatever it takes to help you. I promise you that. Please believe me."

"I do," Jayes said as she jumped out of bed and ran towards the bed pan in the corner of the room. She barely made it before the contents of her stomach violently emptied. Jayes was gasping for air in between spilling her guts when she felt James behind her. He gathered her hair up in one hand and began to gently rub her back with the other.

Jayes had tears in her eyes. She turned around and just held him. She felt so much better just being in his arms. He picked her up and carried her back to the bed. She didn't want to let go of him. He quickly undressed and crawled in next to her

"Are you okay?" he asked.

"I am now that you're holding me."

They laid there in silence. Jayes was listening to the beat of his heart. Her mind turned to Gin, she felt she had to do something to try to save her.

"James, can I ask you a question?" He replied with a grunt, she took that as a yes. "If there were an English Lady, one of good birth, among the cargo, would she be of importance to you?" she asked hoping the answer would be to Gin's benefit.

"Aye, it would. Why?" James half mumbled.

He was exhausted, Jayes realized he must not have slept elsewhere. She smiled.

"There is an English girl. I met her in the prison in Ireland. She was kidnapped when she was on her way to the ship which was to return her to England."

James lifted his head and looked at her. "Are you sure about this?"

Jayes wasn't sure. She was almost jealous suddenly at the interest he suddenly had in an English girl. Of course that made no sense she told herself. She wanted to help Gin. She should be happy that he was interested in her.

"Yes I am sure. Her name is Geunivor or Ginevera, I cannot remember exactly, something like that," she said trying to sound out Gin's given name.

James sat up. "What does she look like? Do you know where she was?"

Jayes gave him all the details she could remember. What Gin looked like, the green and white gown she had worn, her blonde hair. She explained about where they had sat.

James got up. "I'll be right back."

Jayes just sat there staring at the door. She wished she knew what he was thinking. She knew what he was doing. Gin was going to be okay if she was still alive.

She wondered if all Englishmen were like the Queen Elizabeth. They cared of nothing but their precious England. To hell with everything and everyone else. England first.

Jayes laid back down but sleep would not come. It seemed like eternity until James came back into the room. She sat up in the bed the moment the door opened and just stared at him as he undressed silently. She couldn't take it.

"Well?" she asked impatiently.

James looked at her, confused, then realized what she was referring too. "She's alive, she is not well, but she is still alive. She is being tended to." He climbed into bed.

"What will happen to her?" Jayes asked.

"I am not sure. She has no family. She is an orphan. It will be left up to the council in Virginia what to do with her." James yawned, unconcerned and pulled her close to him.

"She could be helpful in making your life easier until I return." He yawned again and gave her a squeeze. "Let me think about it," he said.

Jayes knew him well enough to know by now that this was his way of saying he was answering no more questions, and sure enough, only a few blinks later she heard him snoring. She closed her eyes and fell asleep to the melody of his breathing.

They were awakened early by banging on the door. A man was shouting "land fall – land fall!" James quickly jumped out of bed, taking the covers with him and then tossing them back onto bed. He rushed to the door not even bothering to dress. Jayes had barely pulled the blanket over herself when he yanked the door open.

"Really? Are you certain?" he asked the big sailor on the other side.

"Aye, Captain," he said cheerfully in confirmation.

"I'll be up," James said patting him on the shoulder. "Land

to!" James yelled out.

The man on the other side of the door noticed her. His smile faded briefly before he turned shouting "Land to!"

James closed the door. "We have made it green eyes. Land is in sight. I have to go. I will be late." He was excited, of course he was. He had had no idea if he had been traveling in the right direction she thought. He dressed quickly, leaned over the bed and gave her a quick kiss.

Jayes was not sure how she felt. She was not as happy about the closeness of land as James. He must have read her mind.

"It will be okay," he said and left in a hurry.

Jayes fell back on the bed. She stared blankly at the wooden ceiling. She could feel the ship slightly turning. She could hear the ocean beating against the ship in resistance.

"Our Father, who art in heaven, hallowed be thy name…," Jayes spoke the Lord's Prayer aloud and then silently prayed from her heart: "Please protect and guide me, Amen."

She got out of bed and slowly dressed. She was happy for those below. She knew those who survived would have a chance now, although she was still uncertain what that fate would be.

FIVE
Chesapeake Bay off the coast of Virginia, October 8, 1627

Jayes snuck up onto the deck and quickly hid herself in her usual spot inside the safety of the discarded sails. Land was now nearly on both sides of them. In the distance she could make out James' voice as he bellowed out orders, his voice distinctive above all the other commotion on the deck. The sails were frantically being taken down, some being turned and ropes pulled. The men were running about in every direction following orders.

The ship was beating hard against the resistance of the water as they made their turn, at times the waves would sometimes rain down upon them in downpours. Hidden lightly in the abundant sail, Jayes could feel the water dripping off of her head. She felt the wetness soak her clothing as though she had been standing in a witch's storm.

Slowly they made the turn towards the long opening of water in between the land. The river was wide, very wide, dividing ocean from land. From what she could see the dirt was an odd color, a dark tannish red, a color she had never seen on a shoreline. The grass was tall, almost as tall as Jayes, it hid a good portion of land as it rose from the depths of the water onto the shore. Everything as far as the eye could see was a lush green, topped here and there with bright red, orange and yellow leaves. Some of the trees were of the brightest reds and yellows she had ever seen.

This was indeed a new and different world. Not the tall rocky landscape or the lush green rolling hills of home. Jayes vowed she would never call this new land home. Even though it showed much beauty, she knew even the devil himself could appear as an angel. So too, this hell could appear heavenly.

Thinking of the devil her mind raced back to James. She searched for him on deck and instantly spotted him. She could not help but stare. His height stood taller above the other men on deck. His dark, wavy, near black hair waving in the wind.

She could close her eyes and see his dark eyes staring at her. She realized he was the devil. He was the most beautiful evil angel that had ever graced heaven, and now he controlled hell. He was delivering them to hell.

Jayes smiled, and her eyes widened when she felt a tingle thinking of him. She checked herself, and focused again on the rolling of the ocean.

Jayes had been looking at the scenery all day. It was nearly dusk now, and she had lost track of time. Jayes could hear the sails being turned and James still shouting commands. "Reeve the rope!" He shouted to his left. Men ran to do his bidding. "Ride the anchor!" He shouted behind him, and many other commands she had no idea what they meant. They were guiding the ship into this new land that was to become her prison. It was a bitter sweet feeling.

Under any other circumstances she would be overjoyed to step again on soil. She sighed, she was not normal. She was being delivered to Virginia as her prisoner. Virginia was not her friend; she was her hell.

As they made their way further from the ocean and up river, the beaches became lighter, though they were few. At times the sand sparkled in the setting sunlight like diamonds, the finest of gems. There was less red rock looking dirt and more and more tall grass growing up the sides of the banks to stand tall like a gate of protection to whatever stood behind. Green trees that seemed to go on forever into the distance. The land was flat but seemed go on forever and ever.

Missing were the tall cliffs of Ireland's coast line. The air was heavy and seemed to be unseasonably hot.

This was what they called the New World she thought again. Still in disbelief that she was actually here. The land of Virginia, named after that awful Queen Elizabeth.

Jayes smiled remembering a conversation she had with James late one night when she had called her the "awful Queen."

"Why would you say that? She was beloved by the people. She was a queen who loved England above all else." He had defended her.

"She may have loved England," Jayes replied. "England may have loved her. I assure you that was not the case in Ireland or with my people."

"You mean the Catholics?" he asked.

"Both," Jayes answered.

"Both?" James asked, confused.

"The Catholics or any Irishmen, no matter their faith," Jayes said. "I don't think she liked anyone but the English now that I think about it." Jayes twitched her lips as she gave it considerable thought.

James laughed, touching her lips with his thumb gently. "I love it when you do that," he said. "It's so cute. I see what you're saying green eyes. You may have a point. England First. That was our Queen."

"Damn everyone else. That was your Queen," Jayes countered. James had laughed. She knew these moments with him were gone forever as the ship sailed closer and closer to land. Soon he would be gone and she would be...

Jayes climbed out of her hiding spot. She was no longer curious what this New World looked like, she had seen enough. She knew she would see way too much of it soon enough. She looked at this strange land with its strange colors and red dirt one more time and she wished she could just make it disappear. Yes, she had definitely seen enough.

This was not a dream that she would wake up from. Every day she seemed to realize it was a new reality. An unknown future. Yet everyday she still wished she could just wake up.

There was nothing about her life she could now control. There was not one thing that she could predict~ except that she would fall asleep and wake up. Even that was questionable. She did not want to see land. She did not want to wonder what tomorrow would bring. She wanted to go back to the safety of the cabin. She wanted to fall asleep and dream of Ireland. Dream about her family and running along the cliffs of home.

James must have come back to the room long after Jayes had fallen asleep. The next morning she woke as he was finishing dressing. She just watched him.

"Can I see her?" Jayes asked him.

James turned towards her and smiled. "Who? The girl?" He had not expected that question. He was pulling on his boots and about ready to leave her for the day as usual.

She hadn't told him that she and Gin had become friends, he really had no idea who she was talking about. Jayes rolled her eyes at him.

"I don't know if that's a good idea green eyes. She is quite ill besides, I don't want you getting sick."

"Please, please let me see her. I am sure she is worried about me," Jayes pleaded. "It might be good for her. I promise I won't stay long."

"Okay. How can I say no to you?" James smiled and held his arms out as an invitation.

Jayes nearly leapt from the bed and ran towards him as he stood in the open doorway. She felt a large gust of wind as he led her down the small corridor to a nearby door. Jayes could hear the sails flapping as they caught wind, falling down and then flying again with another gust.

James opened the door "I'll be right back. I'm expecting visitors. I need to make sure everything is ready and prepared for their visit. I'll be only a few minutes then I'll take you back to our cabin."

Visitors? Jayes realized what he meant. They must have reached Jamestown.

"We are here?" She asked in complete shock.

"Yes we arrived early this morning," he answered.

Jayes was in a daze, she felt as though reality had just punched her. She walked through the door and into the room, she saw Gin lying on the bed and stopped suddenly.

Gin was only skin and bones and so very pale. As the door closed behind her she walked closer to Gin and sat in the chair next to the bed. She touched her hand, breathing a sigh of relief to find it was warm, she had been half expecting it to be cold.

Gin opened her eyes, smiling to see Jayes sitting at her bedside. "You're alive," she softly breathed, in shock as she tried to sit up.

"No, save your strength," Jayes said, gently pushing Gin back down onto the pillow. "Yes, I am the only one who survived from that horrible day," she replied with a feeling of guilt.

"Andrew, the little boy, and his mother?" Gin asked, already knowing the answer. Jayes felt a lump in her throat unable to say the words out loud. She merely shook her head. She would never tell anyone what happened that day. Never would she speak the horrors aloud to a living soul.

"That poor boy," Gin spoke softly in her weakened state.

"He is in a better place," Jayes said as she took the ladle next to the bed and filled it with water. She stood up and gently fed Gin. She used the hem of her gown to wipe the few spilled drops from Gin's neck.

"How did I come to be here?" Gin asked. "Did they finally realize I was English or did you have a hand in saving me?

"To be honest," Jayes tried to explain. "I truly wish I would have mentioned you sooner to the Captain." Jayes did feel guilty. "I really wasn't sure what would happen if I mentioned that you were English and of good birth. It could have made your fate worse."

"How could that be? What is to be my fate?" she asked. Jayes knew she really had no idea.

In reality, Jayes didn't either. She could not imagine what either of their lives would be like when they stepped onto Virginia soil. She remembered the chains she saw and was beginning to understand their intended purpose. She certainly was not going to tell Gin, she was too young, too innocent and too fragile.

"I started to trust the Captain, so I told him about you," Jayes said. "I no longer believed that he would harm you and I knew that you were in danger where you were. I merely hinted than an English Lady had been kidnapped by mistake. I had been afraid they would single you out in a bad way. I do believe that was a foolish fear and you are safe now."

Gin's eyes lit up. "Is he going to bring me home to Wales?"

Jayes did not want to give her false hope. "I do not believe that will happen, Gin," Jayes said firmly. "I do believe that your station could save you from much suffering, I don't know exactly but I am sure it will not be as bad as it could have been."

"If that is so I promise that I will become your champion Jayes Mackey, as you have been mine." Gin smiled at her and squeezed her hand.

The door opened and James stood there. Jayes smiled at him, as she stood she leaned in to kiss Gin's forehead. "You rest now. I will visit you soon," she said as she quickly looked at James for permission.

He was smiling also. He nodded his head that she would be allowed to come back and visit. He was not so horrible after all, Jayes thought.

SIX
Jamestown, Virginia – October 15, 1627

Jayes had visited Gin almost every day without James knowing. He was very busy preparing for the 'sale' of his cargo. He had also stopped locking the door, and was no longer concerned she would run away. She had thought that since they had reached shore, that perhaps he would begin locking it again. Relations between them were strained and they had little conversation.

Jayes read the papers that he had been preparing. There were indentured, servitude and prisoner contracts between the unfortunate prisoners and the London Company. Jayes had glanced at them but could not finish reading, it was too upsetting to her.

According to the papers, there was going to be a sale. A sale of 'Cargo'. Jayes had seen the announcements that had been distributed in town. It was a sickening thought what these poor people were going to go through. She was beginning to question again who James really was. Was she right about him, was he good in his heart? Or was he a merchant of flesh? She could not believe that, even with the proof, in writing that was sitting before her. The path to hell was paved with good intentions, he was delivering them to hell, even if it was for the greater good of England, did he just not realize it? How could he not realize it?

The proof was lying on the table she told herself. Yet she still refused to believe it. No, she still refused to think badly of him. She picked up the papers and turned them over. If she couldn't see them, they were not there. She walked away as though they no longer existed and put it out of her mind.

On the fourth day after their arrival, she sensed that something was horribly wrong. She had not slept all night and she knew James had not slept either. They lay in bed together, yet separate, both wrapped in silence pretending sleep.

Early the next morning, before the sun rose, Jayes awoke with the feeling of impending doom. As though revelations were upon her. She sat up in bed sweating and shaking.

James opened the door, slowly closing it behind him. He was staring at the floor for several minutes before he even looked at her. It had seemed like an eternity.

He did not speak, he did not have to, she knew. She somehow just knew. Jayes could not cry. The feelings inside her were far deeper than just mere tears. Every hope that she had was now forever lost. Hope was completely gone. She knew, just looking at him, at his expression that her fate was far worse than death.

Jayes took a deep breath in, and stood up. Meticulously she shook the wrinkles from her dress that she had slept in, and placed her hands out in front of her. "Let's get on with it, shall we," she said in a choked voice.

James did not speak. Again he lowered his head and started at his feet. She could see his hands trembling.

"I understand," she practically screamed at him, not meaning to. "Please, if you have to do this…" she paused, trying to find the words. She couldn't.

He looked at her. "Jayes, I am sorry."

"Of course you are. So am I. Can we please get on with it? Let us get this over with!"

"Jayes, you need to remove your clothes. All of them," James said, reluctantly. She could hear the remorse in his voice.

Jayes was in shock when his words registered. Her legs nearly gave way. She balanced herself quickly and sat back down on the bed.

"Naked?" she asked in disbelief.

"You will not be the only one. They are all naked," James said quickly, grasping for anything that might make him feel better for what he was about to do to her.

"So you were right, you had been honest with me when you said that we are not even as valuable as cattle. Therefore we should be treated as such!" She glared at him with contemp.

Jayes was now angry, no longer shocked, she almost hated him in this moment. She was angry at the world, angry at Mrs. McDougal. Angry at the Judge. Angry at her cow, because she had not produced milk.

She frantically began stripping her clothes off, she heard the sounds of cloth tearing as she carelessly lifted her gown over her head and threw it at James.

"I am now naked for inspection, Sir. Are you happy?" she seethed.

He started to take a step towards her. She lifted her arms to stop him. "Do not come near me," she shouted. Tears of humiliation and defeat filled her eyes.

"I do not belong to you. Is that not what you said? You must sell me because I am not yours? You took me as yours, yet I do not belong to you?" Her words were so full of hate. Yet she did not hate James even though she knew that she should.

"Jayes, I have made the best arrangements possible for you.

I have done everything I can to help you." James was pleading with his eyes for her to understand. "I am going to do more. I am going to come back for you. I promise."

Jayes took two quick steps towards him. She was only inches away. "So I should be grateful, James? Do not bother. I am much better off without your help!" She said with deliberate spite. "Have you lost your mind? Do you think I have lost mine?" She glared at him. "I am not grateful. I never want to see you again!"

She walked to the door and waited. James said nothing. He opened the door and stepped aside. Jayes glanced at him briefly seeing a tear drop rolling down his cheek.

She almost came undone. She wanted to jump into his arms – tell him she understood. She wanted to tell him she would always love him.

She turned and climbed the ladder instead. She told herself he was better off thinking that she hated him.

When they reached the deck Jayes saw the iron chains around the necks of all of the prisoners. In their nakedness you could see almost every bone in their body. They were all so thin and sickly looking. Jayes had never seen anyone so bad off – not even a beggar. She felt guilty, that she had not suffered with them.

"Jayes."

She looked around and saw Gin calling her. She was jumping with her hand in the air trying to get her attention. The sun was beginning to rise.

"Over here, Jayes," Gin said. Then she turned to one of the sailors who immediately came towards Jayes.

"Come here, girl." He followed, yelling at her. "Where are your chains?"

She heard James yelling at the man from behind her. "She

gets her wrists bound. That's it. She has a contract."

The short, round, and dirty sailor grumbled. He looked around and was gone from sight. He reappeared with metal chains in his hands that he quickly attached roughly to Jayes wrists. He grabbed her forearm and led her towards Gin.

"It's going to be okay." Gin smiled. "Thanks to the Captain, I am being given in marriage to a successful Plantation owner. I am sure he will be handsome! I will have my own home!" Gin could not hide her excitement.

Jayes could not get past her nakedness, or that Gin had not even noticed. Then, she suddenly realized Gin was beautifully dressed. The difference between the Irish and the English, Jayes felt ill again.

"Captain James has vouched for my character. I am to marry! Did you hear me?" Gin continued waiting for congratulations from Jayes. "He is making the final arrangements right now. You will be my servant! That should make you happy!"

"I am happy for you, Gin. I am happy that we can stay together." Gin's maid? Is that what James had meant? Jayes was skeptical. Had James really changed her fate for the better? And if he had, why hadn't he just told her what his plans had been?

Suddenly there was a commotion. The prisoners started moving. The round sailor grumbled and they were led down the plank.

As Jayes' bare feet touched the cool, strange colored dirt of this new land, she was shamefully aware of her nakedness.

She was startled when she heard a shot, and jumped forward into Gin. The crowd slowly became silent, she stopped and looked around. She could still see the ship, hear its familiar sounds. They were standing against the banks of the river.

Jayes wanted to retreat back to the ship that she had at one time dreaded.

There were several strangely dressed people and a few tan half-dressed people of which she had never seen before. They were all beginning to approach the chained and naked prisoners that were being lined up near the shore.

There were rattling noises and whistles coming from all around her, as though the trees were talking in this strange land. She was scared, she did not want to be here, and she felt an emptiness, a heavy numbing type of pain. Her body was physically ill and heavy, and her heart beat strangely. Was it a sin to wish for death? Yes, she thought, she knew it was.

"She's a pretty one," a man said as he approached her with an evil smile. He reminded her of Mr. McDougal.

"This one is sold," the round man who had chained her said in his grumpy tone. "Go find sumthin' over there." He pointed to the other prisoners. "Fatten one of them up."

Jayes looked at Gin, she was scanning the crowd. Gin moved closer to Jayes and quickly said, "Which one of those handsome men do you think will be my husband?"

Jayes looked but could not speak. She could not understand how Gin could be so excited. Did she not understand what was happening?

"Gin, do you think you could get me some clothes?" she whispered hopefully.

"Oh, Jayes," Gin said. "I do not think that would be appropriate right now." She seemed upset she had been bothered. "You are, after all, a prisoner, a servant. I think you should just not worry about that right now."

Gin dismissed her and began scanning the crowd again. "He is handsome," she said pointing. "I hope he is the one."

Jayes could not find any handsome man in the crowd,

instead she spotted the man who had approached her. He was now inspecting the teeth, not so gently, of a young girl who looked horrified.

Jayes thought she was losing her mind, she could not stand here and watch her people being treated like animals, naked and inspected like livestock. It was too much for her. Where was James? What were these strange sounds? What was she doing here? Why couldn't she have just drowned in the ocean with everyone else that day and been spared this hell. "I am in hell," Jayes said aloud, Gin just looked at her briefly and went back to scanning for her husband, unconcerned.

"The auction will begin," a man yelled.

Jayes couldn't see him through all of the tears in her eyes.

"Political prisoners from Ireland. Irish servants. A healthy cargo!" There were some guffaws from the crowd. "No murderers or rapists. There are many men, women and boys as you can see. A blacksmith, tradesmen, carpenters, even a silversmith. House servants. A reasonable credit will be allowed and head-rights. The usual contract of seven years. About a hundred suitable workers. Let the bidding begin!"

Jayes felt sick. He sounded as though he was selling oxen, not people. Only one hundred? She knew there had been at least three or four hundred when they had left Ireland. So many had not made it, she wondered if they were the lucky ones. She was mixed with emotions. She was unsure if she should feel bad for them or happy that they were in a better place.

"I'll give you thirty-five pounds of t'bacca for these three on the end," a man shouted out.

"Sold!"

"Forty-five pounds for that man and that girl," another man exclaimed.

"I'll give you ten pounds for this lass," a familiar voice said.

Jayes looked over. It was the McDougal man.

"Fifteen," countered the auctioneer.

"But she's bone. It'll take me that just to fatten her up," the man complained. The poor girl looked terrified.

Jayes couldn't look. She wanted to close her ears but her hands were still chained.

"Fine, fifteen," the man said angrily. "Ya better be worth it," he said as the girl was unchained and released to her new 'owner.'

Jayes wondered...did that make Gin her 'owner'? Is that what James meant when he said, 'I did all I could.' She wasn't actually going to be 'sold.' She would be Gin's ladies' maid? Why couldn't he have just explained?

Jayes saw James walking towards her. He was not alone. He was not smiling. He looked angry.

"Take her chains off now!" James yelled before he was even close. The round man instantly started to take the chains off her wrists.

"Put these on," James said as he tossed her the same gown that she had thrown at him over an hour ago. Had he held onto it this entire time? Why even have her undress at all?

Jayes couldn't look at him. She wasted no time dressing.

"Mr. John Turner, this is Guinever Sinclair," James introduced Gin to a very thin, tall man. He wore an odd black hat. Heavy wool clothes that seemed way too hot in these temperatures. A white fluffed shirt that seemed old and dirty. He had long front teeth, too large for his mouth. Dull, thin, wavy hair that fell nearly to his shoulders.

Gin was obviously not impressed. She forced a fake smile and merely held her hand out to him. He did not take it. Surprisingly, he did not seem impressed either. His eyes went to Jayes and he gave her a genuine smile.

JAYES – 1627

Gin turned to look at her when she realized where his gaze had strayed. "This is my servant. Is she welcome in our home, sir?" she asked her soon to be husband.

"Of course. There is not much room yet, our home is still being constructed, added onto, as well as some out buildings. I have obtained a plantation up the river. I have hopes the land will be fruitful," he said proudly.

"It had been abandoned after the massacre and had shown great promise. It should take no time at all to get 'er rebuilt and runnin' again. Been working on it myself. Day and night and its comin out more than fine ma'am." He smiled. He was obviously proud of his efforts and accomplishments.

Gin smiled happily at that. She asked with excitement. "Is it a large mansion? A large plantation?"

He laughed instantly as though she had grown a tail. "No ma'am, you aren't gonna find that here." He could not stop laughing. Gin was deeply offended. Jayes wondered if this marriage should even happen.

Jayes finally got a look around Jamestown and her surroundings as they started walking. There were several ships docked in the river. The little town was made almost completely of very simple wooden structures. The fort stood near the docks, a triangle shaped fort. Inside was a large church, some barracks, storage houses, and a few private dwellings. Only the church was built of brick. It was obvious it was fairly new and there was still some construction being done on it.

The men started walking in. James reached out for Jayes' hand. He quickly pulled her away. She glared at him. Her heart was broken by the look on his face. He had an expression of deep pain.

Jayes told herself again this was best for him. He would be

better off thinking she hated him if he really did love her. If this was all he could do and he had actually improved her fate, he was still better off.

If he looked pained because he was simply guilty, then he deserved to believe she hated him. She wished she knew which one it was. Perhaps it would make her feel better.

They entered the brick church. She could smell the newly constructed wooden floors, walls, benches, tables, even the rafters still gave off a fresh scent. Jayes had always enjoyed the sweet smell of freshly cut wood.

The wedding was over in a matter of minutes, no formal ceremony, no flowers, no dress. Jayes felt as though Gin had been cheated.

Suddenly James started laughing, and he moved closer to her. Much too close she thought. His lips were nearly touching her ear, she could feel his breath on her neck. He sniffed her. Jayes mistook that and thought perhaps she stunk, she sniffed herself too. James laughed again.

"You're refreshing, Jayes. I love you, do not ever forget that," he whispered into her ear.

Jayes stood there in shock just looking at him. The look in his eyes was full of love, she knew he was not lying to her about that. She wanted to jump in his arms and never leave them, she wanted to beg him to take her away from here. Was it her pride that kept her from doing so? Damn her pride she thought, as she remained silent.

"Next time I will have a feather bed in our room just for you." He smiled.

"Will there be a next time?"

"Yes, Jayes. Be strong, wait for me and believe in me. Do not get near those savages, stay in the house as much as you can," he said taking her hand in his.

"Well, Captain James," Mr. Turner approached him. "Thank you," he said shaking his hand. "If this venture works out I think we will all be better off. It was a pleasure meeting you."

"Just keep your end of the bargain, Mr. Turner," James said in a warning tone.

Jayes so badly wanted to confront him. Find out what bargain he had made. She knew she couldn't. She had to bite her lip.

"I shall see you within the year, Captain James," he said awkwardly. He then turned to Gin, "Shall we? I believe the reverend is waiting for our signatures.

Gin grabbed Jayes' arm. Despite her excitement earlier, she now looked horrified.

Jayes turned back to look at James. He put his hand on his heart and mouthed the words 'trust me.'

As he walked out the doors Jayes cried. She could not stop her tears. She felt as though her chest was hollow.

"I'm scared too," Gin confessed. "Don't worry, I will be fine, he looks decent enough."

Jayes didn't know how to reply.

After signing the necessary documents, they made their way towards the back of the church and down towards the river. Jayes searched for James but she couldn't find him.

She was helped into a small, odd looking boat. The boat rocked back and forth. It was much smaller than the ship they had come in. It was more than half the size and painted with odd colors. It only had two sails and there was barely room to stand on the deck. It smelled of sweet and rot at the same time. Jayes held on to the sides for dear life as she sat down.

Two young men sat in front of her and another two behind her to guide the vessel.

"We're going home," Mr. Turner said to Gin smiling. She

did not reply. Neither of them were smiling now. Jayes brushed Gin's attitude off, she was tired and still not recovered from her time on the ship.

The sun was high in the sky and the rays made the water glisten and the trees come to life in the most magnificent way. Jayes had never seen anything like it. It was so beautiful. Was this a sign from God? Jayes knew only God could create such heavenly colors.

Jayes stared at the shoreline as the small boat slowly made its way up river, Gin sat next to her and laid her head down in Jayes lap. Jayes slowly drifted off to sleep.

Surprised she had fallen asleep Jayes awoke as the sun was setting. Gin sat up and rubbed her eyes, they must have been traveling for quite some time. They began turning back towards shore. Jayes thought they were close, they must be, as they had traveled into the night. As they entered, yet another opening they steered towards what she thought was another river. Darkness was all that surrounded them now. Jayes could see sparkles of light flash and disappear. She was mesmerized with these bugs of light.

A loud rumble came to life from the sky. Lightning flew down and struck nearby with the loudest bang she had ever heard. Gin grabbed hold of her hand. Jayes had to let go of her grip on the side of the boat to pry Gin's grip loose, she had been squeezing so hard her hand was nearly numb.

The boat was rocking hard side to side, rain poured down with painful speed. The water seemed to get rougher, they were soaking wet and cold.

"God seems to have disappeared and the devil has taken over," Jayes said aloud. There was rattling and hissing coming from all around them. Crackling and what seemed like screams filled the air.

Through everything she had endured, except almost being tossed to her death in the ocean, this was the most scared she had ever been. She wished that James was here with her now, she felt safe with him. She closed her eyes and prayed.

Jayes heard shouting and opened her eyes, seeing people standing on the shore guiding them in to a clearing of grass cut out along the bank of the river. Looking at the crude landing she wondered if this was a sign of what to expect? Would they be isolated in this wilderness, living in a roughly constructed dwelling, not the spaciousness of the plantation home Gin was expecting?

The people waiting on the shore were young, most of them poorly dressed. One tall, skinny boy waded out and began to swim towards their small vessel. A large thick rope was tied to him, which he and another man quickly tied to the front of the ship. The people on shore began to pull, slowly turning them as other men were running around, tossing anchors into the water.

"Out," Mr. Turner started shouting. They lowered a plank that led directly to the water.

The men that were sitting behind Jayes walked down and jumped, quickly swimming towards shore.

"You're not going to carry me?" Jayes had heard Gin ask. She turned. Mr. Turner began laughing.

"Of course not, you will swim like the rest of us."

"I cannot swim!" Gin cried frantically.

Mr. Turner laughed again. "Well you had better learn quickly. I do not want to be a widower before the honeymoon," he joked, all the remaining men on board started laughing as well. He then made a show of pushing Gin into the water.

She screamed. Jayes saw her head slip under and she quickly jumped in after her. Gin was thrashing about frantic. Trying to hold onto her, pushing Jayes under.

She grabbed ahold of Gin's hair and swam, yelling at her. "Stop moving or I will let you drown! I am going to grab onto you and swim you to shore but keep your hands off me or we will both drown!"

Jayes grabbed Gin's shoulders and swam backwards towards shore. It was not far but the struggle with Gin had completely exhausted her.

They walked upstream, and finally reached their destination. The sun surely would show itself shortly.

As she had that thought, the little light left began to fade, the sky turning black as the moon completely disappeared. The wind began to blow so hard Jayes found it difficult to walk, the trees started to sway and creek. A Witch's storm like she had never seen before came alive.

As they entered the tiny house Mr. Turner called home, it began to shake. They had made it inside just as the sky lit up with furor.

When the light came she nearly jumped when she saw what looked like wild animals all around her.

Mr. Turner pointed to a small area on the floor.

"You sleep there," he said as he grabbed Gin by the arm and led her out of the room.

Jayes knelt down and nearly fell over when she felt her way to what was to be her bed. She felt fur! She screamed in fear. The sky lit up again and she was relieved to see that it was merely an animal skin, nothing crawling or alive.

She wrapped the fur around herself and then went and hid under the wooden table that was in the center of the room.

Another loud rumble that seemed to go on forever made Gin scream from the next room. It was followed by a big boom and even the table seemed unsteady.

Gin ran out of the room and cuddled up next to Jayes.

JAYES – 1627

"I hate it here. I hate that man. I hate this barn. I hate this land!" she said as she wept on Jayes' belly. Jayes just held her. "I want to go home. I want England."

"It will be okay," Jayes assured her. "James is coming back for me. Maybe he can take you back to England.

Gin sat up. "James?" she asked confused.

"The captain," Jayes told her.

"You mean Tristam? Captain Tristam James, that awful man who sold us?" Gin said angrily.

"Yes," Jayes said absently. His name was Tristam?

"Yes, he's coming back, you fool!" Gin screamed at her angrily. "Not to save us though! He is coming back to get what belongs to him. His land and his slaves!"

"What do you mean? He found us a safe place to stay, the safest place, we are not to be slaves like the others. He did all he could." Jayes was so confused. "He said I could trust him."

"My 'husband' told me all about the 'bargain' Captain James made with him. He 'gave' us to him to use, me as a wife and you as a servant." Gin spat. "We were bartered!"

Gin slammed her fist down onto the floor. "My service is a lifetime beneath that filthy man! I would have been better off sold as a servant! Instead, in the eyes of God, I am bound to that horrible man for life!"

"What do you mean?" Jayes asked, Gin had been so happy earlier.

"We are head-rights you fool! We are these filthy men's workers, their slaves and oh I am a WIFE! Mr. Turner promised to make Captain James' plantation habitable and purchase a certain amount of servants on his return. Only half of which he will claim as head-rights, the other half he will give to my husband for the work he has done. It will ensure Captain James enough land to start his own plantation. In exchange, I am free, his wife to do whatever he wishes." Gin was torn between anger and tears. "Or at least free of charge to him. I will never be free again."

Jayes still did not really make sense of what Gin was saying. She was just angry right now and of course she would blame James. This was not his fault, he had helped them. It could have been much worse, she knew that. Gin would realize that soon.

What bothered her was his name. Was his name James? How could she not even know his name? How could Gin know something like that and not her?

"Tristam?" Jayes said aloud to hear his name.

"May he rot in the pit of hell," Gin spat.

She remained quiet, she could not reason with an angry Gin. Instead she listened to the wind and focused on the sudden cracks of the thunder. She did not want to think about Ireland, Virginia or Captain James. Even thinking seemed to hurt and be painful these days, there were no thoughts that seemed peaceful.

Seven
And so it begins… Life in the New World

The next morning, Mr. Turner came out of the room and walked out the front door without saying a word. The wind and rain was still somewhat strong but the witch's storm had ceased.

A few minutes later he walked back in with two young boys.

"Girl!" he looked directly at Jayes, "Go with them. They will show you what to do. Be quick!"

Jayes jumped up from her spot under the table. She was wrapped and tangled between the fur and Gin. Gin was not being as quick at getting up.

"I said be quick, girl!" he yelled again.

Gin was finally awake and looked around. "I need my maid with me," she said.

"You do not have a maid," he said rudely. The friendly Mr. Turner that she had met yesterday was gone.

Seeing him now, made her believe Gin had been telling the truth earlier when she described him as "awful."

As she left the little house the door slammed shut behind her. She followed the two boys around the house and into the woods behind it.

"Watch where ya walk," the taller of the two boys told her.

They were dressed alike and both were thin. They both had the touch of the sun's glow on their skin, and light blonde hair. Jayes thought they were brothers.

"Why?" is all she asked as she watched the ground.

"There are snakes, lots of them," the shorter boy said.

Jayes stopped walking. The tallest boy turned around and asked, "What's wrong?"

"I hate snakes. I don't want to go in there."

"Ye don't have a choice. Ye take a chance with the snakes or ye will get bit by the whip."

Jayes still didn't move. The word 'whip' hit her like a bee sting.

"The snakes are big. Ye can't miss them. 'Sides," the short boy explained, "they're fraid of us as much and they rattle, you'll see 'em for they bite ya."

"And stink, before they bite, oh do they stink. You'll know they're there. Just watch your step," the taller boy confirmed. "Come on. It's Okay. Better to take ye chances with the snakes than to cross the Master."

Jayes started walking again. "What are your names?" she asked, carefully scanning the ground looking for any movement beneath the fallen leaves.

"My name is Will and that is John," the taller boy said.

"Are you brothers?"

"No," Will said "Are ye Irish?" he asked.

"Yes I am. What are you?"

"English. Well we were Englishmen. I don't think I'll ever see England again."

"Are your families here?"

"No we was orphans. That's why we got sent here. Now we are just here to serve Master Turner along with the filthy convicts," John said.

JAYES – 1627

"Yeah, being an orphan makes ye as unwanted in England as convicts. I'm glad we're not there. England changed with the Stuarts."

Will reached forward and gave him a shove on his shoulder. "Shush your mouth John. Don't say that. England is much better. We had freedom there."

"We will have freedom here."

"No, we won't. We will never be free," he said sadly. After a few minutes he asked Jayes, "Why are you here?"

"I'm a convict, I guess."

Neither boy said anything. They walked in silence.

They stopped in a small clearing. Will pointed to a nearby tree. "Ye go do that one," he snapped.

"Do what? Call me Jayes, not ye," she snapped back.

Will looked irritated as he looked at John with a 'get to work' warning. "I have to show her what to do." He stomped over to the tree picking up an odd looking basket that was laying on the ground.

"See these berries?" he asked her sarcastically. "You pick it up off the ground here, then you put it in the basket. Don't pick up any rotten ones, just the fresh fallen. Can ye do that?" He did not wait for an answer; he went to his own tree.

Jayes wanted to cry. Not even the servants wanted to be her friends. She was completely alone in this country they called Virginia.

Jayes was having a hard time seeing the berries, her eyes were so full of tears. She was surprised when she saw another hand reaching for the same berry she was about to pick up.

Jayes looked and stood up. She knew this must be an Indian. She was a girl! She took a frightened step backwards and stared at her.

Her skin was dark from the sun, much darker than Will and

John. Her hair was black and long. Her clothing was leather and a bit sparse, Jayes noted.

"*Keihtascrooc!*" the Indian girl screamed, quickly stepping behind the tree. Jayes watched, she saw the fear in the girl's eyes and panicked, she turned to run.

"*Keihtascrooc!*" she screamed again, pointing to a pile of leaves near Jayes, the pile moved slightly. She smelled a sweet smell in the air suddenly and tried to remember what the boys had said. *Smell...Snakes*, Jayes' eyes widened, there was a snake near her feet! She was frozen with fear, what was she supposed to do?

Suddenly another Indian appeared, seemingly out of nowhere. He moved so quickly and the snake was dead, headless, before Jayes could blink her eyes.

The Indian stood holding the dead snake's body triumphantly. She was so grateful, that she had forgot to be scared of this *heathen warrior* that she had been warned about.

As she rushed towards him, she was lifted off the ground and in his arms before she took her second step.

"*Mattah, tah,*" he shouted looking down at her. He tossed her a couple of feet away, where she easily landed on her feet. He kneeled down and pointed to the snake's head.

The snake's beady eyes blended with the snakes' dirt like color as they seemed to be staring directly at Jayes. It's mouth wide open. Jayes was shocked to see the two long, curved fangs inside the snake's pink mouth facing up.

She realized that she had been very close to stepping on it, she could have been killed. Shocked, she looked up at the Indian who had now saved her life, twice, in a matter of moments.

"Thank you," she said with genuine gratitude. Jayes was surprised, the Indian did not look pleased. He showed no sign of being proud, more accurately, he appeared to be quite angry.

The Indian girl, stepped out from behind the tree. She was giggling as she skipped forward with a thick stick. She started poking at the snake. When a gold liquid started to drain from the snake's tooth, the girl took a large leaf and let the poison drain into it.

This lasted a few minutes. Jayes took a step closer to watch. When she was done she ceremoniously presented the leaf to Jayes. She had no wish to be anywhere near the snake's venom. She took a step backwards refusing to take the leaf.

This seemed to anger the Indian even more. He grunted and glared at Jayes. He took a step closer and put out his hand motioning her towards the Indian girl.

"To give to Cuttmwa," she said. "You must thank him for your life. Give him *Tascoo* as a gift."

"Tascoo?" Jayes asked.

"Tascoo, the life of the snake," she said as though Jayes should understand.

Reluctantly Jayes stepped forward taking the leaf. Very carefully she turned and walked towards Cuttmwa with the leaf and the poison held as far from her body as she could manage.

Jayes heard a scream and saw John running, not far away. He lost his footing and fell forward every couple of steps he took. Jayes giggled, which shook the leaf. Some of the golden fluid ran onto her second finger. Her eyes widened in fear. The Indian looked impatient, he came forward and took the leaf from her.

"Thank you," she said, wondering if she should say more, or bow. She wasn't sure, and didn't have to wonder long. They both turned and the Indians were quickly out of sight, almost as though they had vanished into thin air.

Jayes looked at her thumb not knowing what could happen.

She quickly wiped it on her dress, then regretted it. She bent over and wiped her dress off in wet mud.

"That will have to do. Please God, spare my life," she prayed. Almost immediately she questioned her request, did she really want her life to be spared? Jayes shook her head, she did not have time to question her request to God or to debate with herself. She took off, running after John.

She found him sitting at the beginning of the trail on his knees, praying. He heard her and ran towards her, quickly embracing her in his arms. John kept looking at her as though he doubted his eyes.

"You're alive! They did not kill you? Or scalp you?" John asked as he put his hand on Jayes head, assuring himself that she still had her entire scalp intact.

"Of course I am alive. Why wouldn't I be?" Jayes asked.

"The heathens," John explained as if that was all the explanation needed. "They collect the hair of the white people."

"Don't be silly John, they're not heathens. As a matter of fact they saved my life!" Jayes said as she started walking down the last of the path. "Where is Thomas? Is he waiting for us at "home?" she asked and stopped.

Home, tears came to Jayes eyes slowly at the thought. This was not her home. It would never be her home. John caught up to Jayes. She looked down as he took her hand.

"We call it the hut," John said. "That's what it is. It is straw and clay and sand. A little wood. It has a nice roof. We sleep there, that's all it is."

John was struggling for more words. Jayes knew what he was doing and smiled to herself. Jayes squeezed his hand "It has tree branches on top of mud walls, would you really call that a roof, or even a house for that matter?"

John looked up smiling, "Naa."

"Thank you, John," she murmured as she bent down and kissed the top of his head. "Race you to the hut!" she yelled as she took off running.

As Jayes came flying through the trees with John close on her heels, a hand reached out and grabbed her wrist.

Jayes body kept a forward motion but was pulled backwards by the grasp on her wrist. Jayes fell backwards in slow motion landing hard on her backside.

"Where have you been?" Jayes looked up to see Gin screaming at her angrily.

"The woods, I was collecting berries," Jayes answered, confused. She began to stand and brush herself off. Jayes felt a hand sting across her face. She looked up at Gin. She had slapped her!

"Why?" Jayes looked at her in complete confusion.

"You should have been back hours ago!" she screamed at Jayes. Gin turned towards John. "You're lucky I don't have you whipped, boy! Go fetch the water, now!"

"What is wrong with you?" Jayes asked Gin, why was she acting so strange?

Gin turned on her. "You! You are what's wrong with me!" Gin gave Jayes a hard shove on her chest with both hands. Her face twisted with hate.

"I know!" Gin seethed. "I know you were the Captain's whore! I was too much of a lady to mention it before. You just disgust me!"

Jayes shook her head in denial. How could she explain? She opened her mouth to speak, before a word even got out Gin slapped her again. This time with such a force that Jayes saw flashes of light before her eyes, there was a sharp pain on her lips. She noticed a large amount of blood dripping from her mouth.

"Tell me Jayes, did you really think if you pointed me out to the Captain he would reward you?" Gin screamed at her unaffected by the blood she had caused.

"No he tried to help you. I did help you Gin, I would never hurt you," Jayes said confused why Gin would be so cruel to her.

"You call this help?" As she quickly moved her hands from her chest downwards. "Do you call that helping me?" Gin asked as she quickly turned and pointed to the clay huts. "That man," Gin cried, "that awful man is helping me?" Gin's voice began to crack.

Jayes moved forward to console her. Gin swung back around. A tear in her eye, but hatred covered her face.

"Do not touch me. I do not need anything from you. You are a whore Jayes Mackey! I curse the day I met you. I would be better off if they had tossed you overboard!" Gin screamed at her. "You are my slave, bought and paid for. You are not my friend. Never forget that!" Gin turned and walked towards the house.

Jayes could not move. She could not speak. She just stood there watching Gin walk away and cried.

Jayes could not eat, her teeth had cut into the bottom of her lip leaving a small hole on the outside and the inside of her bottom lip completely raw and torn. A tooth had penetrated the skin, leaving her lip so swollen she could see it when she looked down.

She could not help but to touch it with her tongue, making the healing slow and bringing a fresh flow of blood that she could taste. Jayes tried to tell herself to not touch it but instantly her tongue returned to massaging the wounds.

Jayes moved her finger up to feel the swollen bottom lip. It felt like dirt, she realized when she moved her finger to wipe the dirt away that she had rubbed off the scab and a new tenderness was instant. She looked at her finger and saw the red blood.

Jayes dared not touch it again, she just lay on her pillow feeling the warmth of the fresh blood and tears as they rolled down her face. She wanted to close her eyes and wake up in Ireland. Please let this be a dream she begged God silently over and over until she finally fell asleep.

JANUARY 1628

It had not been a dream, none of this was a dream and Jayes realized she either had to suffer miserably or try to survive in hopes someday she could find her way home.

Jayes chose survival. She made a private vow to herself that someday she would go home. She refused to die in this place called Virginia. She refused to allow her captors or her enemies to choose her fate. Most of all she refused to let them break her spirit.

She was raised to stand strong against adversity, the Irish had overcome hardships for hundreds of years. She was up to the challenge. She would make her family and countrymen proud.

Nothing had changed between Jayes and Gin in the following weeks after the attack. Jayes realized that she may have misjudged who Gin really was. She had assumed she had been wronged by her Da's family, maybe they knew the real Gin and it was Jayes who had made a mistake in trusting her.

Gin had her scrubbing the floors, carrying buckets of water from the river, sweeping dirt that had been swept, cleaning the chimney. She was working before the sun rose and long after it had set. The weather had turned chilly and cold. Snow, or what

Jayes was told was snow, fell from the sky and had covered the ground for many weeks.

It was beautiful. It was white and covered the trees and the ground. It was so amazing. Jayes could sit and watch it fall for hours, forgetting where she was and just feeling a happiness that had been gone for so long.

Jayes was now sleeping in the small hut with John, Thomas and several other servants. The weather was still cold but it seemed to be getting warmer with each day.

She was thankful she was so busy and too tired to think. As Jayes finished beating Gin's gown and setting fresh water out for morning she made her way to the sleeping hut. She could hear the trickling of the water from the nearby river.

Jayes had worked for days with little sleep. Every muscle and bone in her body ached. Nearly every inch of her skin was raw and bleeding. The bug bites that were swollen, infected and blistered covered her body from head to toe. Even her little toe looked like blisters from a pox.

The water called to her. She knew she would find relief from the sores in the cool water. She turned and made her way quietly down to the river. She had found a long stick to help her through the darkened trail. It also gave her comfort in case there was a snake waiting for her, although they were sparser this time of year.

Jayes found a rock and sat down. She put her feet into the river and felt instant relief in the coolness of the water as it gently massaged her sore muscles and tender skin.

Jayes heard a twig break behind her. She jumped up in fear, nearly falling into the water as she searched for the threat.

Jayes heard a giggle as the Indian girl peeped her head from around a tree.

"You could have killed me!" Jayes yelled in frustration. She turned back towards the river and settled herself back upon the rock. "You should not sneak up on people. I could have slipped, fallen, hit my head, broke my neck and drowned," she mumbled. The Indian girl just smiled and watched Jayes. She frowned when she saw the wounds on her feet and legs.

"I never got to thank you for saving my life," Jayes said. The girl seemed as though she did not understand. Jayes made the hand gesture of a snake slithering through the grass and biting.

"Thank you," Jayes said slowly and put her hands on her heart.

The Indian girl sat down beside her. She also put her feet into the water. She was still smiling.

"You do not understand, do you?" Jayes asked her, still annoyed.

"I understand," the girl said pointing to her own head. Jayes thought that was odd.

"I am Jayes," she said pointing to herself. "Who are you?" she asked.

The girl smiled again "I am Maybran," she giggled. "You are a silly fool," She finished with a bigger smile.

Jayes almost fell off her rock again. She regained her balance and stared at Maybran. Certainly she did not know what she was saying she thought, so Jayes corrected her.

"No, I am a girl. Ir-ish g-i-r-l," Jayes sounded it out.

"G-irl. Jay-ss."

Maybran giggle again and splashed her feet in the water, dipping her hands in she suddenly splashed Jayes in the face.

"Jayes the Ir-ish girl is a fool." Maybran said laughing as Jayes sputtered trying to get the water out of her eyes.

Jayes was actually shocked, she didn't know what to say in reply.

"You are awful mean! Just like the Colonists of this Virginia!" Jayes cried.

Maybran was instantly sober. "No. No I am not like the white skins," she said in perfect English.

"You speak English? You had me believing you could not understand me!" Jayes whined feeling deceived.

"I speak English yes. My village has had many white skins that have lived with us and taught us the white language."

Jayes thought about that. James had warned her to stay away from the Indians. Was this why? He was afraid they would kidnap her and force her to live their heathen life?

"Are you going to kidnap me?" Jayes asked. As she spoke the words she wondered if living with the Indians could be worse than living as Gin and Master Turners' slave.

"We do not kidnap." Maybran announced offended. "Your people, the white skins, great deceivers, liars and kidnappers. You take my people and kill them."

"I am not English. My people have never hurt your people. I was kidnapped, deceived by them!" Jayes pointed down the river towards Jamestown.

Both girls sat in silence thinking about what the other had said.

"In my country when someone thanks you for a good deed, it is polite to acknowledge their thanks," Jayes said watching the ripples form in the water.

"You are welcome. My people do not think it a great deed to save the life of a white skin." Maybran said, also watching the water.

"Is that why that Indian looked so angry?" Jayes asked. "Because he saved me?"

"Maybe," Maybran laughed. "My brother Cuttwma always looks angry."

JAYES – 1627

Jayes could not help but laugh, then remembering her brother she felt such loss a tear fell from her face.

"What is wrong?" Maybran asked.

"I miss my family. I miss Ireland. I miss my brother."

"Where is Ireland?" Maybran asked, "Is it by that Britannia? The country that deceived my people and name this land after their lie?"

"Britain?" Yes, that is England. My land is near England. They named this after Queen Elizabeth," Jayes said.

"Elizabeth no Virgin." Maybran mumbled.

"No, Elizabeth was her name. She never married, so they called her the 'Virgin Queen'" Jayes explained. Not understanding what Maybran was saying.

"I know, she was no Virgin, the Britannia people are deceptive and lie." Maybran explained.

Jayes did not know what to say. She could not speak badly of the dead. And she had heard rumors about the Queen and her lovers, but she did not know for certain one way or the other.

"We have King Charles now. He is a Scottish King, his Da' was Scottish, his grandmother was the Great Queen Mary of Scots, and may God rest her soul," Jayes said as she made the sign of the cross.

Maybran looked at her funny but did not say anything.

"Pocahontas, was my Aunt. She was murdered in England. She lies there still in unholy ground." Maybran said in such a sad and quiet voice.

"I have heard of Pocahontas. She was a Princess. Are you a Princess?" Jayes asked and then remembered her manners. "I am so sorry for your Aunt."

"My people were deceived, the white man came here and made friends. They tell tales of untruth. They smile and then be snakes in the grass." Maybran said. "We do not trust the white skin people," she said.

Jayes wondered if Maybran was trying to decide if she should be friends or kidnap Jayes. Honestly, Jayes was unsure which of the two would be preferable.

After some thought Jayes decided that she did not want to be kidnapped by the Indians. James would not know where to find her, and the children also needed her she thought.

Jayes stood up it was now nearly daylight. She swayed on her feet. Maybran caught her and steadied her with another serious look of concern.

"I am fine, thank you. Thank you again. I hope we can be friends," Jayes said.

Maybran thought for a moment, then she smiled. "Yes, friends."

Eight

Jayes went out of her way to avoid Gin. She could not understand this new hatred that she seemed to have for her, just thinking about it caused pains in her chest. They should be protecting each other, helping each other get through each day until James- or Tristam, she angrily corrected herself, returned. Instead, Gin had turned into her enemy. Jayes decided she could not keep thinking about it, the situation was killing her inside.

Every day she awoke before the sun. She would walk down to the river and carry buckets of water up to the house. Sometimes, John would help her. Together they would gather wood, boil the water and deliver it all before Gin was out of bed.

Gin had found a new girl she seemed to like, and had completely replaced Jayes. Luckily, she rarely even saw her anymore, except when it came to the water, which was too difficult a task for the new girl Elizabeth and somehow had become solely Jayes' chore.

Gin seemed to be happy that the new girl was English. She was very pretty with long blonde hair similar to Gin's, fair skin and a nice smile. Master Turner had purchased her from another ship only days after their arrival. Gin had taken to her almost instantly.

Elizabeth had moved into the main house that night, and Jayes found herself on the wooden floor with the other servants in the flea infested hut. There were 13 other servants in total sleeping in the small room.

John and Thomas were not the youngest. There was another little girl whose name was Arabette. She too was an English girl, although she proudly had the bright red, unruly, curly hair of her Irish mother. She thought she had been dreaming.

Jayes knew this because one night a stranger had come into the hut. Every night Jayes cried herself to sleep despite her sore and exhausted body. She could not help but wonder if her Mother cried for her as well. Did they miss her and mourn for her, pray for her return or had they forgotten about her? It had been months now since Jayes left Ireland.

Through her tears, Jayes saw a dark figure enter the small room. Jayes could only see an outline of a woman as the light of the moon washed over her body.

Jayes sat up, "Mummy. Is that you? Mummy?" Jayes laid back down, convinced she was seeing things. She knew it was not possible.

"I'm sorry, child," the figure spoke softly. Jayes slowly sat back up.

"Are you real?" Jayes asked still disbelieving her own eyes and ears.

"I hope that I am real, would be a shame to find out otherwise," the figure answered with amusement. "What a silly question you ask."

"I thought it was a silly dream," Jayes replied in defense.

The woman walked towards her. As she came forward allowing the light of the moon into the room, she was thin and tall with fiery red hair that curled about her head in an unruly fashion.

"You're Arabette's mother? You're Irish though."

"I am part Irish. I married an Englishman. Arabette is English." The woman sat down on the floor next to her daughter. "I have not seen you here before. You must be new. I am Emmie." She smiled sweetly.

"I suppose I am, I have been here a while though. I've lost track of time," Jayes replied. "The sun, it seems to shines for days here."

The woman laughed. "It must seem to you as though it does," she smiled. "The sun in this land shines longer and the nights are shorter than in Ireland."

Jayes did not quite understand, but she did not want to ask more questions and sound ignorant.

"Were you stolen from Ireland, too?" Jayes asked instead.

"No. My husband died fighting the King's war. His brother tricked me! I trusted him, he betrayed us, and he sold us for coin. He said we were vagrants and placed us on a ship. He took our freedom and all that my husband had left us. He is an evil man." There was so much sadness in her voice.

"He cannot do that!" Jayes cried. "That's not right! You cannot be sold. Go back to England and fight!"

"It's not that easy, someday you will understand. What is your name?" Emmie asked.

"Jayes."

"Jayes, this world is evil. There are evils all around us, especially here in this land. Evil men who help other evil men. All of them doing naught for what is right but only led by greed."

"I don't understand."

"You're young and naïve, you will understand soon enough. There is nothing I can do so I must accept my fate and trust in

God." Her voice cracked and she lowered her head. "And Bette's." She stared down and wrapped her daughter's red curls in between her fingers. She bent and kissed her daughter's head.

Jayes knew she was crying. "Even when you accept your own fate, it can still be so very painful."

MARCH 1628

Jayes had felt as though she had barely slept when Master Turner came barreling into the room wielding a stick.

"Get up. Get up you lazy dogs! It's time for you to earn your keep! Get up!" he hollered as he struck Jayes on the bottom of one foot, causing her to jump to avoid another strike.

She moved quickly towards Will and Arabette pushing them out the door. Both children were moving slowly. "Quickly!" she scolded them. It was too late. She felt the stick land across the middle of her back, causing her to drop to her knees.

Will and Arabette witnessed the attack. They took each other's hand and ran.

John grabbed Jayes by the arm and helped her crawl out. Jayes looked around quickly for the children, they were huddled together terrified.

That is when she saw him.

The largest man her eyes had ever seen, he was as tall as he was wide as an oak tree with skin as dark as the deepest of night.

As Jayes lay on the ground looking up at him, she could see the whip's tails falling about his feet. She saw it move, and then his feet began moving towards her.

Her instinct was to cover her face.

"Up girl!" she heard, from a deep voice which rumbled like

thunder. Jayes looked up and got to her feet quickly, never completely standing. She fell several times, catching herself with her hands on the rocky ground as she went towards Arabette and John.

"Listen," Master Turner shouted. "This is Corzara. He will oversee the fields. You will listen to him or he will force you to!" He laughed as though this was amusing to him.

"Get in line!" the man called Corzara yelled.

Jayes guided the children towards him. She had to push them several times in their reluctance.

Elizabeth came toward the front of the line. The whip cracked in the air – "Move!" he yelled in that deep, terrifying voice. As they moved forward, Elizabeth with a scowl, handed them each a small portion of bread. This was to be all they were given to fill their empty stomachs.

"Jayes I am cold. I cannot eat my bread with my mouth chattering so." The fields were not far away. Jayes finally began to feel the cold as she walked.

"Eat it Bett, you don't have much time, we're almost there. Don't think about the cold and it will not be so bad."

"Where is there?' Will asked chewing on his stale bread.

"The fields, I think," Jayes said. "Do not speak with food in your mouth Will," she scolded him.

"Ya," John said hitting him with his hand on the back. "Have some manners, Will." He laughed.

Bett started laughing, too. They heard the whip crack in the air.

"No talking. Walk!"

The children looked frightened. Jayes knew there was nothing she could do, she just gave them an encouraging grin and kept silent.

Jayes felt sick again. Her mouth began watering, she started nibbling her bread. She knew she was not eating well, not sleeping well. It was too hot, so hot she was having dizzy spells nearly every hour.

"Again?" John looked worried. "If you stop he will strike you."

"I'm not going to stop. I'm fine John," she lied. Only a half lie she told herself.

They reached a clearing in the trees and the sound of the woods finally came alive.

"*Sssshhhhh, chcheheh.*" It sounded like hissing whistling and rattling was rushing towards her.

"I'm scared," Bett cried.

"It's fine Bett," John said to her. Jayes smiled, John was a good boy. He tried to be so strong.

"To work," The dark Corzara demanded.

"What are we supposed to do?" one of the older boys Jayes did not know asked. Jayes thought it was the first time she had heard him speak.

"Make the ground dirt," he said, simply cracking his whip loudly over their heads.

"He likes doing that," John said angrily.

"Shush. You help Will and I will help Arabette," Jayes said and then warned, "Don't say anything to get in trouble."

"Who me?" John joked.

Jayes smiled shaking her head.

They worked day after day. From daylight until dark they toiled beneath the hot, unrelenting sun, turning the hard ground into soft dirt.

Jayes was getting weaker every day, so were the children. She had begun feeding them half of her food. She had no choice, she would rather suffer herself than to watch the children slowly waste away under the grueling pace set for them by Corzara.

Jayes knew her belly was swollen. She was able to hide it under the heavier clothes Master Turner provided the first day it snowed.

"Need to protect my investment," he offered as an explanation for the unexpected kindness. Jayes had learned to detest him, not as much as Corzara, but still she detested him.

Her swollen belly confirmed her fears. She was slowly dying. God was punishing her, even the sick and bloated cows from home did not waste away as slowly as she seemed to be.

Part of her was thankful she had more time, she was worried what would happen to the children when no one was there to protect them. It was too painful to think about.

Jayes heard a whispering sound that seemed so out of place. She hadn't heard birds in months. She tried to ignore it. Today she was working alone. Arabette had been summoned by Gin to assist with the laundry.

The whistling continued, it was becoming annoying.

"Irish girl!" she heard from the woods behind her, followed by another whistle.

Maybran! Jayes rolled her eyes. She searched for Corzara. He wasn't anywhere to be found. Dropping the large log, she was trying to move, Jayes quickly made her way towards the woods.

"Where are you?" Jayes asked looking into the trees. Most of the trees were too thin to hide behind.

There was a loud rustling sound overhead. Jayes looked up and out jumped Maybran.

"Girl!" Maybran said smiling happily.

"Jayes," she corrected her.

"Ah, Jayes, the *Ir-ish* girl."

"Yes. What do you want?" she asked. "I am not going to let

you get me in trouble again."

Maybran must have known that word. Her smile disappeared and was replaced by a scowl. She turned toward the field.

"He is not there," Jayes said. "He is probably searching for that annoying bird that has been whistling for the past hour."

Maybran giggled and let out another piercing whistle. Cuttmwa dropped from a tree behind her.

"Will you please not do that?" Jayes cried holding her chest. "It scares me." She started to feel dizzy again.

Jayes made a circle, found a dry spot and plopped down.

Maybran came up to her, she placed her hand on Jayes' cheek.

Jayes slapped it away. "I am fine," she lied. "I'm just dizzy. No food," she said pretending to eat with her hands.

Maybran looked at Cuttmwa, Jayes followed her glance.

He opened an animal skin pouch he was wearing around his waist. He pulled out some dark red meat and handed it to Jayes.

"Eat," he instructed.

Jayes took a small bite. It was delicious. She did not feel right eating, knowing the others were not joining her.

Maybran shook her head. She must have read her mind. She shoved Jayes' hand closer to her face. "Eat Jayes," she demanded. Jayes took another bite and then a larger bite.

Maybran smiled happily again. It would be so nice to be able to smile like that again she thought.

"Thank you," Jayes looked up at them. "I am sorry," she said to Maybran, she felt bad for being ungrateful to her kindness.

"Gra," Cuttwma mumbled. Jayes looked at him, and for the first time, she realized he was actually quite handsome. How had she missed that before? 'The Snake' her inner voice reminded her, she had been distracted with nearly being killed. Jayes smiled at him.

Cuttwma smiled back at her.

"Why do you cut half your hair and leave the other side long?" she asked him.

He just smiled.

"We honor the Great Spirit," Maybran answered.

"Is your Spirit like our God?"

"No. Yes," Maybran replied.

"No or Yes?" Jayes really was beginning to care about Maybran, but at times she was not sure if she didn't try to confuse her on purpose, it was as though Maybran enjoyed it. She was really beginning to prick Jayes' patience.

"Wahunsonacock, my grandda', was Chief of Powhatan before my uncle Opechancanes became Powhatan. My grandda' was a great man, he longed for peace with the White Skins." She sounded angry and sad. "He accepted your Gods as our Gods. He believed that no matter your names for your Gods, we all find the great light in the other world."

Cuttwma got up and walked away.

"Is he angry?"

"He is always angry." Maybran giggled. "He thinks there will never be peace with White Skins. He does not believe your people have God's and can still be so cruel. He does not want to like you. He does though," She giggled, "and that makes him angry."

Jayes had to think about that. "What is your God's name?"

"Ahone, created the world, the moon and stars, the companions to the stars. Ahone has great powers which makes the sun shine. Ahone is light and life. Okeus, is to fear, he watches all things, and he is in the air and thunder and in the storms. He punishes in many pains, death and destructions if displeased or he brings great feasts to hunters when appeased. He makes Heaven and Earth, he brings us medicine weeds and corn. He guides us when he is pleased." Maybran bowed her head, as though praying.

"Okeus sounds like our devil, only our devil is never rewarding."

"Tell me of your Gods, and this Devil God." Maybran asked. "Tell me why you are not accepted by your people if you worship the same 'Gods' as your Christian masters. Why are the Irish vsqwaseins are you not Christian?" Maybran was truly interested in Jayes answer, she stared at her. Jayes was not certain how to respond.

"Those Christians broke from the true church around a hundred years ago. I think they are still angry; they are scared of the Catholics. I am a Catholic," Jayes said. Maybran wanted to know more, she continued to stare at Jayes and wait for her answer. Jayes sighed. She knew the bible told her to 'speak the word of God to all who will listen so they may be saved'. Perhaps she was here to save Maybran.

"I believe in God the Da', God the Son and God the Holy Spirit."

"You have three Gods? And the Devil God?" Maybran exclaimed. "Four Gods?"

"No!" Jayes said and then thought about it. Of course it would seem like that to an Indian, and they are three separate but one God. "In a way, yes three. The Devil is not a God he is a fallen angel that is sent here to tempt us to forsake God and burn with him in hell." She sighed, she knew she was confusing Maybran. "It is complicated," Jayes admitted. "Perhaps we are not so different after all. Perhaps your grandda' was right."

Maybran smiled thinking now they had found some common ground.

JAYES – 1627

"I will try to explain to you someday, and someday you can explain to me," Jayes said, she would never again judge the Indians as heathens for having more than one God. She giggled, "I will have to tell you about the Virgin Mother Mary, she was the mother of Jesus on earth."

"A Virgin mother?" Maybran laughed as though Jayes was joking until she realized she was not. "Who is Jesus?"

"The Son of God of course," Jayes replied automatically.

Maybran merely shook her head. "You have many Gods. Your Christians only have one. That is why."

Jayes was about to correct her when she heard Corzara. She panicked, she had not gotten any work done! "Go!" She said to Maybran but realized she had already disappeared into the woods.

Jayes grabbed a few sticks and then realized there was already a huge pile made, the area had been cleared as though magically while she was talking with Maybran.

She just stared at the freshly cleared ground, Cuttwma had done it for her.

"You did good girl, now get back there with the others!" Corzara said scaring Jayes with his appearance and the sound of his whip slashing into the ground. Jayes ran as the big man disappeared into the woods searching for other servants.

Jayes had worked from the mornings first light until long after the sun sat every day. Besides clearing the fields, and digging the earth, Jayes had been sent one day to work up the river with the boys in the frigid and icy waters of one of the smaller rivers that flowed off the James. They were instructed to gather large rocks and carry them into the water making a large V.

They were building a trap for the fish, the colonists had learned this technique from the Indians. Jayes had ended up spending weeks filling the river with rocks and later trying to warm her frozen feet by the fire at night. She tried to construct a trap of braided thin wood strips to put into the mouth of the rocky trap.

"You're silly, do you not know how to weave a basket?" Maybran came out of the woods quietly one night spooking her. "Everyone knows how to make a basket."

"I wish you would not do that. It shocks my heartbeat," Jayes scolded her. "You should not be here, what if someone sees you?"

"Ehh," Maybran replied grabbing the thin sticks from Jayes' hands and twisting them together effortlessly into a perfect circle.

"Weave the other sticks into these. It should be wide and narrow, twice as tall as you are," Maybran explained and flittered silently back into the woods.

Jayes sat struggling with the wooden sticks, unable to get them to cooperate. She wondered if Maybran was out there watching, and laughing at her failures, braiding wood was not easy for her.

Jayes gave up, and threw them down onto the ground. She went to lay down and was fast asleep. When she awoke in the morning, she found perfectly woven traps completed. Maybran had obviously finished them for her. Jayes smiled, she was so grateful for her new friend.

Winter here was harsh. The ground remained frozen and ice fell from the sky nearly every day. Bones seemed to freeze from the inside of your body and many became ill. They would take to their beds to never rise from them again. At other times it would warm, only to become cold again.

Clearing the fields was near impossible, the wood seemed to double in weight, hands and fingers became so painful it was impossible to use them.

"Irish girl!" Maybran yelled at her from a branch above her head one day when Jayes was trying to plow the frozen ground.

Jayes looked up and smiled as she jumped from the tree, ran off and came back only a few minutes later carrying a large stone bowl and a smile.

Maybran stuck her hand in, she pulled it out. Her entire hand was covered in a thick greasy white liquid, which dripped in between her fingers then down her palm. "Rub. It will keep you warm." Maybran pointed to her feet.

Jayes sat down, removed her thin leather shoes and covered her feet in the thick ointment.

"What is it?" Jayes asked, not really caring, she would do anything if it would keep her warm.

"*Muminsaqweo.*" Maybran smiled. Jayes cocked her head and gave her that confused look that always seemed to amuse Maybran. "Bear *woraohawk*, fat. Keeps you warm."

Jayes looked at her in disgust. "Are you telling me I am wearing a dead bear?" She asked as she continued to rub the grease over her body, after all the bear was already dead.

Maybran smiled. She pointed to the children working in the field and then disappeared. One by one Jayes collected the children and covered their body in the white thick bear fat. She chose not to tell the children what it was she was rubbing on their bodies. She resisted any visible areas as to avoid any questions from the other servants or Corzara.

That night they all cuddled together and despite the smell, they slept comfortably and warm. Jayes thanked God for giving her Maybran.

The weather was finally starting to warm up a bit, the leaves on the trees starting to grow and fill in. Jayes woke in the mornings to the sounds of new life. Baby birds chirping and learning to fly. The air had a freshness about it.

This was normally always one of her favorite times of the year. The spring, and of course the fall when the leaves would fly about her. She remembered always burying herself in piles and piles of leaves, and then scaring her brother every time she would jump out, Jayes smiled at the memory.

No matter how many times she did it, he always acted scared and scotched. He would tease her hair and smile as he said. "You got me again, Jacey." These were all sad, but also happy memories now. Jayes closed her mind to her thoughts remembering her family, remembering the carefree days.

Jayes was told that she had important papers to deliver in Jamestown while Master Turner acquired the seeds for planting. They were leaving immediately. Jayes was to accompany Elizabeth to Jamestown and they were to find materials and cloth for Gin.

Elizabeth and Jayes spent the night on a small vessel with Master Turner, and two other slave girls who were laughing and drinking. Jayes could hear the sounds of him making use of their bodies all night long.

Jayes tried to tell herself not to judge the girls too harshly, after all they were slaves and had no choice. However, part of her hurt for Gin, her husband breaking their vows of marriage. It was a betrayal Jayes wished on no one.

She thought of James, Tristam, she corrected herself angrily. A part of her would never forgive him, another part of her missed him. Jayes placed her hands over her ears and tried to focus on the gentle sway. She finally drifted off despite the laughter and moans coming from nearby, she came to the conclusion that they were all happy participants.

Jayes did not feel sorry for them, yet she refused to judge them. Not because she had been forced and raped on the ship, they were not like her. It was not the same Jayes kept telling herself. The truth was Jayes was torn, she could not reason the difference yet she knew there was one, she just could not think of one.

Elizabeth and Jayes made the short walk from the dock to town, she could not help but remember the last time she was here. The last time she had seen Tristam, the day he had her strip and left her.

They passed the old fort, the gardens and the many men that were gathered around the blacksmiths. They walked silently towards the tall stone church. Jamestown was bustling with new construction; new buildings had been erected in the short time Jayes had left here. Some of them even with brick that was being made in all corners of the town. Jayes accidentally stepped on one of the bricks that had been placed in the path to dry. She looked down and could see the perfect outline of her small foot in the red brick.

"Hey You!" The brick maker yelled after her as Jayes ran quickly down the path. Both girls giggled.

"I will forever be printed in stone," Jayes said jokingly. "For hundreds and hundreds of years my footprint will remain."

When they neared the church there was a large crowd gathered outside. Elizabeth grabbed her arm. "Come on Jayes! Let's see what all the fuss is about."

"Elizabeth no, my feet are tired. Let's just deliver the letters and go. Please I really do not like this place. It is almost more horrid than the fields." It was no use. Elizabeth was off and moving into the crowd.

Suddenly there was a loud cracking sound and the crowd gasped in unison. Jayes was curious now too and quickly followed. Another loud crack, she moved through the crowd.

Tied to the pillory was a boy, younger than herself. His back bare and bleeding. He was being whipped brutally. Jayes noticed that his ears were nailed to the wooden boards, tearing and bleeding with every jerk his body made from the pain being given by the whip.

Another crack. Jayes closed her eyes and started to move away. A man behind her stopped her and turned her around. "Watch!" He demanded.

Jayes closed her eyes for what seemed like forever until the horrible cracking finally stopped. Jayes was afraid to look at the boy, afraid to see if he was still alive.

"This is the punishment for any servant that disobeys his Master. Idleness will not be tolerated. Disobedience will not be tolerated. We will not tolerate obstinacy anymore," shouted a man in a robe. He was not the man who had whipped the poor boy but Jayes knew he was responsible.

Her body ached for the poor boy. The crowd started to disburse. They had not taken him down. Who was going to tend his wounds? She turned to the man behind her.

"Did they forget to release him?" She asked. "Is he going to hang there to die?"

"No, he is to stand four days. Being whipped each day," he said not even realizing the horror of such punishment.

"What did he do?" She asked.

"He spoke against his master in a slanderous tongue," he said irritated. "He gets what he deserves, it would be good for you to remember that girl," he said rudely with contempt as he turned and left.

Jayes stood there in shock. She could not move. Elizabeth found her, she took her arm. Jayes, you need to let me teach you English. They are much kinder to the English," she whispered. She too was obviously affected by the scene.

"We need to deliver the letters and get back." Was all Jayes could say. Both girls walked in silence into the Church.

"You should have just listened to me," Jayes said. The visions of what she had seen kept flashing through her mind. Horrors that she wished were not in her head, were, visions she could never erase from her mind were adding up. She told herself at least this boy still had a chance of survival.

NINE
Life is a gift, or so they say – April 4, 1628

It was much cooler tonight than the usual cold they had felt lately, and it seemed as though the wet seeped into the bones just as natural as the stars lined the sky. Jayes shivered and rubbed her arms with her hands trying to bring them heat.

Jayes was certain she was going to die tonight. She knew her belly was growing large with the signs of impending death, like the poor cows that died in the fields at home. Their bellies bloated like hers has been the last couple of months.

Starvation, she knew she was starving, the hunger pains moved her belly in horrific ways, begging for food.

She knelt on her knees and prayed to Mary. She needed to make peace, she needed to ask for forgiveness. She was not sure if this was a test from God, or the end. Either way she would remain faithful in her beliefs. Faithful even through the worst of the worst. Like Jesus was steadfast when he was in the desert.

"*Aar, Aar, Aar,*" came a loud cry from the woods behind the hut. Jayes stopped.

"Hello?" Jayes asked, not moving. Trying to move her head as much as possible to see around the hut without moving her body.

"Is someone there?" she asked.

"John, is that you? It's not funny!"

"*Aar Aar Aar,*" the sound came again. Jayes took a few steps but still saw nothing. Smells. She could smell something wonderful. She walked closer to the edge of the woods following the sweet aroma.

The Indian who had saved her from the snake, Cuttmwa stepped out from behind a tree. Jayes stopped, she was not afraid of him anymore.

"Why are you here? It's not safe for you here you know."

He replied by showing her a bowl. The wonderful smells were coming from the bowl. She stepped forward, it looked like some type of meat stew.

He moved the bowl closer to her and grunted. Jayes smiled as her tummy made a loud growling sound. "For me? You brought me food?"

Again he pushed the bowl towards her, this time she reached out her hands.

"*Mamwah,*" he said as he mimicked eating with his hands. "Eh," he said as he motioned for Jayes to sit.

She sat and ate. The stew was delicious and not just because she was hungry. It was actually quite flavorful, perhaps the best stew she had ever eaten. Jayes ate quickly and tipped the bowl to sip the last drops. Cuttmwa grabbed the bowl and disappeared.

She listened to see if she could hear any sounds or hint of him in the woods, there was none. She started to get up but felt sick, she couldn't move, her mouth was watering. She felt as though she was going to vomit, her belly was obviously not used to so much food. She felt a horrible cramp in her tummy and then another. She cried out from the awful pain.

Cuttmwa appeared and slowly came closer, but stood a distance away. He looked worried and very concerned. She looked at him pleading for help, then felt another pain and cried out even louder than before. The pain became increasingly worse.

Cuttmwa put his hand up to his lips. Jayes knew what he was saying.

"I can't. It hurts. Help me please!" she begged him. "I cannot move!" Another pain came, Jayes tried with all her might to cry silently. Cuttmwa came and knelt beside her. He gently lifted her up in his arms and started making his way through the woods.

Jayes put her arms around his neck and laid her head on his shoulder, she cried, she was in so much pain and it was still getting worse.

She watched as the small hut disappeared. She knew she would be in trouble, but she did not care. She squeezed her hands together as tightly as she could behind Cuttmwa's neck as another pain came.

Jayes had no idea how long they had been walking before she could see the faint light of a campfire. She knew this was the Indian village. She knew she should be afraid but she felt no fear. Was it because she no longer feared death?

No, she knew that Cuttmwa brought her here because he was trying to help her. He had saved her life more than once and he would never hurt her.

Jayes heard Maybran's voice. She was speaking her language to Cuttmwa. She could not understand what they were saying but there was urgency in their voice. She lifted her head turning to look at Maybran. She too looked concerned.

The pains in Jayes' tummy no longer came and went. She felt one long continuous pain. She no longer had the strength left to cry out. Maybran touch her head gently with her hand.

"You *vebowchass,*" she said with a worried expression.

"Am I dying?" Jayes asked with no strength or emotion.

"No, not dying, sweating. You have a fever, you are too weak." Maybran grabbed Cuttmwa's hand and led him quickly down the hill to the village a short distance away.

Many Indians began to come toward them even though it was late into the night. The village was well lit with several fires still burning.

Jayes was still being carried as Cuttwma and Maybran walked slowly through the village not speaking. Jayes looked at the Indians who had gathered. Some of their expressions frightened her, others looked at her with concern.

They reached a tall mud hut that was long and stood near the middle of the village. Four Indian warriors stood guard outside. Cuttwma spoke to them and they all entered the hut. Jayes could no longer hold her head up and once again laid it on Cuttwma's shoulder.

The room was divided into two parts by a half wall. The walls were lined with animal furs, the flickering light from the fires, burning at both ends of the room causing them to appear to come alive in her fevered mind. The room was horribly smoky and crowded.

The Indians formed a half circle sitting around the fire with their backs toward Jayes. There was one facing her sitting alone. Jayes tried to focus. He was covered with a large bear fur and it seemed antlers adorned his head. She was finally beginning to lose consciousness and could no longer fight the urge to close her eyes, even though the pain seemed to increase with each breath. She could feel her strength seep from her neck as it fell sideways.

Cuttmwa bent down and laid her gently on the floor in front

of who she could only assume was the chief. That is when she saw the Indian women who were seated against the wall near the door. She looked at them trying to see their expressions. She couldn't focus. Jayes lost the battle and closed her eyes.

She awoke in an extreme amount of pain, even worse than before. She opened her eyes to women gathered around her, pushing on her stomach. She tried to sit up, to get away but quickly realized she was tied down. Both wrists and ankles were secured tightly to the table on which she was lying. She looked up and saw an older Indian woman whose face was old and wrinkled, with black hair sprinkled with white looking down at her smiling. She said something inaudible to Jayes, she had no teeth.

"English?" Jayes prayed the woman spoke English.

She smiled again not understanding Jayes.

"Maybran! Maybran!" Jayes yelled, trying to lift herself enough to look about the room. The old woman pushed harder on her swollen stomach. Jayes screamed out in pain, tears filled her eyes.

"Jayes," she heard a familiar voice. "It is good." Maybran said smiling as she appeared at her side and took hold of her hand.

Good? Jayes thought, "No, this is not good. Are they killing me? Is this how I am supposed to die?" Was she not even to die a Christian death, but surrounded by unbelievers?

"*Bodl,*" the old woman said, "*Bodl,*" and she smiled.

"Bodl?" Jayes had no idea what that meant. Was it supposed to mean 'die'? Go to your God? Jayes began to pray. She closed her eyes against the pain and screamed the words to God in her head.

"O virgin of virgins, my mother, to thee do I come, before thee I stand, sinful and sorrowful…."

JAYES – 1627

Another horrible pain hit Jayes. She screamed, even louder than that tragic day on the ship. The women removed their hands from her belly and began untying her, one of them pushed Maybran out the door.

"No!" Jayes screamed. She did not want to die alone with strangers.

Another woman shoved a cup to Jayes lips as soon as she had sat up. It was a foul, bitter tasting liquid. She kept forcing her to drink.

Two women grabbed her hands and slid her down the table. They all held her as she stood on her feet. The pain was coming back, Jayes screamed. They turned her around and again grabbed her wrists, which still had the ties wrapped around them.

Jayes was forced to bend over the table, the other women were holding her legs apart. As she stood there, she felt a warm liquid rush down her legs. The pain felt as though she was being dismembered.

Suddenly it was gone and she heard the cry of a baby. The old woman who had been standing above her was now releasing her wrists as she smiled her toothless grin.

"Bodl?" she said. Finally Jayes began understanding.

"Baby?" Jayes asked in disbelief. "My baby?" Jayes looked up. "I am not dying?"

"No," one of the women said as she tried to take the baby from Jayes. Maybran walked in, smiling. She asked one of the women a question in her language.

"It's a boy!" she exclaimed. "Did you want a boy Jayes?" she asked.

Jayes just looked at her. She began shaking her head. "I did not know. How? Did you know?" There were so many questions roaming through her mind.

Maybran laughed. "Jayes, did you know you were with baby?"

Jayes looked at her. "Did you know I was?"

"Of course I did. I just thought you were trying to keep it secret, I played along. You white skins have odd ways." She smiled at Jayes, sitting down beside her and touched her hand. "Jayes, give them the baby, they will wash him, feed him. You cannot feed him, even I know that."

Reluctantly she let go of her tiny little boy. She still could not believe that she was a mother. An unwed mother she just realized, she began to panic! "I am not married!"

Maybran tried to calm her. "Jayes it is too late for that now. You have been given the blessing of life. What are you going to name him?"

"I am thinking of Tristam, after his Da'," Jayes said looking at the baby with love as an Indian woman took him to go wash the birth from his little body.

"Is his Da' alive? Is he here, does he know he was going to be a Da'?"

"I do not know the answers, but I know he is not here," Jayes replied, not taking her eyes off her baby.

There was a commotion in the village, a young girl ran in and started frantically speaking to Maybran. She quickly got up and left. Jayes was so sore she could not move. She tried to keep her eyes on her son and try to see what was going on in the village.

Maybran walked back in with a scowl. "You have a visitor. She cannot stay long, she is not safe here." She stepped aside and Emmie walked in behind her.

"Jayes, you're alive," she said relieved. I have been looking for you everywhere. Gin has thrown a fit, she thinks you ran away. There are many looking for you." Emmie's eyes finally scanned the room. She saw the baby, the way Jayes was laying, and the blood on her legs.

"You had a baby!" She looked horrified. Jayes thought she thought less of her. Maybran was ready to defend her friend. "Jayes, they will punish you! They will take your baby and sell it for life! You will be sold and forced to serve the governor for two more years for this! You will be whipped!"

Jayes was shaking her head, no, this cannot be true she thought. The idea of being whipped sent shivers through her.

"You must hide the baby! Why did you not tell me? There are ways, we could have found someone who could have pretended the baby is theirs, and even Gin may have considered it."

"No! No one will take my baby from me. He is mine!" Jayes cried.

Emmie looked so sad. "Jayes, nothing is yours anymore. You do not even belong to yourself, you have no rights, no freedoms."

Jayes listened, she was right. Saddened as she realized Emmie spoke the truth, she began to cry. Why was this happening to her? Why God would give her a baby, allow her to feel such a strong amount of love for such a small thing and then take it away from her she couldn't begin to fathom? What had she done so badly in her life to deserve such punishment from God?

"Leave!" Maybran ordered Emmie.

"I was trying to help. I am sorry!" Emmie cried.

"I know, we will see you safely home. Do not come back, do not tell anyone you found her. You know nothing of this child." Maybran said as she all but shoved Emmie out of the doorway.

Jayes was still crying, she could not think of anything she

could do that would make this better. She needed to escape but she could not swim to Ireland. She could not hide on a ship with a baby that would surely cry. She was desperate. If Tristam James knew he was a Da', would he help her? Would he marry her and take her home?

"The bodl will live here. He will be safe. He will have freedom. He will be loved here, not abused by the white skins."

Jayes cried. "Yes," she said feeling relief and instantaneous heart break.

Jayes stared at her perfect little baby. She was still in disbelief that she had a son, she was a Mother. She knew that she had to do everything she could to protect this child, this gift from God.

Tears came to her eyes, she knew this meant leaving him. The idea of not being with him, not being able to hold him felt like shooting knifes through her body. She began to cry uncontrollably, holding her son as close to her chest as possible. Kissing his tiny face as tears fell upon his head.

The Indian women never left her alone, they did not disturb her or talk to her much. No one pressured her to stay or leave. Although Jayes knew she could not stay. She looked up and asked God why? Why had he left her, what had she done for him to forsake her?

Jayes took in a deep breath, and then another. She sniffed in and then wiped her wet face with her free hand. Jayes looked into the eyes of a tiny angel.

"You are a warrior my little angel. That's it! *Kealan*, mighty warrior, that is your name! I will fight for you, we will fight together. Someday, we will be together again," Jayes cried and kissed her son. "I promise you, I will live every day to get back to you Kealan."

Maybran stepped out from the corner of the room. "Kealan,

I like it, your bodl's name."

"It means mighty warrior. He will grow strong and brave. I will be strong and brave. I will come back for my son; I will change our stars. I promised him," Jayes cried her heart breaking at the thought of being apart from her son.

She handed Kealan to Maybran. "I am ready, there is no reason to postpone this any longer. I need to start adjusting my son's stars, and mine."

Jayes looked at Kealan. "Mummy is going to take you home someday to meet your grandparents and uncle. You will love them, I promise." She kissed his tiny head, wiped a tear and went out the door. How could her heart break so completely for someone so small that did not even exist a few days ago?

Jayes could not stop crying. How could such a strange little being hold such a large part of her heart? This was all new to her. She wondered how painful her being sent to Virginia was for her Mother. Jayes never knew how painful the love of a mother could be until now.

Her baby, her son, in only a matter of days was such a part of her, or all of her. Leaving him was even worse than sailing away from Ireland and all those she had known and loved her entire life.

Jayes, Maybran and Cuttwma made the long walk from the village back in silence. Jayes tried to pay attention to the direction as much as possible, just in case she needed to get back to her son.

They passed two rivers ends, and followed the river's edge. It seemed as though they walked downhill the entire way. Finally, shortly before night fall Jayes saw familiar surroundings. The mulberry, cypress and oak trees on the other side of the river seemed familiar. She stopped, staring at the tall oak that seemed to be in a constant struggle to find life. Jayes had stared at that tree many mornings feeling its pain, feeling its struggle as its branches reached towards heaven as though begging for the divine touch of hope.

Hope, she had to reach deep inside herself to find hope. Jayes told herself she had to believe that it was possible. She would believe from this day forward there was hope, she would believe in miracles, and she would believe that she could find both~ for Kealan.

TEN
With life, we seek hope…

Jayes stopped and stood when she reached the clearing that looked down towards the small Turner Farm. She stood looking at her temporary hell from the shade of the oak trees. She could not will herself to step forward. How could she return to this life as though nothing had happened? She wanted to run back to the Indian village and live peacefully with her son. She knew that she was not welcome there, she would put the Indians in danger, she would be considered stolen or a runaway. Either way, she could not involve them, they had done so much for her and they were now protectors of her son. She could not ask any more from them.

Jayes could see Elizabeth ordering about poor Arabette, screaming at her to stop spilling water. The poor girl could not carry such heavy buckets, Jayes watched her try to lift one and fall under its weight. Jayes rushed forward to help her.

"You!" Elizabeth screamed when she saw her. She lifted her skirts and ran into the small house. Immediately Gin appeared in the doorway. Her face twisted with an expression of hate.

She came quickly towards Jayes and struck her hard across the face. "You are nothing but trouble!" She kept screaming and struck her again. Jayes fell to the ground and tried to block the assault.

Gin grabbed her by the hair and pulled her backwards towards the house. Painfully Jayes twisted and tried to follow, trying to push herself along the ground with her legs.

Gin threw her onto the wooden floor. She jumped on top of her slapping her across the head with the heavy irons that Elizabeth had handed her. Jayes felt burning pain with each blow, she could see the blood dripping down from her forehead falling onto her dress, her arms and the floor.

Gin snapped the irons onto her wrists as she yelled out the door loudly for Corzara, who appeared immediately. His large frame blocking the light into the small room. Everything happened so fast, she was slow to realize what was happening to her.

"Chain her up! Make it tight!" Gin ordered. "Give me that whip!"

Jayes felt the back of her dress being ripped off. Elizabeth appeared at her side, she pleaded with her eyes for help. Elizabeth smiled a wicked smile and ripped what was left of the sleeves off her gown, baring her shoulders before she stepped away.

Jayes felt the sting of the whip on her backside before she heard its hissing sound. The pain jerking her entire body, her knees went week, she was hanging by her wrists that had been chained to the wall. Jayes tried to find her footing and strength to stand, she couldn't before the second lash took her breath away. She cried out in excruciating pain. Trying to stand again, the third lash hit her, she turned her head slightly to see Gin lifting her arm before the fourth struck her.

Gin was laughing, it was such an evil sound. Jayes felt herself lose all control of her body and urinated on the floor. Gin saw this and wielded the whip hitting the back of her legs purposefully as she laughed.

Jayes hung there, giving up on trying to stand, her thoughts drifting to her baby son. He was free. At least he was free, any pain, even this, was worth his freedom. Even death was worth his freedom.

Again and again the whip slashed into her body, ripping skin, blood was flying throughout the room as the whip was wielded, over and over again. Her back, her bottom, her shoulders, her legs. None were spared pain.

The pain was so unbearable she was grateful when she felt herself slipping away. She did not care if she died, she welcomed it.

Jayes awoke laying on the floor. She opened her eyes and saw fire in the hearth burning in front of her. She was disappointed she was alive. Corzara stood nearby smiling down at her, he bent over and picked up a large iron rod from the fire.

"Your awake, good, I have been waiting for this," she heard Gin say. "Take her outside."

The dark man lifted Jayes naked, weak and battered body off the floor with one hand carrying the iron rod in the other. Jayes had no strength as she was dragged across the dirt, re-opening the wounds that had stopped bleeding. He tossed her mercilessly into the dirt.

"Listen! This is what happens to runaways. Be warned!" Gin screamed to the gathered crowd of servants. "Do it!" She ordered Corzara.

Jayes felt a horrific, scorching pain in her shoulder, could hear the singeing and smell the burning of her skin. The pain was like none other she had ever felt, not even the whipping. The pain was so horrific, she could not even cry out, could not breathe or move. She could only lie there and suffer in silence again praying and hoping for death.

"Now everyone will know you are a runaway! She has been branded with the mark of a runaway slave! I am warning you all, if you disobey me, you will be punished!" Gin kicked dirt into her face, as she turned and walked away. Jayes could see her feet and the bottom of her gown as she disappeared into the house.

How could she have done this too her? What had she done to deserve this?

Jayes awoke in pain, an awful burning pain that seemed to consume her entire body. She was lying on the floor, on her stomach in the servant's hut. She looked up into John and Will's teary eyes, her neck twisted awkwardly to the side, trying not to move her body. She tried to speak but the pain was unbearable when she tried to open her mouth. The tears came streaming down from her eyes uncontrollably, she tasted the salt as it ran onto her dry, chapped lips.

"Don't move, it is almost dark, she will be back tonight," John whispered in her ear. "You are doing better Miss Jayes, you are going to live."

Jayes moved her eyes in question, the only part of her body that did not suffer in pain.

"The Indian, she is caring for you," he answered her silent question.

Jayes closed her eyes and drifted off again.

When she awoke awhile later, it was dark. She flinched as she felt someone touching her raw back. She opened her eyes and saw Cuttwma chewing on something. He bent over and spit it into her wounds, the many open gashes that would forever be branded onto her skin.

"Lie still, this is Indian weed, *wisakon*, better than your white skin medicine, this will heal you." Maybran explained. Jayes felt burning as they tended to her, then a sort of relief as the pain began to subside. She closed her eyes again and found peaceful darkness.

Several times Jayes woke, and several times she quickly slipped back into the darkness. She dreamt happy dreams, without pain. Dreams of running alongside the lush, tall cliffs of Ireland. Dreams of holding her baby son and laughing as she played with him. Dreams of being in Tristam's arms, safe, free and loved. They were dreams, mere dreams so far from the realities of her world.

Each time she woke she begged to escape back into her dream world. That wonderful place where there was no pain. A place far from Virginia, far away from Jamestown and this life of hell she had been condemned to endure. She did not belong here, she never wanted to be here. In her dreams, her life was free and happy, she danced and sang, she could laugh with her son. She was not a slave.

Eleven
Life is never a guarantee... – May, 1628

"Caw caw, caw caw," Jayes heard, she knew it was a signal. The boys were still awake. Was there something wrong with her baby?

"Caw caw, caw caw, caw caw." It was such a shrieking sound, an alarm, she knew something was terribly wrong. She could not bear it, she stood up and ran out of the hut, leaving everyone staring after her in confusion.

Jayes ran, she never slowed down, she did not care who saw her. She entered the woods running towards the sound until she saw Maybran. The look on her face confirmed she was right, there was something terribly wrong.

"Is it Kealan?"

"No Jayes, it is worse, you need to leave, take the boys and the children you care for and hide. Hide near the river. Run!!! Go now!!"

Maybran was for the first time showing fear, and that scared her even more than her words. Jayes panicked, she wanted details, wanted to know what was happening.

"Tell me what is wrong!" She begged.

"My people were attacked by yours. My brothers, uncles and their daughters, a great priest, all killed by white skins."

JAYES – 1627

Maybran was upset, hurt and saddened as well as angered by the deaths. She was risking her own safety coming here, Maybran was uncomfortable being here, it was apparent.

Maybran turned to leave, the light from the moon illuminating her. Her face, hands and arms all were painted with grey. She looked at her in question.

"Not now Jayes! There is no time! Go- go now and hurry!" Maybran turned and disappeared into the woods. Jayes ran back to the hut to get the children.

She ran in and grabbed Arabette from her bed, lifting her sleepy body into her arms. She hit John on the arm and whispered, "Get Will, be silent, and meet me outside. Be quick about it!" She grabbed a couple blankets and went outside.

A short time later, John and Will came out. "Pppsssst!" Jayes said to get their attention. "Hurry up, be quiet and follow me."

"Where are we goin?" Will asked.

"Somewhere safe. Do not talk, just walk, walk quickly boys. Keep up with me."

The boys followed quietly, Jayes was not sure how far to go or even where to go when she heard the drums. She turned off the path and began to quicken her pace. There were some fallen trees that was covered with overgrown grass. Jayes decided this would make a sufficient hiding spot.

"In here! Hurry up!" she yelled at the boys. She laid the blankets down. "Be quiet, I am going to fix the grass to cover our trail."

By the time Jayes returned to the hiding spot the drums and chanting was much louder. The boys and Arabette were terrified. "It will be ok I promise," she said.

"Are you sure?" John asked her.

"Yes, I am sure. They will not hurt us, I promise you we are safe." She smiled trying to reassure them.

"You really are not scared are you? The drums, the Indians, the sounds of war, that does not scare you does it?" John studied her face looking for but not finding fear.

"No John, that does not scare me. That is the sound of freedom. The Indians are not our enemy," she said this with all honesty and a straight face. She was scared, she was scared for the safety of her son, and she refused to think about that. She refused to believe that he was in jeopardy.

"Then why are we hiding if that is the sound of freedom?" He asked her.

"John, be quiet," Jayes told him. There was screaming and gunshots in the distance.

Arabette let out a scream and Jayes quickly covered her mouth. She could not see her but she looked at her. "Arabette, boys, listen to me. The Indians do not want to hurt us, I know that, but they will not take the time to see who we are before they kill us. They will only see the color of our skin. You have got to be quiet. Do you understand?"

There was silence. They sat there in silence all night listening to the sounds of battle, of death all around them. Jayes prayed that the Indians would win. She prayed for her son's safety. She dared not pray for freedom, but that too she hoped for. She silently hoped the colonists would all be gone by morning and her life would belong to her again.

"Caw caw, caw caw!" Jayes was rustled from her sleep. Arabette lay limp sleeping in her arms. She looked towards John and Will cuddled in a heap together, sound asleep. She smiled grateful they were all safe.

She laid Arabette on the blanket and made her way out of their hiding spot. Jayes clicked the top of her tongue to the roof of her mouth and made a loud clicking sound. It was not long until Cuttwma appeared from the woods. Jayes shook her head, she would never get use to that.

"How do you move about like a cat?" she asked him.

Cuttwma just chuckled his sideways smile. "Maybran is waiting. I stay and watch children," he said pointing down the path.

Jayes made her way back towards the path and along the river to the huts. Maybran was sitting near the opening in the woods. Her expression was sorrowful and grim.

"Who?" Jayes asked her panicked, "Not Kealan!"

"No, your son is safe." She pointed towards the huts. "Go," She said.

Jayes walked slowly across the bare earth. As she walked, her surroundings appeared in stark relief accentuating the barrenness of the ground between the huts where she and the other servants were sheltered and the main house. Her mind briefly drifted back to the lush, green hills of Ireland, recalling the natural beauty she took for granted before being ripped from her home and brought to this wild, untamed land.

She could still smell the gunpowder, the acrid scent mingling with the harsh metallic scent of fresh spilled blood. The air was filled with smoke from the burning huts. Jayes saw a woman lying on the ground between the main house and the weapons hut. As she walked her steps slowed even further. She turned her over, her body was stiff and unusually heavy.

Jayes immediately realized it was Elizabeth. Sickened she let go and the body dropped back onto the bare earth with a loud thud. Jayes reached down and closed her eyes. She stood up, unprepared for what she had seen and what she knew was to come.

She saw another body lying near the slave hut. She walked over and knew it was Emmie, her red hair blending with the blood that lay around her. Jayes sucked in her breath and fell to her knees. She was grateful Cuttwma stayed behind with the children.

Jayes heard moaning from inside the hut. Slowly rising she quickly walked inside again, unprepared for what she was to find. Bodies and blood littered the small room. Jayes stepped over the body of a boy, she was not sure who it was, and she lost her footing and fell forward.

She went to lift herself up and realized that she was covered in blood. She screamed, a loud shrieking sound. Maybran appeared. She too heard the moaning. It was an older servant, the Irish one that never spoke. His eyes widened when he saw Maybran.

"No! No!" he tried to yell. Jayes crawled towards him, quickly removed his shirt and examined his wounds.

"You will be fine, they are not deep. She is our friend," she said looking at Maybran who stood with no expression. Jayes knew Maybran did not consider them her friend, she was willing to not kill him though for Jayes.

They then heard a curdling sound from the corner of the room. All three turned their heads to see an older girl laying in the corner covered in blood. Jayes moved closer. Maybran reached her first. The girl seemed to rattle in her chest unable to speak. Maybran pulled out a rock that had been sharpened into a blade.

"No!" Jayes yelled.

Maybran solemnly looked Jayes in the eyes shaking her head, and slit the girls' throat. "She was going to die, I helped her to not suffer."

Jayes began to shake. She knew that Maybran had done the right thing, but to take a life, to watch while that life left the body, it was too much for her.

JAYES – 1627

She quickly left the hut, fell to her knees and threw up. Maybran began hitting her on her back. 'No time to be weak! Do you hear that? In there?" She asked pointing towards the house.

"Gin," Jayes whispered and she stood up, slowly walking to the house where she could hear a faint cry. She entered the room, her eyes darting first to the chains secured to the roughhewn planks of the wall. She shivered. She looked to the doorway leading to Gin's room and saw Master Turner. His lifeless body was lying face up. His eyes open in horror his arm was barely attached to his body. The blood.... Jayes turned to leave the room. She heard the cry again, a faint whimper. She looked around the room but could not see anyone.

"Jayes," she heard so faintly. She looked again and buried in a corner, beneath a pile of corn husks she saw a hand. She ran over and uncovered Gin.

She sucked her breath in when she saw her wounds. Gin had a deep gash in her side spilling blood onto her hands where she weakly held the wound closed.

"Let go, let me see," Jayes urged her.

"No, you want me dead, I would want me dead if I were you," Gin managed to say with the last of her energy before she lost consciousness.

"Maybran!" Jayes yelled.

Maybran appeared and looked Gin over. She shook her head and started to reach for her blade.

Jayes grabbed her hand. "No! Wait! We must save her!"

Maybran looked at Jayes confused. "Why? Why would you want to save her?

"She is my friend," was all Jayes could say. Maybran shook her head in disagreement. Refusing to help.

"Please," Jayes pleaded with her. Reluctantly Maybran knelt

down to help. They carried Gin into the other room stepping in cold and sticky blood on the way. Jayes felt her stomach turn. She tried to focus on the task at hand.

They stripped Gin down, the jagged gash was three or four inches long from below her breast across her belly.

"Can we save her?"

"Ugh, *Kanyough,*" Maybran replied in her language. Jayes just stared her down waiting for an answer.

"I know not!" Maybran was torn, Jayes knew she had no love for Gin, which was confirmed when she spat out, "*Keihtascooc!*" Hatefully calling Gin a snake which made Jayes love her even more.

Jayes and Maybran heard a sound coming into the little house at the same time. Both girls stood, Maybran reaching for her blade. It was the tall, dark, giant Corzara, he too had blood dripping from his head and arm.

He saw Maybran and started for her. Jayes jumped in between them screaming "NO!" Jayes ran into him with all of her weight and surprisingly knocked him over.

Maybran ran towards him with her blade, Jayes reached out screaming as the blade sliced her wrist. Maybran stopped instantly.

"Enough!" She screamed grabbing at her wrist. "No more death today!" she cried out. Both of them looked at her in shock. These were enemies, they were not friends. Maybran looked hurt that she had injured Jayes and also that Jayes had stopped her from killing an enemy.

"Today we are not enemies. He can help us move the bodies," Jayes tried to reason with her. She marched out muttering words in her language- Jayes was grateful she did not understand.

Corzara looked at Jayes in confusion. He knew she had no

reason to try to help him. He thanked her silently and stood up. They had just made a silent truce when they heard the unmistakable sounds of others approaching the house. Corzara peered outside and saw two of the house servants.

"Come!" he shouted. Two girls appeared in the doorway. They were the two girls that Jayes had thought lazy, the ones who had both accompanied them on the last trip to Jamestown. Bedmates and favorites of the late master Turner, they had taken advantage of the special attentions he paid them. They had been spared any real work in the fields alongside Jayes and the others. She did not particularly care for them, yet she was grateful they were alive. Their elevated status had spared them the exhausting work in the fields and afforded them better food and shelter. They were stronger and their strength would be useful.

"Go to the river and fetch water," Jayes instructed them. They did not move and looked at Corzara.

"Do as she says!" he yelled at them. They quickly disappeared.

"When they return I will tend your wounds. Can we remove the bodies? The children will be back soon. I do not want them to see," Jayes asked him.

He said nothing to her and left, walking towards Elizabeth. Jayes turned back to Gin. She put her hand on her chest and let out a sigh of relief when she felt the slow rise and fall of breath.

Jayes covered Gin with the coverings available, wrapping her wound as tightly as she could. She went to the trunk of clothes that Gin had been trying to repair and sew. She found some material, some they had purchased during their recent visit in town. She started ripping it into strips.

She went to the hearth, removing the iron pot from the ingle that sat in front of it. She started a small fire. The girls returned quick enough, although their pails were nearly empty. Jayes wanted to yell at them. 'No,' she told herself. 'I will not be Gin.'

"We need more water," she told the girls as she took the wooden pails from their hands and poured the water into the iron pot that hung above the fire. "If you go slowly, you will have less trips to make as the water will not spill from your buckets," she calmly explained to them. "Go, we are going to need much more water."

"Why are you burning the water miss?" The one girl asked not moving.

"What are your names?" Jayes asked confronting them.

The younger, shorter girl replied with a sassy tone. "I am Bekka and this here is Frances."

"Bekka and Frances, I know that you are not ones to be 'quick' about anything. Today, however, lives could be lost if you dilly dally. We do not have time for silly questions," Jayes scolded them realizing that her speech was not motivational. "If you must know, it is something the old woman in our village did. It seems to heal wounds better if the water is hot," Jayes explained. "I am going to do my best to save lives, I need your help. Please go and fetch me water so I can clean Mistress Gin's wounds, she will be grateful to you when she recovers."

That must have registered with the two girls. They must know that they were not Gin's favorite people and Master Turner was no longer around to run interference for them. They quickly headed off towards the river.

Jayes stood over the water for what seemed like hours. She watched as more and more steam began to rise from the pot. She could not get herself to look outside. She did not want to see anymore dead bodies today.

Maybran came in quietly. She carried with her an

assortment of leaves. Without speaking she went to the pot and dipped in a ladle. She put the hot water into a bowl giving Jayes a strange look.

"I do not question your medicine work, do not question mine." She scowled at Maybran, who just smiled in reply. The two girls walked back in, they were leery of Maybran's presence. Jayes gave them a warning look and both girls remained quiet but near the door. Jayes looked inside their buckets. "Ah we are getting better. She took the first bucket and poured it onto the floor to the poor girls' frustration. The second bucket she poured into another cooking bowl and hung it above the fire.

"More," she said to them as they all but ran from the house. Maybran giggled as she sat down and began crushing leaves with her stones.

Jayes took a thick pad and unhooked the boiling water from the metal hook above the fire, replacing the pot with fresh water in its place. She sat at the table alongside Maybran who was furiously crushing her leaves.

Jayes looked in the bark that was laying on the table. It was full of a sticky dark yellowish fluid some solid like rocks.

Maybran tossed Jayes a long smooth rock. "Crush it," she instructed her.

Jayes began beating the yellow rocks that surprisingly seemed to break apart easily. They heard Gin moan from the next room. Jayes got up and went to her, bringing with her the hot water. The bandages that she had placed on Gin's side were already soaked with blood.

Jayes grabbed some of the cloth and dipped it in the pot. "It is still a little warm. I am going to clean this Gin, it may sting," she warned her. Gin's color was quite pale. Her breathing shallow.

"Let me die," Gin moaned.

"No, too many died today, I will not let you die," Jayes told her as Maybran walked into the room with her medicines in hand.

Gin saw her and found her strength. She sat up in the bed as though possessed and let out a piercing scream. Her wound gushing blood uncontrollably. Just as quickly her strength left her and she fell back once again unconscious.

Jayes quickly tried to stop the bleeding. Maybran started to dance around her shaking a rattle and chanting in her language oblivious to Jayes. She watched as she shook the rattle high in the air then slowly brought it down and touched Gin's foot. She dipped her hand into the water and splashed Gin, then began again with the other leg. Maybran did this covering Gin's entire body, singing and allowing the rattle to caress all Gin's limbs slowly.

Maybran then reached into her bag of leaves, chewed them and slowly spit the leaves into Gin's wide gash. Jayes was going to protest but knew that this was Gin's only hope. She stood back and watched.

Corzara carried in the wounded boy. He stopped as he was slowly entering the small bedroom. Laying the boy on the floor near Gin. Both of them staring at Maybran in silence.

Maybran covered her hands in the liquid gold that had once been the rocks Jayes crushed. It was now like a dark golden honey. Maybran covered the wounds completely then packed bark on top, all the while singing what Jayes assumed were prayers. Suddenly she stopped and looked at the boy who looked terrified.

Maybran motioned for Corzara to put the boy on the bed next to Gin. He obeyed her silent order and stood back. Maybran started the ritual all over again.

After quite some time, Maybran looked at Jayes. "I have done all I can do. You can pray to your Gods now." She turned and left the room as though she was exhausted.

"That is the heathen's medicine." Corzara said.

"That heathen is going to heal you too. You should be nice," Jayes replied sarcastically.

"The heathens are the reason we need healing." Corzara spat back at her.

"No! Not the heathens. This is their land. They are victims of the King of England and the men who think they are King. Those men make their own laws taking life and freedom! Those men have no care nor concern for the many lives they destroy through their own arrogance and greed," Jayes yelled at him. "Do you not know anything about freedom?"

"This country gave me my freedom. I am thankful," he said solemnly.

"I am not! They took mine! You, of all people, should have compassion yet you don't!" Jayes turned and left before she said something she might regret. After all, though they may be on the same side at the moment, he was still her enemy, and he could still hurt her and make her life hell. He would always be one of them.

Twelve
We bury the dead...

That day many people lost their lives. Jayes and the children buried Emmie- in a special place near the river's edge in a private ceremony. Mr. Turner, Elizabeth, and five other servants were buried in the graveyard that had been established after what was commonly called the '1622 attack' near the river in a spot they called the Curls.

Gin was recovering well. She had moved Jayes back into the house to be near during her recovery. Jayes had snuck out as often as she could at night to check on the children and spend time with them. Bekka and Frances, the two worthless servant girls were changing their evil and lazy ways and had been quite helpful. Jayes was beginning to almost like them, although she doubted she could ever fully trust them.

Corzara had prepared the graves and then had taken to his bed to recover from his wounds. Maybran had checked on him often, although she refused to do anymore for Gin. Gin had kicked the servant boy, Paedar, out of the house and sent him back to the servants' hut before he was well enough to go. Maybran was furious and refused any aid to Gin 'for eternity and after.'

Gin was being cordial and at times, even friendly towards

her. Although Jayes was unsure if it was because she was grateful for her life being saved or because she was unsure what could happen to her now that her husband was dead and Jayes may be her only friend and ally left in Virginia.

"Jayes!" Gin screamed from her bed, although she had recovered as much as she would, she still pampered herself and rarely left the house. Jayes ran back into the house spilling the bucket of water she had just fetched to try remove the bloodstains from the floor.

"Yes, I am here," Jayes said exhausted.

"I need you to turn this house upside down! I need to find those papers that nasty man signed, the contracts or whatever they were, we need to find them! I need to read them and destroy them! I need parchment and ink! I can rewrite those papers." Gin was speaking frantically as she was running about the house turning things upside down.

Suddenly she stopped and grabbed ahold of Jayes by the shoulders. "Yes! That is what we can do, we can hire a forger. Can you copy a signature?" Gin asked her hopefully. "No, I can do it myself. That way there are no witnesses…"

"I don't know; I do not know if that is a good idea Gin. If we got caught…."

"Of course it is a good idea! If we get caught what it the worst that could happen? We have already lost our freedom. I swear to you, I will never be another man's property again. Never! Honestly Jayes, you should be grateful, I can give you your freedom too. At the very least, more freedom than you have now."

"I will look for the papers. Do you have any idea what he may have done with them?"

"If I knew that I would not have you search for them would I?" Gin asked, screaming in frustration. "Sometimes I worry about you Jayes, sometimes you act like a half-wit."

Jayes rolled her eyes and went in search for the papers. She searched the entire house all day. She found nothing.

"What ya look'n for Miss Jayes?" Will asked in a whisper as he came into the house. Jayes was on her hands and knees in front of the fireplace searching for a loose stone behind which Mr. Turner may have hidden the papers.

"Master Turner had some papers that Miss Gin wants me to find. I don't know where he put them," Jayes sighed getting up and brushing the soot off her skirts.

"His hiding spot?" Will asked with much joy.

Jayes narrowed her eyes at him smiling. "Will, do you have a secret?"

Will smiled happily and nodded his head yes. Jayes smiled. "Do you know where Master Turner's hiding spot is?" she asked him unbelieving, could it really be this easy?

Will smiled an even bigger smile. "I usta spy on Master Turner," he whispered.

"Is that your secret?"

"Yep," he said proudly.

"And when you were spying on Mr. Turner, did you see where he hides his papers?"

"Yep," Will said as he turned and ran out the door. Jayes picked up her skirts and followed. Will ran past the weapon hut, the storerooms and the chicken coup to the edge of the woods. He took a quick left nearly disappearing in the trees. Jayes caught up to him, he was pointing towards a dead oak tree.

"In there Miss Jayes. He puts his stuff in there." Will was so proud of himself. Jayes bent down and gave him a hug and a kiss on the cheek. She turned towards the tree and noticed it had a hollowed out hole in the center of it that was covered by another piece of wood from the inside.

JAYES – 1627

Jayes stuck her hand in and tried to push the wood out of the way, it did not budge. She tried to find the ends of it to lift it out again, she could not get it to budge. Jayes tried to find a stick, she found one nearby, picked it up and tried to bang the wood loose.

"You are not doin it right." Will said so quietly Jayes almost did not hear him over her knocking on the wood. Will reached his hand up and took the stick from Jayes. He walked a little to the right of the tree and stuck the stick into another hole. To Jayes' amazement the wood rolled to the left and Jayes could see bundles of papers inside.

"You are a good little spy! Thank you, Will!" Jayes reached inside and pulled out the papers, and a leather pouch, Jayes shook it and knew it carried coins. She quickly slipped it into her dress.

She bent down to Will's level. "This is our secret Will. Do not ever tell anyone about Master Turner's tree or that we found his hiding place. Do you understand?"

Will nodded his head.

"Ok it is our secret." She smiled at him. "Can you put the wood back in place for me?"

Will ran around happy to help, he stuck the stick in the other side of the tree. Jayes watched as the wood rolled back concealing the hole. Jayes was still in disbelief, she would have never found this. She looked at him and realized she did have family here. Through all the horror and death that she has suffered, there was still happiness and love in her heart.

"How would you like it if I went and found us a big fat chicken and cooked it up for dinner tonight?" Jayes asked him smiling. Will's eyes got really big and he licked his lips in excitement.

"Yes! Yes! That would be," Will stopped and looked upset.

"What?" Jayes asked him wondering what could possibly change his expression so quickly.

"The Indians killed all the chickens," he said sadly.

Jayes laughed. "No they didn't silly, they missed a couple."

"But what about Mistress Guinever? She won't let us have chicken."

Jayes reached out and messed his hair. "Well Miss Guinever will be so pleased that you found Master Turners hiding place, she will certainly reward you with a good chicken dinner."

"I thought you said no one was supposed to know."

"You are right!" Jayes smiled happily, he was such a smart little boy. "I will tell Miss Gin. You are not going to tell anyone though okay."

"Oh, ok!" He said happily. "I am going to go find the fattest chicken for my reward!" He yelled as he took off. Jayes watched him run shouting for John. She couldn't help but laugh out loud.

That night Jayes sat at the table reading the papers under candlelight. Gin sat across from her reading and every once in a while she would let out a growl and stomp her feet. As Jayes read she did not feel anger, she felt pain.

Everything Gin had said the night of the storm was true. Until this moment Jayes had not truly believed it. She had refused to think that it had been true. There was no denying the truth now. Captain Tristam James had sold her.

She believed that he had cared for her at the very least, maybe even loved her. She had believed that he was coming back for her, that he was going to rescue her. It was all a lie. She was such a fool to believe him. She hated herself for falling in love with a man who raped her, stripped her naked for all to see and then sold her to the highest bidder.

Jayes started to cry. She still loved him. She hated him, but she still loved him. He was her hope. She couldn't believe that her only hope, her son's only hope was a deceitful monster. How could she have not realized she meant nothing to him?

As she stared at his signature, a tear fell, landing on the paper. Jayes still felt a ray of hope from deep inside her. She still wanted to believe that Tristam would come back and rescue her, he would take her in his arms and he would carry her back to his ship. Together, with their son they would return to Ireland and live happily with her family.

She did not want to see the truth, she wanted to believe in him. Believe that he had done what he could for her given the circumstances. Life could have been worse, she could have been sold to that nasty man who had approached her on the shore, how was she to have known that Gin would have mistreated her as she did?

As she stared at the papers in front of her, she still refused to believe he did not care about her. "I am my only hope now," Jayes said to herself. Her heart though still refused to believe in reality.

"What?" Gin asked looking up and staring at her.

"I spoke my mind. I am sorry," Jayes said as she stood up. "I am sorry I doubted you. I thought you were lying about the Captain the night of the storm. I was wrong." She walked over to the fire burning in the inglenook.

Gin jumped up and ran towards her. Grabbing the paper from her hand. "What are you doing?" She screamed.

"I am burning it!" Jayes said as she tried to grab the paper back from Gin. "I saved your life! Are you going to make me your slave? Are you going to whip me again?"

To Jayes surprise Gin looked hurt. Tears came to her eyes. "I am sorry. I was wrong and horrible. I am sorry. I do not deserve your forgiveness." Gin sat down and began to cry.

"You cannot burn the papers. We need to change them. We need to change our fates. We need to copy the signatures, you cannot burn the papers, not yet."

Jayes stared at her. She was trying to understand what Gin was saying. "Change them to what?" she asked confused. "How can we change our fate? Our lives do not even belong to us!"

Gin looked up. She wiped the tears from her eyes and gathered the papers together. She started sorting them out and handed one to Jayes.

"They stole our life; we steal it back! Governor Yeardley is dead." Gin said pointing to his signature at the bottom of the contract. "He died in November. Captain James is nowhere to be found, hopefully he is dead," she said as she pointed to his signature. "Sir John Turner, dead, buried face down as he deserves." Gin said hatefully of her late husband pointing towards his signature.

Jayes' eyes widened. "Face down? Oh Gin you didn't!" she said shocked. Yes, Master Turner was a horrible person, but to be disrespectful of the dead? "Gin, it is not your place to judge."

"Oh Jayes, I don't care, I am not talking about that with you, that is not what is important right now. Do you not understand what I am saying?" Gin asked as she laid the papers on the table and ran her fingers over all the signatures. Stopping on her signature and Jayes. "We are the only witnesses alive to testify to the validity of these contracts," she was smiling happily. Gin ran quickly into the bedroom and emerged with another sheet of paper and handed it to Jayes.

She read aloud, *"In the name of God Amen, January the third in the year of our Lord 1627, I John Turner..."* Jayes looked up. "It is his will, where did you find this?" Jayes asked as she scanned the rest of the document.

JAYES – 1627

'Leave to my brother Thomas…All my patents and land 1000 acres…12 white servants… one Negro servant…4 cows.'

"Gin this does not benefit you. It leaves everything, including me, to his brother!" Jayes said panicked, who is this brother? What if he is even viler?

"Jayes!" Gin said exasperated. "You do not understand. Who witnessed his Will?"

Jayes looked at the bottom signature. "Thomas Crowe."

"He is also dead!" Gin said happily. "We change the will. We change the contracts." Gin smiled so pleased. Jayes finally realized what she was saying.

Jayes looked at her. She knew it was wrong to lie and change the documents. She also thought that it was wrong, what had been done to them. The circumstances of her being here were so very wrong. Jayes was so torn. She heard what Gin had said now, and completely understood- and agreed. We steal it back.

"Do you have paper; do you have ink? What if the signatures do not match? What if we get caught?" Jayes asked.

Gin ran up and hugged her knowing that Jayes was now a willing participant in this scheme. "You will not be a servant, we will make you the Captains fiancé and 'overseer' of his lands, the ones he owns from the head-rights. Of course I will be the beneficiary of my husbands will." Gin smiled at her.

Jayes knew this was Gin's way of apologizing and trying to make things right. She accepted it. Once again they were in this together.

They spent the entire night forging papers. Gin was now a contracted bride, brought over to the New World after the unfortunate death of her Da'. Her marriage contract had been formed between Captain James and her Uncle in Ireland; her passage having been paid to the Captain as well as Jayes' his fiancé for their transportation to Virginia. This made her and Jayes free women in the colony and not contracted to service for their transportation.

Mr. Turner's will had left everything and all household goods to his wife, Guinever. This included his servants, and all land which would equal 1000 acres of land. Including the head rights of 11 servants.

"Gin, they are not going to just hand over a thousand acres of land to us," Jayes told her.

"They have no choice; it is due to us." Gin brushed off Jayes worry and continued with her forgery. "The laws are different here, or they are right now. There are many widows that maintain their own property here in Virginia. It is not like England. Woman have rights here, they have yet to make the laws to take those rights away from us." Gin explained when she saw the worried look on Jayes face.

"One night, Mr. Turner had held a meeting late, I think it was a secret meeting. There were three or four of the ancient planters here." Gin whispered, kind of like Jayes had whispered secrets to her brother even though no one was ever around to hear. She called it 'the secret voice.' "They had been talking about a letter that had been received by King Charles." Gin sat her feather quill down and crossed her arms. The King was considering allowing a Mr. Amis to import 500,000 pounds of Spanish tobacco into England." Gin said as though it was such a horrible thing for the King to do.

Jayes did not understand why that would be so bad, she thought that would take the pressure off of her and all the other servants in Virginia, so how could that be bad?

"You do not understand. If England was to buy or begin to plant the Spanish tobacco the price of our tobacco, not to mention the demand would fall so low it would devastate and destroy us!" Gin explained. She stood up furious. "King Charles knew this too! He had said in his letter, might it be said," She mimicked King Charles in a high pitched squeaky voice. "That the plantations was wholly built on a weed that made smoke, it could easily disappear like air if either tobacco was permitted to be planted or Spanish imported."

Jayes was delighted, "He threatened to destroy Virginia? If he succeeded, we could go home! There would be no need to have us here!"

"Jayes, do you really think they care that much about you, or any of us for that matter? Do you believe that they would go to the expense of the Kings pockets to take you back to Ireland? No. That would never happen. They do not even plan to return the dark skinned people." Gin said as she sat down again. "My husband and his conspirators talked about that too. They said that they did not want them here, but because of their skin and their endurance to the summer heats they are good- for now. They do not want them mixing with good English blood, so when the time comes, they plan on eliminating them, and you!"

Jayes had heard about the summer heats, surely they could not be like the heats that she felt upon the ship on the way here she thought. She hadn't thought of her skin, was the sun here closer? Jayes had never even thought of that before.

"They plan on eliminating them when their work is done Jayes! Just like they would eliminate us, only they would just leave us here and let the Indians do it for them!" Gin was obviously upset. Jayes had no doubt that what she said was true.

"So, what happened? Did the King buy the Spanish tobacco? Does England no longer have use for Virginia? Are we going to rot and die here?" Jayes cried worried as she stood and began to pace the room.

"No, that's over now." Gin said calmly.

Jayes turned to her angry. "Then what was the point of this story? You had me scared to death!"

"Oh, my point was with the Governor dead, and the new government all at odds with each other," Gin began tracing signatures as she spoke. Jayes wanted to wring her neck. Sometimes Gin made no sense and just talked to get a rise out of people. "Well, that Captain West, the new governor, he is worst of all ya know. He is a snooty gentry's type." Gin looked up making a face of disapproval of Capt. West.

"Just explain! I don't care about how snooty or how not snooty he is. Explain how this, lying and forging papers is going to get us 650 acres of land. We are women!"

"That is what is so wonderful about this new land! There are no laws saying that a woman cannot be a landowner, not yet anyways. We will need to be especially nice to Captain West of course. That should not be a problem for you, you are even friendly with the heathens. We will need him on our side or he is gonna be a problem, he doesn't really like women either, we don't have to go to him right away. And they're not gonna really care what we are doin. They're too busy with business and compromising with the King. They promised not to sell to anyone but England and the King," Gin paused and finally took a breath as she looked up. "Well, the King promised not to buy from the Spanish fields. They're all busy now compromising on price, and Indians and of course labor. They said the King is sending more men to farm." Gin looked up happily. "And salt! Oh I forgot about the salts and sturgeons."

Jayes had heard enough. She didn't care about the King, and she could care even less about salt. She thought that Gin was ignorant, nothing she was mumbling about had anything to do with forging papers. All she could think about was feeling the whip against her skin again. She was scared. She did not think this was a good idea.

"I need to go check on the boys and Arabette," Jayes said.

"You care about them don't you?" Gin asked not looking up from the paper.

Jayes thought for a moment, she did not trust Gin completely but she answered, "I care about them very much."

"I will let you keep them. They can be yours." Gin said as she looked up. She expected Jayes to thank her and be happy.

Jayes forced a smile. "Gin, how do you know so much about the business of the King?" she asked.

Gin looked up, her smile gone. "My husband and his friends were enemies of some of the members of Virginia's Council. There have been lines drawn and sides taken. They chose to meet in private to stay neutral, you do not want to show your true allegiance until you know the victor." Gin looked down again. "If ever asked, I know nothing. My knowledge though has bought us some powerful friends Jayes."

Jayes understood what she meant. Perhaps, Gin was not as daft as she pretended to be. Maybe she was not daft at all, she just did not focus on conversation or words well. Jayes smiled and walked out the door letting it close behind her. She would never understand Gin, she had to respect her in a way, despite her selfishness she survived and adapted, even if it was just to save herself.

She wanted to tell her that they were people, you cannot own people, and you cannot sell yourself so save it and be saved. The children were not Gin's to give away, but Jayes would hold her to that, she went quickly through the dark to the little hut. If this worked the children would be free too. She would make certain of that.

"Jayes. Jayes, wake up."

Jayes opened her eyes to see Gin standing above her. She was gently shaking her awake. Jayes looked around and realized she was in the small hut. Arabette was cuddled in her arms. She looked at Gin in question.

"Is everything alright?" she asked as she gently moved Arabette and sat up rubbing her eyes.

"Yes, I need to show you something." Gin said and she gently stroked Arabette's hair. "She is a sweet little girl." Gin said with so much affection it shocked Jayes.

"Yes, she is. This is Arabette. Her Mother was killed in the Indian attack," Jayes said standing.

Gin looked up at her. "She is an orphan then?"

Jayes regretted telling Gin. She wanted to take Arabette away from here, somewhere safe, even though she had no idea where that might be.

"She shouldn't be out here after such a shock." Gin said. "Pick her up, bring her into the house. She can sleep with me."

Jayes felt panicky. She did not want to turn Arabette over to Gin. She knelt down and picked her up. As they were walking towards the house, Jayes thanked Gin. "Thank you for giving me the children and for caring about Arabette as much as I do."

Gin did not say anything. Jayes was worried. When they got to the house Jayes laid Arabette down. Gin sat on the bed next to her.

"Go read the papers on the table. I need you to tell me what you think." Gin did not take her eyes off Arabette.

Jayes went to read the papers. They were perfect! The signatures were identical as well as the writing on all the documents. The only difference was the contents of the documents themselves.

JAYES – 1627

To Jayes astonishment, she picked up one document that was new, it was signed between the former Governor Yeardley and Captain Tristam James. It was for a tract of land of 3000 acres, 1500 acres guaranteed immediately on the plantation known as 'the curls' to be planted and used at his convenience on the condition that Indian corn be planted as well as tobacco. That the buildings would be repaired and within 3 years an additional patent would be granted for an additional 1500 acres granted for the head rights of passengers delivered to Virginia.

Another was the contract between Mr. Turner and Captain James that stated that Mr. Turner was hired to oversee and prepare his property during his absence and in return would be delivered 25 servants of healthy and viable men, women and boys with their head rights attached.

Jayes had read this contract and knew it was a variation of the original. The only difference being the deletion of the return of a servant, Jayes Mackey. Jayes saw the original document lying under it on the table. She picked it up, walked toward the fire and watched it burn.

Jayes picked up the land contract to Captain James and went into the room. "What is this?" she asked Gin.

"Your land. Your land to 'oversee', until and if your Captain comes back. I do promise that the 50 acres that I can claim of you will be yours. You will have to work it but you will be free. I am sorry Jayes. I do not know what happened to me. I hope someday you forgive me for all I have done." Gin said with more sincerity than Jayes had heard even the first night she had met her. The night in Ireland when she had been sobbing uncontrollably in an Irish jail cell.

Jayes remembered that Gin, the child that had begged to go home. She looked at Gin stroking Arabette's hair and knew she connected to her as an orphan. Jayes knew she had lost

Arabette to Gin. She had a strange feeling that Arabette would be well taken care of.

Jayes smiled, thankfully. "If this works I thank you. I am grateful. We are friends Gin, always. I forgive you." She turned and went to lay down with the boys in the hut. Nothing more was ever said. Jayes did forgive Gin, however the scars left by the lash of the whip on her back along with the brand on her shoulder, would never allow her to forget.

Thirteen
New beginnings in a new world…

Spring came swiftly with the warm winds. Trees began to fill with vibrant colors of new life. Pinks, purples and reds. Flowers began to bloom in the marshes and the grasses grew tall, taller than any grass Jayes had ever seen. There was new life all around, even in the trees baby birds began to sing.

There was a sweet new smell in the air, a smell that at one time would have sent Jayes into the hills dancing and celebrating the new season. Picking flowers and dancing on the cliffs singing songs of joy to God.

The singing of the birds did not even cheer her. Jayes was focused on freedom. Focused on making a life with her son. Focused on winning this battle that she had found herself fighting.

There was no doubt this was a battle. Jayes laid awake at night thinking and knowing she would do whatever it took to win it. She would not lie down and let these English Colonists win. She was not their prisoner, she was their enemy, and she was prepared to fight for her life.

Today was a day that would bring her one step closer to her freedom. They would put on the nicest dresses they could come up with given the few materials they had at their use. Jayes finished making the final touches to her hair and donned a white bonnet upon her head.

"Are you ready?" Gin asked her unsure and worried. "You need to be strong, you cannot falter or show weakness today."

"I am ready; I will not show weakness to my enemies," Jayes said with strong determination. Gin looked at her oddly for a moment not understanding her meaning but satisfied with her answer.

"Corzara!" She yelled. "We are ready!" Corzara ducked through the doorway with his big frame. Taking his cap off as he entered.

"The boat is ready Miss Gin." He turned and smiled at Jayes. "I have John and Will ready to make the trip. The boys are excited to be allowed to accompany you and spend the day in town."

Two weeks ago a messenger had arrived from a ship that arrived in Jamestown. A total of three ships had recently docked at Jamestown, one from Ireland and two from England. All bringing new servants, men and women of all ages. Most were prisoners who had been sentenced by King Charles to service in Virginia.

Jayes smiled at Corzara. He had become a new person since the Indian attack. No longer was he feared by the servants. He was kind and no longer cruel. Arabette described him as her big, black bear. That had become his new nick name.

Corzara worked just as hard as anyone else on the plantation. Surprisingly, Gin had started pitching in. Everyone had begun to work together, and they did work hard, sometimes from sunrise to sunset. Life was still not easy by any means, teamwork and peace made it bearable.

Gin gathered the papers together. "Let's go get us some

tobacco farmers." She smiled. Jayes was very happy she did not call them slaves or servants. The people they acquired today would be the lucky ones, of that Jayes was certain.

As they neared Jamestown no one spoke. Jayes barely making out several ships anchored in the river. From the distance she could not tell if any were Tristam's, she had gotten to know what the top sails of his ship looked like from her days hiding on deck.

She was a little disappointed but also relieved. She really did not know if she wanted to see him again.

When they reached Jamestown, the town was bustling with activity. Four large ships were anchored near shore, a new one had recently docked. Jayes scanned hopefully for Tristam's ship and realizing with certainty it was not there, she felt disappointment in her heart.

She heard Gin laughing. "If it was there, I would have to tie you up."

"Why would you do that?" Jayes asked her.

"Well, I am going to kill him one day, not today though. I have a feeling that when I do, I will have to go through you. Since I cannot kill you to get to him, I plan to tie you up while I do the deed." Gin was half joking, half serious. Unfortunately, both girls knew she was more than half serious.

Jayes and Gin walked accompanied with both boys and Corzara. Jayes was surprised at the shocked faces of so many people when they saw that large black man. There were other Negroes in the colony, though not many, and very few compared to the size of Corzara.

Jayes walked along the shore and up the little hill along the banks to the remains of Fort Jamestown. The Church was hard to miss, it stood tall inside the wooden walls of the fort.

As they walked along the path, a few settlers were selling

their wares. Woven baskets, blankets, sewn dresses, hats and gloves. Jayes did not take the time to stop and look, she missed the days of going to market at home but it was not the same.

At one time in her life, a time so far forgotten, those had been some of the happiest days of her life. She loved bargaining with merchants, it was a game to her, one she had often won.

As they approached the church, Jayes marveled at the brick. There were very few brick buildings to be found in Virginia, and this one was magnificent. Most of the dwellings were made of wood or mud. To find glass was almost unheard of. Although they had constructed a glass making house for that purpose, the glass so far was reserved for governors, council members and some ancient planters, and of course the church. The church mesmerized Jayes, it just seemed so out of place. The only sense of civilization, a feeling of real life in Virginia. This foreign place that at times seemed so far from the world Jayes had known.

As they walked past the small graveyard and alongside the church, her eyes were drawn to three servants that had been publicly hung. They had obviously been dead for several days. Their bodies being picked apart piece by piece by large birds.

A small crowd stood to look, they all stopped horrified.

"What did they do?" John asked a tall man standing nearby.

"They ate their masters' dog," the man said before he walked off.

"Let's keep walking," Jayes instructed the boys. She felt sick to her stomach, suddenly she was having second thoughts.

As she walked under the tall arch of the church, Jayes noticed that inside it was full to capacity, there was standing room only. Jayes had never seen this many people in Jamestown before, not even the day she arrived and was 'sold'.

She had a flashback of the day in court, the day her life changed forever. She had been so certain that day…She was uncertain of what they were about to do. She could picture herself hanging outside these walls, becoming bird food.

Jayes paused, she began to back up. She was about to turn and run. Corzara looked at her, smiling, he placed his hands on her shoulders.

The big, gentle, black bear, who rarely spoke, said: "You are a fighter. You have a purpose: you must face your enemies and battle them. I know you are ready. You are strong, you have shown that."

Jayes thanked him with her eyes, turned back around, and walked forward.

Jayes did not recognize any of the men in the room. Most of them were much older, and some even wearing powdered wigs and robes.

"Mrs. Turner, is that you?" One of the powdered, red lipped and rosy cheeked gentlemen asked Gin.

Gin immediately turned on her English charm. She approached the gentleman and kissed him on both cheeks without contact and then gave him a hug without the hug. Jayes watched and rolled her eyes, she would never understand these English ways.

"Captain West!" Gin exclaimed. "Oh, how happy I am to see you have made it safely through such horrors." Gin bowed her head, Captain West took his cue.

"I was so sorry to hear about your husband. Such tragic news," he said taking her hands in sympathy.

"I think I may have begun to love him. We will never know." Gin said as honestly as she could. "I have recovered from my wounds, there was a moment I thought I would join him in heaven." Gin said with such drama.

Jayes had to cover her mouth with her hand, she could not keep a straight face. She started to turn and walk away but thought better of it.

"You were wounded?" Captain West asked in surprise. "Not bad I suspect, you're standing here."

"Oh, no! It was bad!" Gin was now showing Captain West where her cut had been. "It was from here to here, and so wide! I nearly bled to death. If it hadn't been for my dearest friend Jayes, I surely would have bled to death." Gin turned to Jayes.

"Oh, my manners! How silly of me!" Gin exaggerated. "Captain John West, may I introduce you to a longtime family friend, Miss Jayes Mackey."

"How do you do Miss Mackey," Captain West was confused, Jayes seemed somewhat familiar to him. "Have we met?" he asked Jayes.

"Oh no, unfortunately when we had the pleasure of your company, Miss Jayes was out in the woods. She likes to gather her herbs and weeds you know." Gin laughed. "Thankfully, she saved my life! I will never speak ill of a weed again."

They all laughed. Jayes rolled her eyes. She was impressed with the way that Gin could easily adapt to their world. It should not surprise her, after all she was one of them.

"Well, Widow Guinever, our Colony is founded on a weed now, and been quite good to us too." Captain West joked.

"Ooh, let us hope it does not go up in smoke!" Gin countered and again they laughed.

"You are such a witty creature Guinever," the Governor said. Jayes silently excused herself and walked over towards the small window that faced shore. Jayes looked outside, she could see hundreds of new prisoners, naked and lined up for inspection. Cattle, Jayes told herself feeling anger.

Gin interrupted her. "Jayes, do you have your papers with

JAYES – 1627

you? It seems that there are no records." Gin said acting unconcerned.

Jayes walked over to the table that had been set up as a makeshift desk for the Governor, handing him her papers.

"Is there a problem?" she asked with her best English accent.

The new Governor was flipping through a ledger. "No, I am sorry, my deepest apologies ladies. It seems that your arrival was so near to Governor Yeardley's illness and his death." Governor West said absent mindedly with his face buried in the ledgers. He finally looked up. "It seems he did not have time to record you into the records."

"Captain West, surely this is not a problem? Oh, my apologies, I mean Governor," Gin said with her 'woe is me', damsel in distress voice. She put her hand onto his arm. "You are the Governor now, surely you have the power to set things right?" She asked with a smile.

"Of course I do!" Governor West assured her smiling, patting her hand. "And I will, I assure you!" he said. "Your documentation seems to be legal, I will enter it this very minute," he said as he grabbed his pen.

Jayes read as he wrote:

Guinever Sinclair, England, arrived a freeman on October 20, 1627, granted 50 acres of land at the Curls, Married Thomas Turner, Widowed, entrusted through his will with 1000 acres of land, all his household goods and servants.

Jayes Mackey, England, Arrived freeman on October 20, 1627, granted 750 acres of land entrusted to her by Captain Tristam James of England for the head-rights granted him upon passage of servants near Diggs Hundred Upper James.

Governor West closed the book and returned it to its place in the 'archived ledgers'. "Problem solved," he smiled at Gin, who gave him such a look of admiration, it was amazing he did not fall to his feet and propose marriage there on the spot.

Jayes had to give it to her, she was a very good actress. She had missed her true calling.

"Now on the matters of credit." Governor West handed them both vouchers which could be used at the sale and in town for goods.

Jayes did not bother to look, from Gin's reaction she knew that it was a very generous amount.

As they made their way down to the auction, Jayes felt as though she was becoming the enemy. She was going to purchase slave servants. She could not help but feel she was becoming one of them. She never wanted to be one of them.

A bugle sounded and the auctioneer began shouting. The crowd livened up and prospective buyers stepped forward to bargain with each other. Jayes was shoved forward violently by a giant of a man with blond hair and burnt skin.

"Watch where ye stand girl, you might find yourself under my boot if you don't!" He said angrily as he continued forward. Jayes followed his gaze.

Standing there was a young girl, naked and crying. Her long blond hair covered nearly half her body to her knees. The brute walked up, brushed her hair aside and cupped her breasts with his hands.

"I like this one, I have a special place for her," he said loudly, the crowd laughed. The poor girl started to cry louder and he slapped her violently across the face. "I like it when they resist," he said, then he turned, looked into the crowd and said. "They don't resist for long."

"One hundred pounds of Tobacco for her," Jayes shouted stepping forward. "I have a place for her too!" She smiled, turned towards the crowd and said. "In my kitchen!" The crowd laughed again.

Gin started to pull on Jayes' arm. "What are you doing? We need help in the fields, not the kitchen!" Jayes ignored her and broke free. She could here Gin make a huff as she turned and walked off.

"One hundred ten," the man said glaring at Jayes. Jayes glared back, she would make certain this girl never became his property.

"One fifty!" Jayes shouted. "I can go higher, sir," Jayes said looking directly at him.

"Take her, she is too thin for me anyway," he said giving Jayes a look of hatred. "The wench would more than likely break in half under me anyways," he said as he walked off and disappeared into the crowd.

Corzara stood nearby her. Jayes finally noticed him there. She gave him a look of gratitude realizing that it was more his presence that saved the girl than Gin's credit.

Jayes looked at the girl. "What is your name?" she asked.

"Persis," she said quietly, not looking up.

"Persis, go stand with that man, he will give you a blanket to cover yourself with," Jayes said pointing her towards Corzara. The girl looked over to Corzara then quickly looked up to Jayes fearfully.

"He will not hurt you," Jayes whispered. "I promise you."

The girl walked off towards Corzara. Jayes purchased two more men from the auction. She decided to go to the local farmers and purchased some cornmeal, a couple chickens, flour, an iron pot, some fabric and a few other supplies that she was certain she would need for her new home.

Jayes was just about to walk to the church when Gin found her.

"Where have you been?" Gin asked irritated. "I have been

looking everywhere for you. Captain West is waiting for us; he needs to record our purchases."

"Oh, ok, Corzara, could you take these supplies and the servants back to the ship?" Jayes asked him.

"He cannot take the servants. They need to place their signatures on their contracts," Gin said. "Well their thumb prints. Captain West is very thorough."

"Oh, well then, can you take the chickens and these," Jayes said to Corzara unloading the items she was carrying into Corzara's arms. Will and John, you take these."

"Oh!" Gin exclaimed. "I almost forgot. The Captain had been so kind as to give us tenants! They are free!"

Jayes shook her head. "They are not free as in 'you own them type of for free' Gin. They are free-men. They have worked off their contracts and are trying to make their way in this new life. They rent from you while they help you farm your land and they farm theirs." Sometimes Jayes just could not understand how Gin's mind actually worked.

"Oh, well they work for free. He has four for you today. He is giving me special tenants that he will deliver in the next couple days," Gin said proudly. Jayes was certain she would not be there when he arrived, she already started making plans in her mind to go explore her new Plantation.

Jayes remained silent, she was at a loss for words and did not want to open her mouth and offend Gin. Jayes did not really think that Gin meant ill will, she honestly believed that Gin did not know any better. Gin had been raised with privilege, she had been taught from an early age she was one of the 'betters'. Better than most.

Inside the church was even busier than before. Men were shouting, standing in a much unorganized line trying to get the Governors attention, new servants in tow. They had not stood there very long when a young and well-dressed gentleman came up to Gin.

"Widow Guinever?" he asked.

"Yes?" Gin turned, not sure if she should turn her charm on or not. Jayes watched the dilemma on her face and could tell the moment that Gin had decided, when in doubt-turn it on.

"Governor West said that you can go. He knows you have a long trip home. He said to tell you that he will finalize Miss Mackey and your purchases when he visits later this week," the man informed her.

"That is so kind of him," Gin said with so much emotion, it did not even seem real. The man was not immune to Gin's near tearful gratitude.

"Well, a Lady like you should not be standing around in the company of people like this." He motioned the occupants of the room with his hands. "Please allow me to see you safely to your boat."

"How kind of you," Gin said, for the first time Jayes realized she was not completely acting. As they passed under the arch of the church, Jayes made a secret sign of the cross, it was only respectful.

"Allow me to introduce myself, I am Daniel Geoken the Second," he said.

"Lovely to meet you," Gin said. "I am Guinever Sinclair Turner; my friends call me Gin. This is Miss Jayes Mackey." Gin turned allowing introductions for a brief moment. "Do you live near Governor West? He is my nearest neighbor you know," Gin said.

"Unfortunately I am not. My land, my Da's land is near the ocean and on the other side of the River James. It is quite beautiful." He smiled. He was a very polite and charming man. Jayes almost felt sorry for him. She knew though that Gin was not a fan of being a wife. He was more than likely safe.

The docks were very busy. Gin saw a small opening where the grass was not tall. She decided to take the shortcut, leading Mr. Geoken. They took a couple steps onto the bank of the river. Gin raised her hand to get Corzara's attention and suddenly her feet fell out underneath her. Gin went flying onto her backside taking the poor young man with her.

"Help!" Gin shouted, trying to stand back up only to lose her balance again. The mud was a dark red color and extremely thick. Gin and Mr. Geoken were painted in it. Jayes took a step forward to try to help and felt her foot begin to slip. She quickly stepped back away from the mud. The red mud was like walking on glass, no traction what-so-ever.

Jayes looked at Gin helplessly, who was still screaming. She was on all fours trying to stand, her hands slipped and she fell face forward into the red mud. She was now covered head to toe. Mr. Geoken had given up, he was lying on his back watching Gin and laughing!

Corzara and the boys had maneuvered the boat nearby, they too were all laughing. Jayes turned around, and realized every one of the new servants were laughing too. Jayes rolled her eyes, she knew Gin was going to be angry. She looked at Gin who had also just realized that she was the subject of great entertainment, Gin started to yell something, lost her balance and rolled into the James.

Jayes could not control herself anymore, she succumbed to spontaneous laughter.

Gin was wet and angry the entire trip home. No one really spoke. They all sat on the deck huddled together, Gin had taken several blankets that had been brought for the new servants. Jayes sat next to a tall, black haired handsome older man who had a very thick Irish brogue.

He was one of the new tenants. He was one of Gin's least favorite new people. He had not stopped giggling since Gin's disaster with the slick mud. Gin started complaining and he started laughing, Jayes gave him a nudge with her elbow. "Shush!" She said trying not to smile, his chuckles were contagious.

"What is yer name, lass?" he asked Jayes.

"Jayes, and yours?"

"Rory Annesley, at yer service," he said putting his hand out. Jayes giggled at his cheerfulness and shook his hand. "She is not going to like you," Jayes warned.

"Well," he whispered back, "I never suspected she would, I do not have a Sir in front of me name ya know." He actually winked at Jayes. She had to bite her lip.

Jayes decided she was better off not speaking with Mr. Annesley during the rest of the trip home, she did not want to start giggling and ruin the friendship she was working on with Gin. Instead he chatted with another new tenant sitting on his other side. Jayes tried to ignore them, however it was difficult, and they did not seem to mind the nasty looks Gin was throwing their way.

The next few days were spent in preparation for the day's journey to the new Plantation. Jayes spent time mending and making alterations to the clothes of those they had buried. Master Turners came in very handy for the new servants, although most of them were too short. Jayes gathered as much as she thought Gin was willing to separate with, or as much as Jayes thought she would not notice.

There was no avoiding Governor West, she had to complete the legal paperwork from the auction. The idea of buying people still did not sit well with her conscience. Jayes assured herself that she had more 'rescued' them than bought them.

The travel delay was good, it allowed the new servants to rest and recover from their horrific journey. It gave them time to adjust to their new circumstances. Jayes thought if she would have had time to rest when she arrived, she may never have met Maybran or Cuttwma.

The Governor arrived late that afternoon with five healthy men, two women and three small children. Jayes was relieved when one of the little girls seemed to attach herself to Gin. Perhaps she would not have to worry about Arabette now.

Persis and Jayes prepared a fish stew with fresh corn bread. They had made plenty for everyone, Persis had left to deliver the rest to those who ate outside. Gin was in her element of entertaining; she was a very attentive hostess.

"Did you prepare this, Miss Mackey?" Captain West asked. "It is delicious. Thank you."

"I wish I could take the credit, Persis, our new girl is good in the kitchen," Jayes smiled.

"Speaking of credit, I do need to get your ladies signatures. Miss Mackey, your contracts will stand for a period of seven years each." He smiled as though that would please her. "Same for you my dear." He smiled at Gin. "All we need is the thumbprint of each servant."

Jayes jumped up finding a way to excuse herself. "I will take care of that," she said as she snatched up the papers and ink jar, turned and walked out the door leaving Gin and the Governor alone.

Jayes went out to the servant's hut, which was overcrowded now to get the prints. Rory and another tenant was sitting outside stirring the fire.

"That was the best meal I have had in years. Thank you,"

Rory said sincerely.

"You should thank Persis, it was her idea. The boys caught the fish," Jayes said.

"They are good boys. Yours?" Rory asked.

Jayes laughed. "No!" Do you really think I started birthing children as I learned to walk?" Jayes rolled her eyes, shook her head and headed into the hut. She could hear Rory sputtering apologies behind her as his friend laughed.

The hut was dark, and quiet. Jayes saw Persis sitting on her blanket weaving a basket. "You seem to fit in here quite well. I cannot make a basket, I have tried and failed," Jayes joked, although she was quite serious. She looked at the papers in her hand.

"Persis, I need your thumbprint." Jayes hated having to ask. She jumped at the opportunity to escape, she now wished she would not have volunteered for this painful task.

Persis took the paper that Jayes had handed her. She read it slowly in the dim light.

"You want me to sign that I agree to be your slave because you purchased me?" Persis asked simply, without anger. "How can you purchase me when I was never for sale? When those that took me had no right to take me and even less right to sell me? I did not belong to them and I do not belong to you."

Every servant sat up as they listened to Persis, waiting to hear Jayes reply. Jayes looked around the room, she was not the enemy. She felt as though she was, and it was an awful feeling.

Jayes started to untie the front of her dress. Slowly she removed the sleeve from her arm and slipped down the back of the dress. She turned so everyone in the room could see the scars from the whip on her back and shoulder. She could hear gasps.

"I was sent here against my will too. I did not deserve the

fate handed to me either. I am not your enemy. I do not want to own you," Jayes said as she re-dressed and tied her dress.

"You do own us," one of the men that Jayes had purchased yesterday said from behind her.

"I do not agree with the rules, I have to abide by them though and so do you," Jayes tried to explain. "I will promise you that I will never treat you like a slave."

"You will not treat us like an equal, I know people like you," the man said hatefully. Jayes was angered and turned on him.

"What is your name?" Jayes asked walking toward him. He was reluctant to reply.

"Alastar," he finally replied.

"Alastar. I do own you. You are in the New World, where they make their own laws. You are at their mercy, and they do not tolerate disobedience or insolence; they whip it into submission!" Jayes was angry she was being accused of being one of them. "I have to play by their rules, too! I am not one of them. I will never hurt you or ask you to work harder than I am willing to work."

"You're going to force us to work!" Alastar cut in.

"Of course I am!" Jayes looked at him as though he was daft. "If we do not work we do not eat! If we do not work, we cannot go home!" Jayes nearly shouted. That seemed to get their attention. Jayes looked around, everyone seemed to be waiting for an explanation.

"I want to go home, I do not want to stay here. I need your help. We have land, we have seed and we have an opportunity to change the path of our stars. I cannot do it alone. I need your help, if I did not need help, I would never have purchased any of you." Jayes could hear her voice crack, she was about ready to cry.

"I will help you, I believe you. I know these people in this colony, she is not like them. You are lucky that this woman bought you, very fortunate." Rory said from the doorway.

Persis stood and took the ink jar from Jayes, she placed her print on the paper. Alastar stood and Jayes handed him his contract. Jayes handed Persis the contracts to the servants that Gin had purchased. She prayed that Gin had learned her lesson on how to treat people, she knew that from here on out Corzara would be kind.

The only contract left was for the other boy about her age that Jayes had purchased. He sat in the corner with a frown on his face watching Jayes. She looked at the contract, the name on it read Liam McDougal.

McDougal! Jayes immediately looked up at the boy, looking for any recognition. She did not seem to remember ever seeing him before. The glare that he was giving her though....

"Liam?" Jayes asked looking at him and holding out the contract towards him. The boy slammed the shirt down that he had been holding in his lap as he sat cross legged. He stood up, stomping towards her and snatched the paper from Jayes.

"This paper is a lie, you will never own me!" He said as he turned his back on Jayes.

"I do not want to own you," Jayes said with tears in her eyes, realizing this boy hated her as much as she had hated Mr. Turner. Jayes stood there watching with regret as one by one each servant applied their print to the documents that agreed to surrender their freedom for seven years of labor. In return they would receive a pair of shoes, some food and new clothing. No land was offered under the laws of King James, they could become freemen and tenants. It was an unfair bargain, Jayes knew many never lived long enough to ever be free again. Most servants, died in service to their master.

That would not happen with hers, she would take care of them and not work them like oxen until they fell and died. Jayes looked to Rory and mouthed the words 'thank you.'"

As Jayes was walking back to the house she heard Rory call her name, she turned.

"You do not have to thank me. I would never lie to those people. I just hope you are who I think you are," he said.

"Who do you think I am?" Jayes asked him.

"A desperate but determined woman with a kind and loving heart," he said studying Jayes.

Jayes looked at him, repeating his words in her head. "You are very perceptive, goodnight Rory." Jayes started walking again.

"Miss Mackey?" Rory called her again. "What time do we leave tomorrow?"

"Morning light," Jayes said over her shoulder still walking. Rory was a challenge she thought. She had never really met anyone quite like him before.

The next morning Jayes opened her eyes as the sun slowly rose. She laid in bed watching as the sun moved across through the openings between cracks in the logs that made the wall. Jayes just stared at the bright light that shone through, like staring into the flame of a burning fire. Even through the wall Jayes could see the heat in the glowing light of the morning sun.

Persis packed food for the journey. Everyone was loaded with supplies, even Arabette carried two empty buckets for water. Jayes was unsure of the exact location of Tristam's plantation, now her plantation. Governor West had given directions on a rough map he had drawn out. The plantation was northwest of Gin's, along the river. They walked west and followed the river north. Jayes was about ready to have everyone stop and rest when a clearing came into view. Jayes thought it looked like an old corn field, with a small gate around it, more than likely to protect the corn from wild animals.

"Look, it's a path!" John shouted, everyone turned, the men patting him on the head for being a 'good scout'. Jayes waited as everyone followed John down the path. There were now eleven others besides Jayes that were going to call this new place home. Eleven whose fate depended on the soil, and most of all, that Tristam James did not come home.

Fourteen
Fate is a funny thing…

For weeks they had worked from sun up until way past the sun setting. They took small breaks in the hottest part of the day, and tried to cool down at the river's edge, washing the dirt from their bodies that had turned them red. The heat at times was unbearable, leaving them drenched from the skin out with sweat, dropping from their brows as quickly as they could replenish it with drink.

It seemed as though they had made no progress, clearing trees, brush and grass. Today, Jayes stood at the edge of the newly open ground and could finally see progress, she could see the dark red pebbled dirt.

"We have accomplished much." Rory said as he came to stand next to her, tying his river soaked shirt around his neck. Jayes looked at him, he was half naked, a sight she was no longer offended by, but would never get used to.

"It has taken us so long. Our tobacco seeds should have been planted months ago. Do you think the plants will reach their full growth in time?" she asked, afraid of the answer.

"Have faith Jayes, God has blessed you this far, he will not abandon you now."

"You think God has blessed me?" Jayes thought it was

funny. "Blessed me with what?" she asked.

"You have your freedom. You have land. You have your health, hell half this country is dying, yet we all survive." Rory took a piece of grass and started chewing it. "We should plant tomorrow. I will gather the boys and we will start planting," he said shaking his head and smiling as he walked off.

Jayes started walking too. She felt a presence, she was starting to sense when Maybran was near, or when Maybran had Kealan near. She walked into the woods, looking behind the trees.

"I cannot find you. Where are you? I know you are here," Jayes yelled into the trees.

To her surprise, Cuttwma appeared. Jayes immediately thought something was wrong with either Maybran or Kealan. She looked at him in desperate concern.

"They are fine, I was nearby and I have not seen you for a long while." He smiled at Jayes admiringly. "You look well."

"Do I look well because I am painted with earth?" she teased.

"No, well yes, it does suit your complexion. I meant you look healthy."

"Much better than I was last you saw me." Jayes just realized they were having a real conversation.

"Your English? You have been learning?"

"Yes, I have been spending time with my sister. She has been teaching us."

"Us?" Jayes asked, why had Maybran not mentioned this to her?

"Those that want to friend the white skins, or trade, some of the children," he replied.

"The children?" Jayes asked.

"The White Skins will pay them well to interpret and teach

them the language." Cuttwma explained.

"There have been strict laws placed. The Colonists are not allowed to trade with the Indians," Jayes said.

"It is not trading, they pay for services." He laughed.

"Ah, yes, there is always an interpretation of the laws." Jayes smiled at him. "I am happy to see you Cuttwma," she said. "I need to thank you."

"For what?" Cuttwma asked, embarrassed.

"For what??" She giggled spinning around and pointing towards her fields. "For that. Unless the spirits have set out in the dead of the night, working on moving trees and branches." Jayes turned back towards him. "Do spirits make chickens and supplies appear in my barn?"

Cuttwma could not resist laughing. "Perhaps." He smiled.

Jayes stared him down, smiling.

"You are welcome," he said. "I must go, until I see you again." Cuttwma turned and quickly disappeared.

Jayes turned and began to walk back to the field, she walked right into Rory's broad chest and nearly fell backwards. He reached out to steady her as he laughed.

"How long have you been here?" She demanded, not giving him a chance to reply. "You should not spy on people!" Jayes remembered Cuttwma, her eyes wide as she studied Rory.

"How long have you been standing there?" she asked.

"Not long, I did not see the Indian you were talking to." Rory said with a straight face.

"Oh good," Jayes said as she started to walk past him, the words slowly registered. She stopped dead in mid stride, lost her balance and shouted 'you saw him!' as she fell.

Rory was laughing uncontrollably. "Did you really think I did not know?" he asked her as he gave her his hand to help her up. Jayes was in shock, she did not know what to think.

JAYES – 1627

"How long?" Jayes had so many questions but those were the only two words that she could get out of her mouth.

"How long?" Rory repeated and looked up in thought. "Well, I would say days within meeting you, well the first day that we came to the plantation." Rory said.

"How? They even avoided me when you guys came? You're fibbing." Jayes did not believe for a moment he knew that long.

"Tools in the barn for farming? Chickens in a coop that had been abandoned for years, half wild hogs roaming nearby as we arrived. Beddings conveniently lying about behind the houses. Should I go on, oh and the pottery!" Rory was chuckling.

"Yes, I suppose that looked a little suspicious. They were gifts you know," Jayes said biting her lip. She knew that Rory had friends in Jamestown, there were strict laws about associating with the Indians.

Rory must have read her mind. "Your secret is safe with me. You can trust me Jayes."

"I know, I am sorry. It is not that I do not trust you, I just didn't know."

"How I felt about the Indians?" Rory finished for her.

"You were here when..."

"When they massacred nearly half the colony?" he finished again.

"Yes." Jayes put her head down. She could not defend the Indians for the massacre, she would never defend anyone for killing children.

"I was here, actually, I was not living far from here." Rory pointed south, "I was living almost directly across the river." Rory sat down, he patted the ground next to him and Jayes sat. "The Indians were provoked. There was a lot of wrong on both sides. The Indians had been thought weak, they had been treated poorly, their crops and supplies stolen, their women raped. They took a stand, a deadly one."

"So you do not hate them?" Jayes asked him.

"I do not hate them anymore than the men who wear wigs and wield their bibles in one hand and their whips in the other," Rory said with pain in his voice. He stood up. "You can trust me Jayes, we are on the same side."

"I am sorry I lied to you," Jayes said as he helped her up.

"You did not lie to me. There is a difference, you did not trust me with the truth," he said.

"I will trust you with my life," Jayes said.

The planting began, rows and rows of seed. A little prayer with every part of the planted ground. Jayes had been on her skinned and dry knees for days, her shoulders and back burnt. Her body ached, her shoulders so painful from her bent over position that it was painful to try to stand.

The boys had been catching fish day and night. Rory and his team planting on the other side of the field. Persis had been given the duties of cleaning, cooking and watching Arabette.

Jayes finished planting her last fish with the remaining seed, thankful the Indians had taught the white man this trick to ensure a strong, healthy crop. She would have to take a break and wait for the boys. The heat was getting worse with each day. Normally Jayes would walk down to the stream and soak her feet and knees. Today she was too tired. She walked over to the tree line, found some shade and laid down. She had not closed her eyes for long when she heard a sound, she opened her eyes and looked up. Maybran was standing above her with Kealan in her arms.

"You are not going to get your planting done while you sleep." Maybran teased. Jayes jumped up and took her baby in her arms, kissing him.

"I ran out of fish," Jayes said absently.

"Fish?" Maybran asked with a wide grin.

"Yes, the fish, the fish helps the seed grow. Something like that, it's called fertilizer, it helps," Jayes said, surprised Maybran did not know about fertilizer.

Maybran started laughing, dramatically. She threw herself on the ground rolled onto her back and grabbed ahold of her tummy. "I cannot believe it's true!" She laughed.

Jayes had no idea what she was talking about. She was actually annoyed that Maybran was taking her attention away from her son.

"It is a, how do you say? A farce? A jest?" Maybran was still laughing.

"What on earth are you talking about?" Jayes was irritated now.

"You are short, the sun is getting to you." Maybran laughed harder.

"Short? Maybran that makes no sense! Explain! What is so funny?"

"You do NOT plant your seed with fish. You do not bury your seed. It takes much more time to grow." Maybran said as she snatched the small bag of tiny seeds next to Jayes and began running into the field.

Jayes ran after her careful not to trip with Kealan in her arms. Jayes watched in horror as Maybran reached into the bag, took a handful of seeds and began dropping them as she ran down the rows prepared for planting.

Jayes realized what she was doing. She began screaming. "No! No!" Jayes was horrified! Her heart was painful, breathing difficult. Kealan began crying. Jayes fell to her knees crying. Her dreams had just been thrown into the dirt of what was her hell.

Maybran came over to her. "Are you hurt?"

"Do you know what you have done?" Jayes cried. "You destroyed every hope I had of ever going home! Of ever being truly free." Jayes buried her face in her crying son's hair. "I am so sorry," she said to him. "I am so sorry."

Jayes finally looked up at Maybran, she was smiling. Rory and the other three tenants were standing there too, all silent, unaware of what was happening. They all had worried expressions.

"Your seeds will grow," Maybran said kneeling down and taking her chin in her hand.

"You did not plant them, you threw them," Jayes said not believing Maybran knew what she done.

"No, the seeds will take root. We lied to the white skin. The fish was all a farce, they believed it and we laugh, all tribes from ocean to ocean laughed at the white skins and their stinky fish and the extra weeks only the lucky seed need to find the sunlight." Maybran was adamant that she had done nothing harmful, her smile was reassuring Jayes.

"I have farmed many fields and never planted seed with dead fish. I never planted tobacco." Rory said trying to ease Jayes mind.

"She did not plant it though," Jayes said sniffing and wiping her eyes, the tears still leaking out.

"Trust me." Maybran said.

Jayes looked up at her. She looked at Kealan. Maybran had never done anything to hurt her before. Jayes had no reason to believe she would hurt her now.

"She has no choice but to try and trust you now." Liam said aloud. "We all have to trust you. Our very lives depend on those seeds." Liam turned and walked away.

"What do you want me to do with the rest of these seeds?"

JAYES – 1627

Rory asked Jayes. Jayes looked up and in the distance saw John and Will coming with a bucket of fish.

Jayes looked at Maybran, who was no longer smiling, she too was waiting for Jayes to answer. Jayes was so torn. She looked at Kealan, she remembered the chickens, the gifts and all of the work that Maybran and her tribe had secretly done for her, never asking for anything in return. Nothing but her trust and friendship.

"Spread them out on the soil. Do not plant them, we will do what Maybran has taught us," Jayes said as she kissed her sons head. Maybran smiled and for the first time, she gave Jayes a hug.

Rory smiled, he turned to walk away, stopped and turned back to Jayes. "Are you bringing your son and friend home for dinner tonight?"

Jayes looked up in shock. She just realized that Kealan was in her arms. "How did you know?"

"He has your green eyes." Rory winked at her and walked back to the other side of the field to 'toss seed.'

The next two weeks Jayes walked around in a daze. Tears came easily to her eyes. She wanted to believe, she wanted to trust Maybran with all her heart. The doubt was killing her slowly from the inside. She told herself her heart was untrusting and that it was wrong. She should believe in Maybran, but what if she was wrong? The possibility was impossible to even think about; it would be devastating. Every time Jayes thought about it, her throat constricted, her chest hurt and tears streamed down her face.

Jayes worked on watering the corn, tending to the vegetables and helping to repair the roofs. She was avoiding the bare tobacco fields. She knew it would be weeks before they knew if the seeds were going to grow, the wait was going to be unbearable.

Jayes once again went to bed crying, she cried silently. John and Will knew something was terribly wrong. Arabette was as usual all smiles and joy, which made Jayes cry even harder.

"Wake up!" Jayes heard a man's voice, she thought she was dreaming, it was quite persistent though. "Jayes wake up!" She heard then she felt a tug on her hair.

"Ouch!" She opened her eyes, Rory was standing there. "Did you pull on my hair?" she asked him angrily.

"You would not wake up," he said defensively.

"I do not want to wake up yet, why are you waking me up anyways?" Jayes asked, confused. Rory had never come into the house and woke her.

"Come with me, I have to show you something." He seemed very happy, Jayes knew there was nothing wrong.

"Now? Why?" she asked, not wanting to leave the comfort of her bed.

"Get up now Jayes Mackey that is an order!" He demanded.

"Now you are being funny, ordering me about. I do not take orders. I will amuse you though," Jayes said. She moved Arabette aside and climbed out of bed, she was in her nightgown. She looked up at Rory.

"I won't look, besides, it covers you from neck to toe and we don't have time." Rory grabbed her wrist and pulled her through the house.

"Where are we going?" Jayes asked as they passed the barn.

"You ask too many questions Miss Mackey, just be quiet for once and follow me." Rory said, still holding onto her wrist. The sun was barely up, it was barely dark, that dimness before the sun peeps his head out.

JAYES – 1627

They reached the fields. Rory stopped. "Wait for it," he said with a silly grin. They stood in silence for only a few minutes, the sun started to rise in front of them. As the sun came up, Rory's smile got bigger. Jayes was confused only a brief second until she saw it.

The field was no longer red, it was speckled with tiny, tiny leaves of green, everywhere! Jayes gasped, the happiness inside her came out in a loud scream as she jumped up and down. Rory grabbed her and spun her around as they embraced each other in pure joy!

"Oh, thank you, God, thank you!" Jayes screamed.

Rory sat her back down on her feet. "She was right. Your friend, she saved us weeks of waiting! It is a miracle, a blessing. I cannot explain it, there are farms that planted two months ago and they are just now seeing their leaves!"

Jayes could not believe it. She was so happy, she wanted to run and find Maybran and give her the tightest squeeze she had probably ever had. "She was right! I should never have doubted her. I feel so bad; I am just way too happy right now to feel bad though! We are saved!" Jayes screamed.

"We were all saved the day we met you." Rory whispered.

That morning was a morning of happiness and celebration. Jayes made a large breakfast and declared it a day of rest. She promised John they could go swimming and walk up to the small waterfall.

"We have things to do, I am not that fond of the water." Rory had said. Today was the first day they had all sat and ate together. Jayes normally fetched water, did her morning chores and then ate alone.

"I think I will stay and help too." Liam said as he stuffed his mouth full of eggs. Jayes gave him a warning look to mind his manners, he laughed and a few pieces of egg fell out of his mouth. The boys started to laugh.

"I will stay too." Rory's other friend said.

"No. You will not stay; I do not even know your name. We have never talked. We have all been so busy, we need to spend time getting to know each other," Jayes pleaded.

The man looked somewhat shocked.

Fifteen
What you sow you reap…

They had a wonderful time. It was a one of the most enjoyable days Jayes had spent in Virginia.

When they finally arrived home that night Gin was waiting and she was not alone. She was with a very thin boy that Jayes recognized from the day the servants had signed their contracts. He was thin and poorly dressed, he did not even have shoes on.

"Gin? It is so wonderful to see you! We have great news!" Jayes said as she ran towards Gin.

"Where have you been? I have been waiting for over an hour." Gin said testy.

"We went up to the falls today," Jayes explained.

"Jayes, this is not a land of fun and play. It is a land of hard work or die." Gin lectured.

Jayes rolled her eyes. "Gin we do work hard. That is why we decided to have a happy day." She refused to allow Gin to ruin her mood. "Why are you here?"

"Well, I had dinner last night with the Governor. I told him I would deliver this to you." Gin handed Jayes a letter.

"Everyone is to observe the Sabbath, it is rumored, that you have not, I gave my word to Captain West that you are a

Christian, you should be thankful for that. I expect you, for my sake, to observe the Sabbath." Gin warned her. "Your servants too. It is a crime not to. You will be punished if you do not follow the new Virginia laws."

"We do," Jayes said.

"Twice a week," John lied. "Wednesdays too, Miss Jayes reads the Bible to us every day."

"No she does not!" Arabette argued with John. Will hit Arabette and a fight broke out between the two children.

"Okay that is enough children," Jayes warned. Persis scooped up Arabette and took her in the house, but not before she kicked Will hard on the shin.

"There is a missing servant girl." Gin said. "I told Captain West, the Governor, I would look around to make certain that you were not harboring her. I know you would never do that, you of all people should know about runaways." Gin said glaring at Jayes.

"Do you honestly think I would?"

"Well, you do have a soft heart when it comes to those people."

Jayes got up close to Gin and whispered quietly in her ear so no one else could hear. "We were those people, or have you forgotten?"

Gin swallowed and stepped back. "She is the Governor's girl, he is more than a little upset about it. I do not think you would do that, but I have been wrong about you many times. No one in their right mind would do that, I hope you are smarter than that."

For some reason, Jayes knew that Gin really thought she would find the girl here. "Well, if you promised him to look around, please search. We have nothing to hide here.

Gin turned and the boy walked to the barn. Jayes followed

Gin as she walked around exploring.

"Mistress Guinever! I found her!" Jayes heard the boy shout from the barn.

Jayes was shocked. Gin was furious and yelled at her. "How could you! How could you put your reputation and mine at risk! I vouched for you! I gave you your freedom. You cannot help but be a thief!" Gin turned her back on her and walked to the barn.

Jayes was speechless. She had no idea the girl was there. She did not know what to say. She was hurt and angered by Gin's words. Rory was standing nearby. Jayes looked at him.

"Did you know about this?" She accused him.

Rory looked as shocked as she did. "No, I did not, I swear to you."

Gin came out of the barn with the girl and holding a plate. "Someone has been feeding her," Gin said as she held the tiny crying little girl. She was about Arabette's age, and her face was horribly bruised.

"Let go of her!" Liam screamed running toward Gin.

Gasper grabbed Liam before he reached Gin. "She is not worth it," he said trying to calm the boy who was kicking and screaming. "She is my sister! She is my little sister, he almost killed her!"

Gasper took the boy into his strong arms and held him tight. "Your sister will be fine, the other one is not worth losing your skin over."

Gin laughed an evil laugh, Jayes had heard it once before. "Oh, he will lose his skin, it is too late to try to save him now." Gin threw the girl onto the ground.

"You are a cold hearted, little bitch!" Gasper released Liam, stood and faced Gin. Liam ran towards his sister who was lying in a heap crying.

"How dare you speak to me like that?!" Gin yelled back, directing her anger at Gasper now. Jayes started to intervene but Rory grabbed her shoulder. And whispered 'don't'.

"Yes you are the bitch that I thank God daily I did not get stuck with!" Gasper had his own evil laugh. "Do you know we drew grass to see who would get stuck with you? Thank the Good Lord I won, I think I would have murdered your black heart by now."

Gin was furious. "You want to lose your skin too! You are not allowed to speak to me like that."

"I am a free man, lady, and I do not think you are anywhere near being a lady. I can and I will talk to you, however I please." He was seething with contempt. Jayes had never seen Gasper act like this, he was always smiling and quiet.

Jayes looked at Rory, he was smiling. She nudged him with her elbow. Do something. She whispered to him.

Rory gave her a wide eyed head shake. "Ugh," Jayes growled.

Jayes stepped forward. "Enough! Gasper, go!" she ordered.

"Gin, I had no idea the girl was here. It is obvious that she was abused and her brother was merely trying to help her," Jayes said calmly. "This is really not as bad as it seems."

"Not as bad as it seems?" Gin repeated, angrily. "Your boy stole the Governor's servant! Trust me on this, it is bad."

"He did not steal her, you make it sound like he stole chickens or a cow, she is his sister, and she was hurt."

"She is the Governor's property, he stole her! He will face judges for this! It is a crime, and it is punishable."

Jayes was frustrated, she did not know what to do. "Can we just fix this, return the girl? You can say you found her in the woods, she is obviously very ill."

"I will not lie for you again Jayes Mackey!" Gin screamed.

"He stole her, and he will have to answer for it. He can come with me now, or I can send the Governor to come fetch him later."

Rory stepped forward. "We will deliver him to Jamestown ourselves, to answer for the charges."

"Fine, this is the most reasonable thing I have heard since I got here." Gin grabbed the girl, dragging her towards the river. Gasper once again took hold of Liam who fell apart in his arms.

"What are we going to do?" Jayes asked.

"That is a good question." Rory answered.

Jayes had no idea what to do. She did not even know who to ask for advice. After the children went to bed that night they all gathered in the kitchen. Liam sitting in the corner in a chair looking like a trapped rabbit.

"What were you thinking?" Gasper asked him.

"She came here, she showed up. She is my sis; I was nae gonna send her away." Liam said staring at the floor as though it would open up and swallow him.

"You had to have known it was not a great idea. If you knew it was not wrong, you would not have hidden her, from all of us." Rory said.

"What were you thinking?" Gasper asked again, not directly at Liam, he was speaking aloud as he paced the short length of the room.

"Liam," Jayes said with such pain. "I do not know if there is anything that we can do to help you. Do not misunderstand, we are going to try."

The next morning Jayes, Gasper, Rory and Liam made the trip to Jamestown. They did not have a boat for transportation and without it the journey took two days on foot. Jayes knew that Maybran was staying nearby the plantation to keep an eye on the children left in the care of Persis.

Cuttmwa was following them, although he kept his presence unknown. The summer was in full heat. They quickly decided they would follow the James River to Jamestown. There were several times while walking Jayes just wanted to get in and swim the entire way.

They took a break near the river, Jayes did not think twice about jumping in.

"Come on Liam, get in," she yelled from the water. "It feels so good!"

The men soaked their feet in the water and splashed their faces, no one joined her. "We should probably think about finding a place to camp for the night soon." Rory said.

"I think we should sleep in the water," Jayes said loudly as she splashed around, finally cool.

"I think that sounds like a very bad idea." Rory replied with a chuckle. "I have seen West in action, he has an evil heart when it comes to the people he believes is below him. He thinks little of them."

"That is being kind I would say, he has no feeling for us. I have seen what he is capable of for crimes even less than this. He killed a boy once, nailed him to the pillory for four days, gave him no water and whipped him to death." Gasper said, still pacing. "He had accused him of not releasing him from his contract that had expired three years before."

Jayes felt as though she was going to faint. That was the boy she had seen in town that day. That man she had seen was Captain West! How could she have not recognized him? No wonder he had thought Jayes looked familiar. Their eyes had met that day! Jayes looked over to Liam.

He was sitting on a rock, his knees to his chest, rocking back and forth crying. She gave Rory a look and quickly got out of the river and went to him.

"It is ok Liam," Jayes soothed him as she took him in her arms and held him tightly. "It will be ok."

"I don't care about me, I am worried about my sister, and she is just a baby." Liam was crying onto her shoulder.

Jayes was terrified for them both, she had to be strong for Liam.

Later that night Jayes finally broke down, thinking of poor Liam and that pretty little girl. She could be strong in front of Liam, she was weak in the privacy of the moon.

"I wish I knew something to say that could give you hope." Rory said as he sat down next to her. "We need a miracle."

"I think I am all out of miracles," Jayes replied as she wiped the tears from her eyes. "Do you know what happens to runaways?" she asked.

Rory did not reply. They both sat in silence. The silence was the answer that Jayes was afraid of hearing. She began to cry again, unable to hide it. "And Liam?" she asked.

"Unless you have the coins to pay his fines, it will come off of his back." Rory reluctantly answered.

Jayes looked up at him. "How much is the fine?"

"Fifteen maybe twenty pounds." Rory said. "An impossible amount."

"It will be okay. I will not allow anything to happen to Liam," Jayes said. Jayes looked up to the sky, why was God testing her so much? Jayes had always thought she knew what was right and wrong. Since she left the shores of Ireland right and wrong did not seem to be as simple as it used to be. Jayes realized in that moment the difference between right and wrong was your perspective of the situation. "Interesting," she thought "how the things that happen in your life can open your eyes to a different outlook on life."

"Rory can I ask you a question?" Jayes asked.

"Of course, ask away."

"If you were given a gift, not from a person, a fateful gift of luck," Jayes said then decided that was not quite right. "A gift from God; and this gift could help you better your life in great ways, but then God gave you a choice to help someone else with the gift. You know that this other person could suffer much more without the gift, is it horrible to want to keep it for yourself?"

"That is some question." Rory joked.

Jayes reached over and playfully hit him. "Just answer the question. It is serious."

"Jayes, you already know the answer." Rory said. "You would not be asking me if you did not know the answer."

"I am asking you because I don't know the answer! If I knew the answer I would'na be askin!"

"You are serious. Your Irish is comin out." Rory laughed, then answered her seriously. "Jayes you know the answer. You're not asking me because you want the right answer, you're asking me because you're hoping I don't."

Jayes thought about it for a moment, she realized he was right. Jayes felt a moment of loss, then she told herself she was being selfish.

"I think I am going to take a swim, cool down before I sleep," Jayes told him. Rory took the clue and got up.

Jayes lifted her dress as she walked into the river, feeling the mud slide in between her toes. As soon as Rory disappeared Jayes jumped out and ran a little way down the shore.

"Cuttmwa! Where are you? I know you're here!"

Cuttmwa came out of the tall grass and walked towards her smiling. "You called?"

"I need your help……"

SIXTEEN
Jamestown, Virginia – June 20, 1628
Fate is a funny thing…

They reached Jamestown in the early afternoon. Jayes had to ask around where they could find Governor West and was directed to a brick house not far from the Church. They passed the cemetery and several other small brick houses that were located behind the fort. The trees had all been removed and there were actual roads. Jamestown really was beginning to resemble a small town.

Jayes knocked on the door of the largest two story house. A black woman answered and showed Jayes into a small sitting room. Jayes was amazed at the beauty inside. There was glass everywhere, even hanging from the ceiling, a small chandelier that held small candles. There was china that adorned the table as though they were about ready have a grand party. Jayes had never seen such fancy carpets, drapes and furniture in her life. She did not expect to see it here, where they lacked most modern conveniences.

"Miss Mackey, I see you have brought the prisoner?" Governor West looked directly at Liam. "I must admit; I did not think you would."

"If I say I am going to do something, I do it," Jayes countered.

"Traits of a gentleman in a woman, you do not see that often." He chuckled looking at the three men Jayes just realized were standing behind him. They all laughed at his jest.

"You do not find that in all gentlemen either," Jayes countered, the Governors smile diminished.

"Well, Miss Mackey, thank you, I can take care of him from here. You may leave now," he said dismissing her and turned to leave.

"Actually, I would like to be a part of that. I would like to speak with you, privately?" Jayes asked trying to smile. How does Gin do that? Pretend.

"Well, I do not know if that is proper Miss Mackey. Besides, you have no business in men's government. We will take care of this criminal according to our laws." He laughed again, the men behind him laughing with him. Jayes wondered if they really thought he was funny or just laughed on cue like Gin.

"Governor West, I am not asking for the type of meeting you have with the Widow Sinclair, I just want to discuss business, not government, this unfortunate situation that our servants have created for us is my business. I also believe the circumstances involved with my servant were not of a criminal intent," Jayes said in her best English accent.

The Governor must not have realized that Jayes was very much involved and determined to be heard. She had always been so timid in front of him, her attitude luckily peaked his interest.

He cleared his throat and for the first time took her seriously. "I am a busy man, I have only a few minutes. We can talk in the dining room." He turned and Jayes followed him.

"I have already made up my mind. They will both be punished. We cannot let them get away with this, it gives a bad example to the others. We do have laws and they must be obeyed by those people."

"They are so young, and they are brother and sister, were you even aware of that?" Jayes asked.

"Of course I was," he said irritated.

"If your sister was ill and came to you for help, would you turn her away even if you knew it was wrong not too? No, you would not. Even you know that you would help her."

"That has nothing to do with it. They are servants!"

"It most certainly does! They are *people* Captain West!" Jayes was trying so hard to control her temper.

"They are servants!" He yelled slamming his hand onto the table.

"Fine, how much? How much did you buy her for? I would have bought her had I known they were related, I would not have separated family. She is so young, and she certainly cannot be much help to you anyhow." Jayes tried to remain calm.

"You have no more credit Miss Mackey," he said with a wry smile.

"I do not need credit Governor," Jayes snapped gritting her teeth.

That shocked him, he gave her his full attention and stared at her, studying her face. "What do you mean, 'you do not need credit'? I am not interested in bartering with you Miss Mackey."

"How much!" Jayes demanded.

"Forty pounds." He laughed.

"In the real world, how much?" Jayes glared at him.

"Twenty-five pounds. I am not desperate to rid myself of

her." He glared back at her.

Jayes took out the little leather purse that Will had found in the tree with the documents. She had sent Cuttmwa home to retrieve it. Jayes pulled out Twenty-five pounds and tossed it on the desk. "We are done here, where is she?" Jayes asked.

"I am afraid we are not done. Your boy still harbored a runaway, that is a crime," he said smiling with the same evil grin he had the day that poor boy was whipped to death.

Jayes paused, she had not thought of that. She had thought if she bought the sister, his crime would no longer be valid if she owned her.

"What is it you want?" Jayes asked, feeling defeated.

"Why do these people mean so much to you? Enough for you to part with good coin?" he asked her curiously.

"I am determined to have a good field. I need them. I need them healthy and I believe if they're happy, they work harder," Jayes replied honestly.

"Interesting, a female's view on servants," he said thinking. "Do you really think it will help?"

"It has certainly helped. They are happy, they are healthy and my plantation is thriving," Jayes answered wondering how this conversation took such a turn. "Captain West, excuse me, Governor. I need that boy, I do not have much help and I wish beyond all wishes to repay you the credit I owe, I need him to do that. And I am certain you want to be repaid?"

This he seemed to consider. Of course he would consider it, it benefitted him. Why hadn't she thought of that sooner?

"If you had coin, why did you need credit?" he asked her, that was a good question.

"Honestly, Widow Sinclair made those arrangements. I have kept my coin's a secret, even to her, in fear of my safety," Jayes answered.

JAYES – 1627

The Governor seemed to accept that answer. He looked at her smiling. "That was wise of you, you live in such a vulnerable and isolated area. Very wise indeed," he said. "Of course, your safety now will be in jeopardy, I will have to divulge that you paid the fines, I cannot let anyone think that I just turned my head."

"Of course," Jayes said, maybe it was not the greatest answer after all.

"How many coins do you have?" he asked.

Jayes looked at him in shock. He turned to pour himself a drink. "Would you like one?"

"Yes, please," Jayes answered. "I am afraid I only have five pounds left."

"Perfect!" He turned and smiled, "That is the exact amount of the boy's fine, and now you have no worry of robbers trying to steal your coin." He turned and handed her the glass of gold liquid that reminded her of the poison from the snake. She took the glass from his hand. He turned up his palm and Jayes put the coins in it.

"Cheers," he said clinking his glass with hers. Jayes drank it, and held it down barely.

"Thank you, Governor West, it was a pleasure doing business with you. I am so glad that we were able to work this out to the benefit of us all," Jayes said smiling flirtatiously, the liquid helped.

"Me too, Miss Mackey," He smiled back in a wicked way that gave Jayes shivers. "Me too." He led her to the door. Jayes took her free hand and placed it over the pocket of her dress that held the coins, she did not want them clinking.

They were directed to the old fort, Abbey, Liam's sister was being held there.

"Is this where you're taking me? Are they putting me in

prison there?" Liam asked scared.

"No Liam, we are going to go pick up your sister. She is coming home with us," Jayes said smiling. She felt wonderful about what she had done. She would have to work much harder to buy passage home now. She knew without even a blink of doubt she had done the right thing.

Jayes looked over at Rory, he was scowling at her. She was taken aback. Why was he mad, was that not the answer he had given her? Well, he was wrong then Jayes thought, she was very disappointed in him.

As they neared the military quarters Rory grabbed ahold of Jayes' arm, she came to a forced stop. Rory grabbed the paper out of Jayes' hand that the Governor had written the release for Abbey and handed it to Gasper. "Get her," he said as he forcibly led Jayes around the building near the fort walls and out of sight.

"Did you give him your gift?" he asked her angrily.

"Of course I did. I could not let him hurt them, I had to, it was the right thing to do." Jayes could not understand why he was so angry. Did he not like Liam?

"So you whored yourself out!" He released her as though she had burnt him.

"Yes! I mean- WHAT!" She slapped him. "How dare you!" Jayes could not believe he would think that she would do that!

Rory touched his cheek. "What else am I supposed to think?" he asked her.

Jayes thought about it, she saw his point. "Last night after we talked, I talked to Cuttwma."

"Cuttmwa? The Indian?" he asked surprised.

"Yes, he had been following us. He has this thing about protecting me. He thinks I am a danger to myself or something like that," Jayes said as she rolled her eyes.

JAYES – 1627

"You are. He is a smart Indian." Rory said with a grin. Jayes glared at him.

"Anyways, I asked him to go and retrieve this bag," Jayes said, holding up the leather pouch. "I found it, it was a gift from God," she said, she would never tell him how she found it, or that it did not fall from heaven. The details would never leave her lips.

Rory looked so pained, the guilt of his accusation slapped him in the face as she had. "I am sorry, I thought…"

"You thought I was talking about me? Do you think that I am so vain that I would refer to my body as lucky? This is not a lucky body, I don't know where you are from but..." Rory took her face in his hands and kissed her. Jayes stood there in shock, she could not kiss him back.

"I am sorry," he said embarrassed.

"Sorry for calling me a whore or sorry for kissing me?" she asked.

"You're impossible," he said and walked away leaving Jayes standing there. She still did not know what he was sorry for. She decided that she would not ask again though, the question seemed to irritate him. Although she still wanted to know if he was sorry for kissing her, she hoped not.

She felt a twinge of guilt and then lectured herself. She should not feel any sort of guilt when it came to Tristam James, for God's sake, the man never told her his name before he bedded her and stole her virginity.

Jayes told herself, she can kiss anyone she wants to kiss. Her heart however, was not in agreement with her stubbornness. She loved him, she was not going to admit it though… Jayes started lecturing her heart as she caught up to Rory.

They left Jamestown right away, they had not made it very

far before they had to bed down for the night. Liam was beside himself with joy, tears were a constant presence in his eyes.

"Liam, you have nothing to worry about. It is over, and your sister is with us to stay," Jayes explained, trying to comfort him as he sat near the fire.

"I can never repay you. I put you and everyone else at risk of a whipping and you're not even mad. I do not deserve your kindness Miss Jayes," he said tearing up again.

Jayes took his hand in hers. "First of all, you can start by calling me Jayes, just Jayes. I don't care much for the miss part," Jayes teased him. Liam smiled.

Second, I made this choice. I am part to blame, I am after all the one that separated you from your sister.

"The men in England are to blame for that." Liam said.

Jayes was curious, how did they come to this country?

She had to ask. "What men Liam?"

"There were men, they promised us food. My Mum and Da had lost their jobs, we was working on the streets by the tower. Doin what we could." Liam explained. "These Lords came and they promised us a hot meal and a job. So we went with them. They put us in this room, and kept us there with lots of people. Then they loaded us on the ship and that is when we met you. They sold us."

Jayes could not believe what she was hearing, yet she knew it was true. She somehow just knew.

Was Virginia's tobacco worth the stealing of innocent children's lives that important? She knew it was, at least for them and for England. It made her hate tobacco, it made her feel guilty for who she had become. She was one of them, but she would never act or become heartless and immoral like them.

"I am sorry Liam. I am so sorry. This new world is a strange and cruel place. Someone had once told me that someday I would understand.

I understand now, but we have each other and I promise you, we will get out of here and far away someday," Jayes said with tears in her eyes.

"How?" Liam asked.

"We will have to work hard. We have to buy our passage home. Not to England, to Ireland. You will be free and happy and you and Abbey can be children once again. We will all be a family," Jayes said determined that what she was telling him, would someday be a reality.

Jayes tucked Liam in next to a very tired and still not well little Abbey. Two children to take care of now she thought, Lord help her.

Jayes made herself a little bed next to the fire. She looked around for Cuttwma, she could not hear him tonight although she knew he was near. Rory was avoiding her, which she was certain of when Gasper came back to camp without him.

Jayes was not really sure what to think of Gasper. He acted tough but she believed that was all it was, an act. She believed that he was much softer inside, he just did not let anyone see the truth in him. She was unsure though if anyone would ever get a real glimpse of that softness.

"What you did today, was admirable," he said sitting down near her.

"What do you mean?"

"The money. You could have bought your passage home. You could be back in your beloved Ireland, and now you're further away from it than ever before," he said stirring the fire. "Why did you do it?"

"I did not have enough to buy passage for me and the children. I could not have left them here, I could never live with myself if I did that." Jayes stared into the fire. Did that make her a bad mother? Was she supposed to sacrifice everything and everyone for that of her child? Put his wellbeing above that of all? Jayes was uncertain of the rules. "I have you, and Rory and some strong men that will help me grow tobacco, we will get home, it will just take a little longer than I had expected," Jayes said with a positive tone.

"A little longer? You know that life is short here. One out ten will live a year and those are generous odds. One out of us will die, what if your sacrifice was for naught?" Gasper asked her.

"Well, if it was for naught, when I meet my Da' in heaven, I will have a clear conscience," Jayes said with finality as Rory walked up.

"None of us are meeting our maker, not yet anyways, not unless it is in our dreams. We have too much left to do. Go to bed Jayes." Rory said.

Jayes wanted to ask him who had made him boss, but she kept quiet and went to sleep.

Seventeen
The definition of faith…

Jayes woke early as she did every morning. The only time she had to be alone with her thoughts. The sky was its usual gray like every morning, the only time she could be outside and free from the heat, the morning's air cool and damp.

As she made her way to the river she felt as though there was something different today. The tides were rolling in with an unusual quickness. Jayes ran towards the shore and saw a ship. A ship here in the curls of the river was unusual, the larger transportation ships could not maneuver well in the turns so far up river. Jayes knew they were preparing for Virginia's harvest, and the shipping of the tobacco from the fields. Several Captains were trying to make private deals for transporting the leaves and selling illegal labor on the side, although it was highly illegal and punishable. The Burgesses seemed to turn their backs at these crimes, depending on who was involved. However, not show up for Sunday service and you were likely to lose some skin off your back.

That summer Jayes was convinced that Virginia was most definitely located somewhere near hell, if not hell itself. She had to be living south of hell, the heat in hell could not be much worse than the heat in the Virginia Tobacco Fields. As the sun rose you could feel the heat from the devil's breath as though he sat above you, breathing down, the water pouring from her body as though she had been swimming in the James. Even the water gave only a moment's reprieve from the sweltering heat. The sun was sitting high in the sky for what seemed like days on end. If she had thought this was a foreign world before, summer made it only clearer this was a world far away from any she had ever known.

They all worked hard, side by side together in the fields, watering, nurturing and removing the weeds that could suck the life from the plants that were valued as much as life. These plants represented life, without them, there was no surviving Virginia. Without these oily large leaves, that were valued more than any jewel, there was no hope.

Farming tobacco was a tough job. The fields were hot. The weeds grew wild and it was a constant battle to keep them from suffocating the precious tobacco leaves. The stalks were as hard as an oak tree and harvesting was a backbreaking job. You could never leave the field without your skin turning dark from the tar of the plants and the dirt covering your sweat slicked skin. The James was a welcome sight towards the end of a long day. The cooling waters of the river soothing a body aching from its labors in the fields, burnt from the sun and exhausted by never enough rest.

They also repaired roofs and sat out storms that brought winds and torrential rains, some could last for days, threating to destroy their crops.

They were all exhausted and tempers high in the men. Gasper and Rory seemed to have drifted apart, Jayes had no idea why.

Arabette and Abbey had become best friends. Baby Abbey

JAYES – 1627

so happy and always cheerful. Will, Liam and John seemed to never be far apart. The boys had taken to making log boats, they had planned on selling them at harvest time in Jamestown.

Jayes had never felt more alone. She rarely saw Maybran or Cuttmwa anymore, although she had seen his handiwork around the plantation that he had magically done in the dead of the night.

Jayes knew they were preparing for winter, she wondered if they were prepared for winter themselves. There were times Jayes would just lie in bed at night wondering if she was leading them all astray, what was she doing? She could not take on the responsibility of all these lives, what if she failed?

Jayes was working in the field, today they were diligently trying to hack down the weeds that were starving the life from the green leaves of the Tobacco. Jayes heard a rumble, she looked into the sky but only saw the bright hot light of the sun. She stood up, wiping the sweat from her eyes. The sound vibrated the ground, the roar coming closer and closer. Out of the trees birds began to flee. Jayes could see a dust storm stirring in the near distance.

She realized the boys were working near the woods. Rory realized what was happening about the same time as Jayes.

"Get out of the way! Get out of the field!" Rory screamed as all the men ran towards the boys. Jayes couldn't move. She stood frozen.

Buffalo appeared, dozens of them, running directly towards the children. Jayes heard herself scream at the same moment her feet finally found footing.

"John!" She screamed.

The dust storm blocked Jayes view, she could hear the rumble and taste the dirt in the air as they ran past her not far away.

"Noooooo!" Jayes heard Rory cry out. She stopped. She walked slowly in the direction the boys had been, unable to see through the thick air of dirt.

As she neared she found herself standing in front of Rory. He was holding a limp and bloody Liam.

Jayes dropped to her knees and cried, they were all gone, the boys, trampled.

Her cries were uncontrollable. "All of them?"

Gasper appeared with Will in his arms, and John was standing near his side. Jayes fell at Johns' feet thanking God. She stood and looked at Will.

His leg was bloody and disfigured, he had a nasty gash on his head.

"I am being brave, Liam saved me, and he pushed me out of the way." Will cried looking at Liam in Rory's arms.

"Take him home, take him home now," Jayes said. "Rory, give Liam to Paedar. Paedar, I need you to take him home."

Rory started to argue, Jayes gave him a 'don't you dare look.'

"Come on Paedar, come on John." They started to leave. Rory immediately turned on Jayes.

"What the hell are you doing?" He screamed at her.

"Shut up and do not question me this one time for God's sake!" Jayes screamed back at him. "I need you to go with me to find Maybran, Will needs her."

Rory surprisingly did not argue with her, they took off into the woods together.

They had not gotten far when Cuttmwa appeared to Jayes surprise.

"Who?" he asked jumping out of a nearby tree and scaring the Jesus out of Rory. Jayes had to fight back a giggle which made her feel awful given the circumstances.

"Liam. He is gone. I need Maybran, Will is badly injured."

"I will bring them, go, get leaves, smoke them."

Cuttwma instructed them as he began to leave. Jayes stopped him.

"Will smoking bring him good spirits?" Jayes asked confused.

Cuttwma looked at her as though she had gone mad. "Do not smoke it!" He said putting his hands to his lips, smoke it." He made a flutter of his fingers like fire. "Dry, dry leaves Jayes," he explained laughing and disappeared.

Jayes looked at Rory who was covering his face with his hand. "It is not funny," Jayes spat.

"Oh but it truly is." He laughed.

"Oh posh, you thought the same thing."

"Oh, you are wrong. I knew what he meant."

"Liar." Jayes glared at him. Rory just laughed. He was so irritating at times.

Jayes woke early as usual. She had already fetched the water and set it to boil. She took a stroll this morning towards the crops and stood looking at the fields of green. Her tobacco had grown faster and fuller than any other near Jamestown. Maybran had been right. The plants were nearly full grown, they were beautiful and healthy. Jayes knew she had done well.

"They are saying you're a witch you know." Gasper said startling her. Jayes turned towards his voice, he was standing a few feet behind her looking at the field.

"Who is saying that?" Jayes asked him.

"Who is not saying it?" he countered.

"Okay, who is not saying it?"

"No one, they are all saying it, and if they are not saying it, they are thinking it."

Jayes swung around facing him. "Are you serious? Why on earth would people think that?"

Gasper said nothing and pointed with both hands towards the tobacco.

"What?" Jayes asked.

"Do you really not know?" he asked her bewildered. "Jayes, your tobacco is thicker and fuller than anyone else, even ancient planters that know how to grow tobacco. You have twice as many plants that rooted than anyone in Virginia."

"So? We have good soil," she said, "We got lucky."

Gasper laughed. "It is easier to believe you are a witch."

"That is unfair! I am no witch! Are they really saying that?" Jayes was upset, do they burn witches in the new world?

"Aye, they are." Gasper said. "Tell me Jayes, how did you get such a good crop? I have farmed in Virginia for eight years, this is the best field of tobacco I have ever seen."

"You really want to know?" Jayes questioned.

"Are you going to admit being a witch?"

Jayes laughed. "No! I am not a witch!"

"Yes, I want to know." Gasper said sitting down in the dirt.

Jayes sat down beside him. "This may sound odd."

Gasper chuckled. "I thought it might."

"Maybran, the Indian girl that I am friends with," Jayes began explaining, "she took the seeds from my leather pouch one day and just began throwing them on the ground."

"I recall a little bit of that. I do not think I knew why," he said.

"Maybran said that the Indians taught the early settlers to plant the seeds in the earth, with fish," Jayes said.

Gasper nodded his head.

"It was a farce. The seeds need light to grow! The Indians

wanted the settlers to fail, the crops to fail. They wanted them to go home."

Gasper finally realized what Jayes was saying. "It was a lie?"

"Yes!"

Gasper started laughing. He was laughing so hard he rolled onto his side and made the fetal position, holding his stomach.

"No one realizes this." Gasper said as he was finally able to control himself. "The Indians have a sense of humor. They must laugh at us!"

"Maybran said they do, from ocean to ocean actually." Jayes giggled finding the humor in it now.

"You cannot tell anyone." Gasper said seriously.

"They think I am a witch!" Jayes exclaimed. "What if they try to burn me?"

"They don't burn witches anymore." Gasper said chuckling.

"Good," Jayes said.

"They hang them," he said.

"I have to tell them!" Jayes swung her head quickly her eyes wide.

"No one is going to accuse you. They are too afraid." Gasper said. "I cannot believe this. I cannot believe that no one has figured it out."

"I did," Jayes said proudly as she stood.

"Well, that is because you're a witch." Gasper poked at her.

"Not funny," Jayes said, and hit him.

Jayes and Rory were unsure what leaves to pick, the larger leaves from the bottom of the plant or the moister smaller leaves from the top. They compromised and took two leaves from each.

They built a fire and Jayes sent Persis and Paedar to get fresh water. Gasper was consoling the boys and tending to Will.

Maybran showed up before dark with two elderly Indian women. Both of them Jayes recognized from her time in their village when she had given birth to Kealan. The one woman took Jayes by the shoulders and kissed her, she was the only who had stood over Jayes smiling and trying to comfort her that day.

"Thank you," Jayes said to her with such emotion, this woman who was there for her second time in need.

"Bodl?" she asked.

"Yes, he is in there," Jayes answered. Rory did a double take.

"How much time have you spent with the Indians?" he asked shocked she understood what the old woman had said.

Jayes looked at him with a mischievous smile and did not answer.

Maybran cleared the room of the surprised and fearful faces. Rory did his best to assure everyone they were safe. As worried as John was for Will, he cooperated with the instructions and did not argue.

"Please make my brother well," John begged Maybran.

Maybran smiled at him and touched his cheek.

"Ahki," Maybran said. "Ahki!" Maybran pointed to Rory and Gasper, she stooped down and picked up a handful of dirt and ran into the small house and threw it on the floor. "Move!" She yelled as she kicked the table in the middle of the room. Rory and Gasper ran to do her bidding. John began gathering dirt and the three of them made a pile in the middle of the floor.

Persis and Paedar came with the water which Jayes set to boil. Maybran placed piles of wood on top of the dirt and started a fire in the middle of the room.

JAYES – 1627

The two elderly women carried Will out from the bedroom and laid him on the floor next to the fire. Maybran lit sage and the room filled quickly with smoke. The two women began to close the shutters as they hummed a lulling song.

Jayes was terrified the house was going to burn down, she quickly went outside and told everyone to grab buckets and go fill them with water, only to find out she too had been kicked out.

It was a long night. No one slept, no one talked. When morning light finally came, there was nothing but smoke seeping through the walls of the small house.

The sun rose high in the sky before the door opened. The toothless Indian women came out smiling, hot and soaking wet. The heat inside the house was radiant and hit Jayes although she was still some distance away.

"He lives?" she asked.

"Okad," she said with a pained face. Jayes eyes widened.

"Okad?" she asked scared that meant no.

Maybran walked out, also dripping sweat. "His leg, his Okad, we do not neegoniwabungigaywin."

"You do not know? He will live though?" Jayes asked hopefully as John came up next to her, leaning against Jayes awaiting the news.

"Only great spirits know what is in the future, the mushkeekiwinum do their healing, he should live." Maybran said.

Jayes was getting frustrated. She knew Maybran could speak better English, whether it was the Indian women or her frustration she was not doing a good job speaking now when it mattered most.

"Thank you," Jayes said releasing the breath she had been holding. "Please stay, do not leave, what if he gets a fever, I need you."

"He will be fine; I will be near." Maybran said as she and the two women made their way down the trail leading to the woods.

"You have some explaining to do missy." Gasper said once the Indians were out of sight.

Jayes spun around. "I have no explaining to do. And you will not say another word, they just saved Will's life and I will not hear a word out of you." Jayes walked into the house. "Help me carry him to the bed."

Jayes spent the day sewing a burial gown for Liam. Gasper dug a grave, Paedar and John built a casket. Persis made lunch and the fields were far from everyone's mind.

"There is a lot of damage to a good part of the crop." Rory said from the doorway sometime later. Jayes had forgotten about the stampede. She had forgotten or not even considered the damage that could have been done.

"I do not want to hear about it right now. This is not the time," Jayes said.

"What do you mean? Liam is gone, we are still here. We must survive, those fields are our survival." Rory countered.

Jayes knew he was right. Why did this have to be such a constant battle? Why could there not be one day of peace, one day without worry or struggle? Jayes finally collapsed. She fell on her knees and just wept. A long awaited cry of the pain that had been building since leaving Ireland, since the betrayal of Tristam, of Gin. Of leaving her baby and not watching him grow every day. Of the blood and blisters on her hands and feet. The burns on her skin from head to toe. The death of an innocent boy. It was too much. Jayes wept.

That night Cuttwma appeared with another Indian. His head was shaved except in the front which was cut very short and then long down the center of his head. His face was painted black like a raccoon type face. He wore a deer skin with the hair still attached that seemed to attract bugs. He was quiet and did not speak. He carried a tall stick that was attached to an assortment of animal tails.

"The Kwiocos, will bless and bury your boy," Cuttwma stated.

Jayes was not going to argue, she would make sure that Liam had a Christian burial as well, Gasper on the other hand began to protest.

"He will not..."

"We are honored Cuttwma, thank you. We would like him to be buried as his Christian beliefs allow too."

Cuttwma spoke to the Indian Kwiocos, he nodded his head and walked into the hut where Liam's body was laid.

They heard him chanting in a deep tone, Jayes began to pray Our Heavenly Father, over and over again.

She did not want to offend the Indians who so kindly protected her son, she also did not want to sin and lay any false Gods above her one true Father in heaven.

Who was she to judge though? The bible says, judge not lest ye shall be judged. Jayes decided this was double safety and respectful.

Gasper was angry. He left after giving Jayes a look that left chills down her spine.

"Do not let him get to you, he is going to go work it off in the fields." Rory said.

"Work what off?" Jayes asked.

"His urge to strangle you more than likely."

"You are not serious?" Jayes asked shocked.

"I think I am." Rory said. "I will go talk to him. The last thing we need is for him to go off to town and tell them we are conspiring with the Indians. You are not exactly the Governor's favorite citizen at the moment, half the town believe you are a witch, and I think the Governor is thirsty for fresh blood to show his power."

"Well, he would be disappointed, I am not a witch. Go talk to him, but I am not offending the only people who have shown me kindness," Jayes said adamantly. "Gasper would be best to just realize that will not change, even if it jeopardizes my throat."

Gasper was not present for Liam's funeral. Will was unable to go and Jayes thought that was best for him, he was too weak and needed his strength. His leg was badly broken; it would take weeks if not months for it to heal, the funeral could have set him on an emotional slide backwards.

Three days later Gasper finally came home. With him was a beautiful stone marker for Liam's grave.

~LIAM MACKEY ~
~ CHILD OF GOD ~
~ AUGUST 14, 1628 ~

Jayes gave him a big hug when she saw it, she could not help but cry. Perhaps she had not realized how close he had been to Liam.

"Did you make this?" Jayes asked him surprised.

"It is no big deal." Gasper said as he not so gently dropped it, causing a large crack in the beautiful marker.

Jayes could have sworn she saw a tear in his eye before he turned and once again disappeared.

Eighteen
October, 1628 – The Jayes

Captain Tristam James finally cleared the shores of the Chesapeake Bay and steered his sails into the James River. It had been a year since he had left Jayes in the hands of John Turner. Not a day had gone by since then that he had not thought of those green eyes.

Tristam had sailed directly for England the first chance he had. He had testified against his old partner in a private audience with King Charles. England was in such an upheaval over the disappearances of so many innocent children. Mothers were so terrified to even send their children outside alone, it had come to the Kings attention and an investigation had begun.

King Charles demanded that strict indentured contracts be signed and he removed any and all head right rewards for transportation of bodies to Virginia. King Charles was determined to only send convicts and political prisoners, his hopes that illegal transportation would be squashed. He did not have the same personal vendetta against the Irish that his Da' had, and although some would disagree, Charles was not as rigid and stubborn as James. Personally, Tristam and many others would disagree with that belief.

"The winds are in our favor today Captain."

"Yes they are, they are not blowing us there fast enough though," Tristam replied.

The seaman misunderstood. "I heard there ain't fancy ho' houses in Jamestown Captain, it ain't matter, it is only land we get to enjoy tonight."

No, I get to see my green eyed angel tonight. Tristam thought smiling as he yanked on the rigging giving it a good yank back and forth as though it would make the ship sail faster.

As they neared Jamestown, Tristam instructed his quartermaster to take over the duties of the ship. Tristam was normally the last off the ship when they arrived in port but it had been a year. He could not waste any time at all to see Jayes, it had been way too long.

They lowered the small boat into the water, as they started to row ashore, Tristam could only imagine how happy Jayes would be to see him. I promised I would come and rescue you, I am here now. He said silently into the wind giving her fair warning.

The new Governor, Captain West, met them on the docks. The two men had never been the greatest of friends, Tristam had no intentions of dilly dallying around making small talk.

"Ehh, I knew you would come back soon. Couldn't leave that little bride to be all alone with those men on the plantation." Gov. West said mockingly.

Tristam took the bait. "What men?" he asked, knowing it was Jayes he was talking about. So she spoke of him? Of course she did, how else was the Governor to know about them if she didn't. She must have been pining about him every day for the last year, longing to have him come and save her. What men though?

"The tenants that I assigned to help work your plantation. I thought there was a chance that the widow Guinever could be wife material. Not sturdy enough, too needy." West said shaking his head. "I gave your girl the handsome ones, didn't need the competition myself."

"Widow?" Tristam asked, his heart sinking. "Guinever? So John Turner is dead?"

"Yup, your plantation and several others were attacked. Heathen savages, killed plenty. Happened in May I believe, been awhile. I am convinced they're probably getting ready for another one, bout that time. Hope you brought firepower with you. It's a law now you know," he said proudly. "I do not allow any wastefulness of gunpowder, need it for those savages."

"Guinever's maid, her servant girl?" Tristam asked, he knew by the face the Governor was giving him.

"Poor girl, dead. Killed her and six others there. They were the lucky ones, got nine across the river."

Tristam felt sick, his heart sank, and he felt as though he was going to vomit. "My plantation?"

"One of the lucky ones again. Your plants seem to grow bigger and faster than all the others. Tell me Captain, you want to sell?" West asked joking.

"Yes, we can talk about that later. I need to go. I need a ride; I need to go see things for myself." Tristam wanted to see Jayes grave, until he saw her grave he could not leave. He had to see her one last time.

Governor West made arrangements to take Tristam to his plantation. Tristam was numb. He was too late, five months too late. If he would have just sailed back. If he wouldn't have taken a stand against the flesh peddlers and kidnappers. He could have saved her, or died with her. He felt half dead now.

"Happy to be home?" one of the men asked as they finally

arrived near the shore of his plantation.

"This will never be home. Tell the Governor I will be back in a days' time to discuss the sale of my property," Tristam said as he gathered up his supplies.

Tristam hated Virginia, he hated himself, most of all he hated the Indians for closing the most beautiful green eyes forever, eyes he longed to see and never would.

"I have got it from here. Thanks for the ride," Tristam said as he made his way to what was going to be his home, his home with Jayes.

Tristam had not gone far when he saw the broken gravestone. Mackey, child of God……

Tristam fell to his knees, he laid down on the freshly tilled grave which had broken stone crumbling around it. He knew this was Jayes.

"I told you I would come to get you. I told you to wait," he cried.

Tristam heard a sound. He knew it wasn't a bird, he knew it was an Indian. Tristam reached into his pocket, he was going to get his revolver.

No, I will die right here with her, they killed her, and they can kill me.

JAYES: HARVEST CELEBRATION

Jayes had prepared a huge meal for the celebration of their harvest. The crop had yielded some of the best tobacco in Virginia. Jayes knew that she owed all of their success to Maybran, had it not been for her, the seed would not have been properly planted and certainly would not have grown as well and quickly as it did.

Maybran, Cuttmwa and several Indians from Maybran's

tribe were at the celebration. Kealan was there, he had started walking, and oh what a handful he was turning out to be. He was blessed with his dad's dark hair and complexion. His eyes he inherited from her, and what a bright green they were, they sparkled. He was such a happy boy! And so mischievous Jayes thought as she grabbed a chicken out of his clenched fist that was squawking and flapping about.

"No, Kealan, food. You do not play with your food," she said laughing. She sat her little Indian boy down. He was dressed in a little leather skirt, tiny moccasins on his feet.

For the celebration, Maybran had made him a little crown of feathers and shells that decorated his tiny head. Jayes thought he was adorable; he was the most adorable baby in the world she thought.

"Cawcawcaw," Jayes heard from near the river, it was Cuttmwa giving a warning.

"Take the children!" Jayes shouted as she scooped up Kealan, handing him to Maybran.

Jayes ran down the path to see what was wrong, Rory and Gasper right behind her. Jayes stopped dead in her tracks.

Lying on the ground next to Liam's broken stone was Tristam. Cuttmwa above him ready to attack.

All at once both men saw her. Everything happened so fast. Jayes screamed, Cuttmwa must have thought she was scared he went directly for the throat. Tristam at the same time drew his own weapon.

"NO!" Jayes screamed. "Stop! Please stop!"

Both men froze, neither took their eyes off each other. "Tristam?" Jayes asked, still not believing it was really him.

Her words broke the trace. "Cuttmwa, no!"

Cuttmwa stood up but did not lower his dagger.

"You're alive, they said you were killed." He looked at

Cuttmwa. "By the heathen savages," he seethed.

"This heathen savage has been more kind and loving to me than you ever have been!" Jayes shouted. How dare him! He sold her! Cuttmwa had saved her, many times!

Tristam was taken aback. He could not believe that she would defend and side with a savage.

About that time, Rory and Maybran appeared. Maybran had Kealan in her arms. She sat him down and he ran towards Jayes. "Mama, mama."

Tristam stood. He looked at the boy.

"It is no wonder you love the savage, you had a baby? You're just a whore." He looked at Kealan with disgust.

"Hey!" Rory shouted, Jayes stopped him.

"Yes, and he is the only good thing that came from being your whore!" Jayes screamed as she scooped up Kealan. "Go ahead and kill him Cuttmwa, we are better off without him," she cried as tears filled her eyes. Jayes ran back to the house.

"So you're the Da'? Now I see why she never mentions you," Rory said, he took Maybran's hand and turned to follow Jayes.

Cuttmwa knew enough English to laugh. "Wish you were dead now? I can help," he said and he also left, leaving Tristam standing there alone.

Tristam looked at the stone. Mackey. If it was not her grave, then who was the Da' of this child? He knew his instincts were right, she had had a baby with someone else.

That Indian? That other man? Of course it was one of them, maybe both of them. They certainly came to her defense quick enough! Did the Governor know she was on friendly- even hospitable terms with the savages?

He would most certainly put a stop to that. This was his plantation!

JAYES – 1627

Tristam made his way up to his house. Jayes was standing near a large table full of all sorts of delicious smelling foods. Some he had never even seen before. And he had thought she was suffering, starving even? He had been so wrong about her! About everything apparently.

"We need to talk. Now!" He said.

"No, I am going to eat. I am not going to let you destroy my dinner party!" Jayes said defiantly.

"Dinner party?" Tristam was staggered. "A dinner party? Do you even realize you're in Virginia? Since when do slaves throw dinner parties?"

Jayes jumped on him, hitting his face, slamming her fists into his shoulders. "I hate you! I am not a slave! I have never been a slave and I will never be a slave! I hate you!"

Tristam took this opportunity to carry her in the house and slam the door behind him. "What is wrong with you? Have you been around them so much you're becoming a savage?" He tossed her into the nearest chair in the middle of the room.

"You are the savage! You're the murderer, you're the man that sells innocent people and steals children," Jayes screamed going after him again. She wanted to scratch his eyes out. She did not even realize until this moment how much she hated him for leaving her.

Leaving her. Jayes stopped. She did not hate him.

"Why?" She looked up at him. "How? How could you have done this to me? Why are you back?" she asked, those damn tears filling her eyes.

"Jayes, I did not want to leave you. I thought about you every day. There was not a moment I did not think about you," he said. Sitting down. Tristam knelt and helped Jayes sit up in the chair next to him. "They said you were dead. I wanted to die with you."

"Who said I was dead?"

"Governor West, he told me about the Indian attack. That John Turner and Guinever's servant were dead. Why are you letting an Indian hold my child?"

"Not now, I am not arguing Indians right now," Jayes said. "That was Elizabeth, Gin hated me. She wouldn't have anything to do with me. She blamed me for ending up in bed with that man."

"And the Indians?" he asked calmly, Jayes decided she would answer.

"They saved my life. Twice! And helped me, they saved that little boy and Maybran even saved Gin," Jayes said, she couldn't even name all the things that Maybran and Cuttmwa had done. "They saved your son. They protected him from being a slave. They have raised him."

Tristam stood up suddenly. "They are not raising my son!"

"And I thought Rory was impossible. Is it all men?" she asked standing and began pacing the room in irritation.

"Who is Rory? Is that your lover?"

Jayes stormed over and slapped him. "I do not nor will I ever have a lover!"

"You belong to me Jayes, you will not have any lover but me. You are mine!" Tristam yelled angrily at the idea of her being with another man.

"I am not yours!" Jayes screamed back at him

Jayes had to think. The papers that they had forged, they had Tristam's signature on them. He was not here. Who was to know? He is here now; did it matter since the papers have already been legally recorded? She wished Gin was here so she could ask what her options were. Could Tristam change everything? Could he take her son if he wanted to? Slaves didn't own themselves, let alone their children.

"Fine, I belong to you. I do not have to like you. You're pig headed, you're mean, and you left me!" Jayes yelled.

"Do you not understand why I left you?" Tristam asked baffled. "Jayes, I spoke with the King. I told him what was happening. I did everything to keep children from being stolen. I gained you your freedom back, and Guinever. I testified that you were illegally transported. I told you to trust me."

"How was I supposed to trust a man that did not even tell me his real names, James?" Jayes did not know what else to say. She did not know if she could trust him either. The last time she trusted him she was standing naked in Jamestown. Had he ever been honest with her?

The door opened slightly and Kealan came running in. "Mama, mama!"

Tristam remembered the other grave, the other child. He tensed.

Jayes saw him tense and assumed it was because of Kealan. She instantly got defensive and scooped up her son protectively.

"He has your eyes," Tristam said.

"He looks like you, you cannot deny that," Jayes replied.

"I never denied it," he said. "Who is the other child? The one in the grave? Who did that child look like?"

"I have no idea, I never met his parents," Jayes said without thinking.

"What do you mean?" he asked as he narrowed his eyes, searching for truth.

"I bought him, it was Liam. He was a servant, he was killed by a herd of buffalo one day when we were working in the field. No one knew his last name, he took mine," Jayes said realizing what Tristam had been thinking.

She walked to the bedroom and placed Kealan on the bed,

then she went back and once again slapped Tristam. "You really thought I was a whore! You thought I had another baby? There was not even enough time for me to have two children you—you blockhead!"

Tristam actually took a moment to do the math in his head. She slapped him again, turned back to the bedroom, grabbed Kealan off the bed and headed out the door.

"I am done talking to you right now. I am having a dinner party," she said and was gone.

She was right, Tristam thought. Why had he not realized it was an impossibility? The math did not add up! His instincts were off when it came to her. This was not turning out to be the night he had imagined. And why wasn't she grateful?

Tristam watched the celebration from a distance. He was the object of curiosity. The old Indian woman who had helped deliver Kealan brought Tristam a plate of food. She smiled her constant toothless grin and it was the first time that Jayes saw him smile.

Jayes watched Tristam as he watched Kealan play, when Kealan grabbed and tried to strangle the chicken again he ran towards him laughing and proud. "That's my boy!" Tristam had yelled.

Kealan had a handful of feathers that Tristam was trying to pry out of his fingers, Jayes went to help.

"He is a strong one," Tristam said like any proud Da' bragging about the strength of their son. Jayes smiled.

"He is not living with them! My son belongs with me not the savages," he said next, infuriating Jayes.

"My son belongs with me, not you! They are not savages either!"

"Oh? Has he been with you? Were you raising your son?" he countered her. Jayes turned to leave taking Kealan with her.

Tristam reached up to stop her but accidently got the fabric on her shirt, ripping the shoulder.

Tristam stood staring. Jayes looked to see what had shocked him, thinking a spider or tick was on her. She went to brush it off and saw the scars. The scars from the whipping that had permanently marked her skin.

"What happened to you?" Tristam asked in a deep breathless growl, he looked deathly white, his face held no expression. "Who did that to you?"

For the first time, Jayes was terrified of Tristam. He looked so cold, so dangerous so full of hate. She was afraid to answer him.

"WHO!" Tristam demanded. Rory stood up protective, ready to come to her defense.

"Do you know who did this?" he demanded, facing Rory.

Rory took a step forward.

"Gin," John blurted out, he too was terrified of Tristam. Jayes knew he was trying to protect her; afraid his anger was aimed at Jayes. "It was Gin who whipped her. Maybran saved her that time too," John said pointing to Maybran.

Tristam looked at Maybran. "Thank you," he said. He looked at Rory. "Where is Gin?" he asked with deadly calm.

"No, what is done is done," Jayes said. "I have forgiven her and you will too." Jayes reached out for Tristam.

"I will never forgive her," he said.

The dinner party did not go well after. No one smiled, no one spoke. Tristam was kind to Maybran, he even held her chair for her when she sat.

The Indians blessed their food in their custom, Rory said a Christian prayer in theirs. After dinner, Jayes disappeared with Kealan.

"Maybran, take him," Jayes pleaded.

"No, you know that he will be angry! I do not need him showing up accusing me of accosting his child," she was adamant.

"Accosting? When did you learn that word?" Jayes asked, her eyes widened. "You have been talking to Rory!"

Maybran refused to answer, instead she had a big smile on her face she could not hide.

"Tell me!" Jayes wanted to know, how long had they been talking, was it serious?

"Fine! Give him to me." Maybran grabbed Kealan out of her arms and turned to leave.

Jayes yelled after her. "We are still going to talk about Rory!"

"No we are not. There is nothing to talk about."

Jayes laughed, Rory and Maybran? No, they would kill each other. She shook her head; he is old she thought. Handsome, yes. Kind, yes. Jayes was deep in her thoughts and did not hear Tristam approach.

"Where is my son?" he asked.

"He is my son, and he is gone."

"No, go get him!" Tristam demanded pointing towards the woods.

"No! He is better off right now with Maybran. No one in Jamestown knows I even had a baby, so if you were thinking about bringing him with us to town-"

"You are not going to town," Tristam interrupted.

Jayes laughed out loud. "Of course I am. A ship will be here in the morning. We are bringing the tobacco to town to be loaded on the awaiting ships. The boys are selling their boats too."

"You are not going," Tristam said with no emotion. "That is final."

"Who do you think you are? You have no right! Go to hell!" She screamed at him, surprised that this brought a smile to his face.

Tristam picked off a long piece of the tall grass and sat down. His arms resting on his knees. He looked up at her, still smiling. Jayes was nervous.

"Should we talk about my rights?" he asked her.

Jayes pursed her lips together and gritted her teeth. Her mind racing. Her mind was not coming up with a good reply.

"I did not quite understand, actually, I thought it was in error when Governor West mentioned my fiancé." He was still smiling; he knew he had her cornered with just his words. "What Jayes? No explanation? No telling me to go to hell?"

Jayes thought for a moment. "No, go to hell," she said and turned to leave. Tristam got up and grabbed her elbow.

"Explain Jayes. Do not get me wrong, I had every intention of making you my wife," he said. "Had." He turned and walked away leaving Jayes staring after him.

He had planned on making her his wife?

SEPTEMBER 19, 1628

Early the next morning the ship arrived from up river as scheduled. It took three hours to load more than a dozen hogsheads full of tobacco leaves, the crew giving Jayes odd looks the entire time. Stepping away from her, out of her path and making sure they did not touch her.

Jayes was laughing inwardly. Tristam had not said anything more about her not going to Jamestown.

Tristam however, could not understand the way the men that arrived on the transportation ship seemed to be terrified of Jayes. He was determined to find out.

After all the tobacco had been loaded, the boys carried on the five log boats that they had made, and planned to sell in Jamestown.

One of the crewmen was still sitting on shore, alone taking a break, Tristam decided this was his chance to find out what the hell was going on with Jayes.

"Is this the last plantation? Looks like the ship is filling up?"

"Most planters don't have that much to load. We have one more. Half of this load probably."

"Bad soil further down the river?" James asked him sounding ignorant, he needed to change the subject to Jayes.

"Not bad soil. Only the witch grows abundance of plants. Her spells or whatnot, who knows how she does it. I don't want to know." He looked at Tristam with a concerned face as he was shaking his head. "You would take care to get away from here before something bad happens to you," he said as Jayes turned her head and stared at them.

The poor man darted off so quickly he actually tripped and fell into the swampy bank of the river. He turned towards Tristam. "See, I told you. She is a witch!"

Tristam followed his gaze and saw Jayes standing there glaring at the man, who looked terrified of her.

"Her? She is the witch?" Tristam asked shocked pointing towards Jayes. He began laughing.

"No, no man," he said terrified, shaking his head adamantly he turned to Jayes. "I do not think that. I am sorry. You are no witch." He was so scared he started off towards the ship running and falling.

Jayes laughed. "He thinks I am a witch! Boo!" She shouted towards the poor man who looked back and fell hard into the James with a big splash.

Tristam stood in disbelief. A witch? A witch and a savage

lover. What has happened in a year to his innocent sweet girl? A witch?

Tristam used all his willpower not to confront Jayes then and there. He was not really certain why he didn't, he told himself it was not because he was afraid of her.

She was as much a witch as he was the sea God Poseidon. That was worth laughing about, he did not however, feel like laughing. He was angry.

Jayes knew something was bothering Tristam and as much as she wanted to tell herself she did not care, she did. She was fuming from the inside. She knew that short, fat, little man that could not even take two steps without losing his balance was to blame.

Jayes also knew, that was the least of her worries right now. They were on their way to Gin's plantation to pick up her hogsheads. Was it too much to ask that Gin would be absent. That she would be off visiting someone and leaving all the work to her servants as usual?

Jayes stared downriver, she could see the river disappearing and curving off to the left. She knew that they were near Gin's. She looked, it was not long until she saw Gin standing on their newly built docks, dressed as though she were going to a dinner party in London. Of course, she would not miss a trip to Jamestown. Jayes closed her eyes in a silent prayer.

"Is that her?" She heard Tristam ask from behind her.

Jayes spun around, pleading him with her eyes. "Not now, please not now."

Tristam stared at her, she could tell from his softening expression the exact moment that he had given in to her pleas.

"I will have my revenge on that bitch! She scarred and hurt you, you belong to me! She had no right!" He said angrily.

Jayes narrowed her eyes and tilted her head ever so slightly looking at him, studying him. She knew she should be offended in some way by his edict. She was just not sure if she liked his ownership, it was however, in a very odd way, caring and possessive. It did make her want to smile. She could not help but feel maybe a little bit loved, even if he had never acknowledged anything of the sort. Still, she knew she should have the appearance of being offended.

"Not today though. Thank you. Play nice, Captain James," Jayes said.

'James' she smiled, she had a brief flash from the time they had spent on the ship. She had not called him James since Gin informed her of his true name. She frowned. That is a conversation they would have someday, if they survived today. Looking at Tristam, she would count her blessings if he was not charged with murder in the next few hours. How on earth was she going to get these two to get along?

Jayes was the first off at Gin's dock. She gave Gin a stern warning look which seemed to irritate Gin.

"I see you did not bring those heathens with you today. That was a wise decision," she said saucily.

Jayes was about to reply when Gin's eyes widened. Jayes turned to see Tristam standing directly behind her. If looks could kill, those murder charges would be being filed shortly.

"What is he doing here? I thought you were dead." Gin was obviously worried. Not for the reasons that Tristam assumed.

"I have no doubt that you wish that. The feelings are mutual my dear," Tristam said with hate in each word.

Gin was speechless. Jayes could not remember her ever not having a comeback before.

"Gin does not wish you dead Tristam, you were gone so long, and with all the ships that crash, and you left right before win—"

"No, I wished he was dead. I am sorry to see it tis not so," Gin said smiling and turned to direct the loading of her hogsheads. Tristam walked into Jayes. She pushed against him turning, holding him back.

"I want that wench's neck."

"Stop it. Not here," Jayes pleaded with him.

"Who does that little bitch think she is? I cannot wait to see her face when they rip those clothes off her and put her up for auction. I am doing her no more favors." Tristam pushed Jayes off him, turned a couple circles and proceeded to pull his hair out.

"You cannot do that!" Jayes whispered loudly horrified.

"The hell I can't," he said. Jayes grabbed him by the collar, forcing him to look her in the eyes.

"Tristam James. If you expose Gin, you expose me! If I am a slave, our son is a slave for life! That is how it works. That is the law! FOR LIFE!"

Tristam looked at her with a horrified expression. Jayes watched as her words registered and he slowly processed the gravity of the situation. She knew the moment he realized, he had to deal with Gin, he could not call her out.

"She gave me my freedom. That is more than you did. Can you not forgive her?" she asked him.

"I will never forgive her! She branded you!"

Jayes felt shivers remembering. "If I can forgive her, you should too. I do not trust her. I never will. She does not know about Kealan. I do not want her to ever know."

"Know what?" Gin inquired, interrupting their private argument. Jayes turned towards Gin. She was playing with a small curl of hair that hung down over her shoulder.

Jayes turned ignoring Gin. She looked out and stared at the James River. The river was so large, it looked a little brown today. The waves hitting the dock in perfect unison. Jayes looked out and watched as the waves began to roll, turning white and coming nearer and nearer.

"Do not tell me then, English do not keep secrets or talk behind friends' backs," Gin said snidely. "You should work on that Jayes if you are going to try to impersonate us." Gin was bumped from behind by one of the workers loading the hogsheads.

"Sorry, Ma'am."

"Watch where you are going. I could have fallen in!" Gin said. She was a good ten feet from the water. Jayes rolled her eyes and began watching the water again. She was praying she could relax; the anxiety was beginning to get to her.

"You win. I will not kill Gin. I do not like her. I will have some type of retaliation. I will just be discreet about it," Tristam said next to her as he stared out at the river.

"You will keep me informed what you are doing?" Jayes asked.

"Is that an order?" he inquired smiling.

"No, just a request. I want revenge too. I do not want to hurt her though. I would not mind seeing her squirm a little bit," Jayes said.

Tristam laughed. She laughed. They looked at each other. "Something we can finally agree on," Tristam said. He looked handsome when he was amused Jayes thought.

Jamestown seemed to be growing more each time Jayes was there. The streets were crowded like never before. There were benches set up outside under the trees for resting, church pews near the well with a continuous service. There were vendors everywhere, selling everything from sugar to glass.

Tristam and Rory helped the boys unload their boats and then helped supervise the unloading of the hogsheads. Jayes and Tristam walked quietly with Gin to the Governors house. He was now living fulltime in Jamestown.

"Captain James!" A young blonde exclaimed as she opened the door. Jayes looked at Gin to see if she knew who this blonde was.

Gin's eyes were big, she smiled slightly and was shaking her head 'no.'

"Millie, when did you get here? I would have brought you on my ship had I known you were heading here," Tristam said with a much sweeter tone than Jayes would have liked. He then kissed her on both cheeks. That was Jayes' cue to step in.

"Millie is it?" she asked sweetly stepping in between them, she turned to Tristam and hit him hard on the chest. "Tristam, you never mentioned 'Millie' before! Shame on you!" Jayes said turning to Millie. "I am Jayes, so lovely to meet you. I am the Captains fiancé."

Millie's eyes widened. "Oh it is true? I did not believe it!" she exclaimed. "You two are in a little bit of boiling water with the Gov."

Jayes and Tristam looked at her simultaneously. Gin turned to leave.

"Where are you going? We are in this together." Jayes grabbed her before she got her foot on the first stair.

The three of them sat in the foyer, silent.

The Governor and Millie entered the room, after what seemed like hours. There were four other gentlemen in the room that Jayes had never seen; none of them, looked pleasing. Two of them wore the white wigs of the English, she thought they were out of place and somewhat stern looking.

"Captain, nice to see you again," Governor West said as he shook Tristam's hand. Everyone went through the proper welcome and niceties.

"Well, let us get down to business," Captain West said pulling out his papers and laying them on the table. He made a deep sigh and stared at Jayes.

"Miss Mackey, I am sorry to have kept you long. I was waiting for a report on the quality of your crop. It seems to be above quality and quantity, and as I do not believe you are a witch, how did you do it?" Every eye focused on Jayes.

Tristam nearly choked laughing. "Excuse me? Did you say 'witch'?"

The Governor cleared his throat. "Well, uhh, yes. There has been some talk. Your uhh, fiancé, umm, we need to discuss that as well, she had extraordinary good luck growing tobacco."

"Luck, she has good luck, I could have told you that John," Tristam said laughing still. He took note of the men standing around the table. He realized the men were safely across the table from Jayes.

He realized, not one of them had properly greeted Jayes, they had all given her a nod. "You are not serious. You people really believe this slip of a girl is a witch? I will take that as a personal insult!"

"Oh stop it, enough of this! This is ridiculous," Jayes injected. "Fine, I will explain. This is not going to make any of you happy. And had I realized the importance, I would have spoken up before now."

All eyes were on her. Jayes wished she had prepared herself for this.

"One day during planting, I had run out of fish. I had sent a couple of my servant boys to fetch more for planting," Jayes explained. "I had fallen asleep in the shade of a tree. When I awoke, I realized my seed pouch was missing."

The men's faces seemed to say they could care less what Jayes had to say, chances were they were not going to believe her. She sighed and used one of her mother's old tactics that never failed to get her Da's attention.

"The Indians think the white planters are idiots. They lied. They laugh at you. All the tribes laugh."

"What do you mean they laugh?" one of the men asked angrily. Jayes had his attention now.

"According to an Indian girl, the one who stole my seeds, the Indians had told the colonists how to plant many years ago?" Jayes asked them, playing as though she was unsure of the whole story.

"Yes, yes." One of the men said, urging her on.

"Well, they did not do that to help! They did that in hopes the crops would fail and you would go home! The seeds need light to grow and root. Burying them in the ground delays their growth," Jayes said smiling. The faces these men were making; she couldn't help but smile. She tried to maintain a straight face, she couldn't.

"What about the fish? The fish fertilize the seeds," one man argued.

"No, the fish stink. That was what the fish was all about," Jayes said trying not to laugh.

Tristam was having a much harder time than Jayes. He began laughing. She gave him a glare that was not going to help.

"Let me get this straight. You all have accused her of being a witch, because her tobacco is better than yours?" Tristam asked, directing the question to Governor West.

"How do we know what she is saying is true?" the Governor asked.

"I have seventeen hogsheads. How many do you have?" Jayes blurted out in answer, realizing it was not going to help either.

"I have been planting tobacco for seven years. I am friends with the Indians. I do not believe a word of it!" one man yelled. "She is either a witch or those savages did something to her crop to make us ask. Next year we will take lead and nothing will grow. Mark my words," he stormed out of the house yelling.

"It sounds as if he is friends with the savages. Perhaps they are not as senseless as you think they are," Jayes said to the Governor.

"How did you plant your seeds, Miss Mackey?" he asked.

"She sprinkled them on top of the soil. It was only a few weeks later we saw a field of tiny green leaves. I am telling you the honest to God truth, Governor West," Jayes said.

"Ok, well, other matters. This matter of the two of you living together. It is ungodly," he said sternly.

"We are not living together!" Jayes raised her voice.

The Governor looked to Tristam. "Are you still of a mind to sell?"

"No, Sir," Tristam smiled.

"I didn't think so, not with a crop like that. Are you planning on living on your ship?" he asked.

"No, Sir," Tristam's smile was ridiculous. Jayes glared at him, wondering. It did not take long.

"You shall marry then, today. I will not have my people living in sin," the Governor said and left the room.

Jayes was in shock. She stood there shaking her head as she watched him leave the room. Unable to say anything she turned to Tristam for help. That smile!

"You knew he was going to say that!" she yelled at him approaching him quickly. He grabbed ahold of her hands before she could hit him. He was laughing! Jayes growled and threw one of Gin's temper tantrums.

Gin started to giggle. Jayes turned on her. "You think you will not have to marry! Think again, Gin! They're not going to want a female living all alone so far from town… I can hear it now. Then the shackles will be on you!"

Gin quit giggling.

"Shackles? You do not know what marriage means to me. Oh darling, I will not need to shackle you," Tristam laughed.

Jayes tried to break away from his grip so she could hit him. He laughed, holding her hands all the way to the church pews set up under the trees. "Seems like a nice spot to say our vows."

Nineteen
When you think it cannot get worse…

Married! She was married! Jayes could not think of a single thought other than the words, wife or married repeating over and over in disbelief in her head.

Tristam had not stopped grinning. Jayes wanted to fall asleep and wake up and realize this is all just a horrible dream.

"It is a dream," she said aloud.

Tristam laughed. "Wait 'til tonight. Tonight you are going to think your dreaming," he said with that grin she wanted so badly to smack off his face. He still held her hands tight. She knew, he was amused by her anger. She hated him, she hated him even more now than ever before.

"I hate you! I will never be your wife in more than name!" she seethed.

"I made an honest lady out of you. What is so wrong with that? We have a child together; we should be married," Tristam tried to reason with her.

"We should not have had a child! You gave me no choice! I did not even know I was having a child! That is how innocent I was!"

"How did you not know?" He laughed.

"I thought I was dying, I thought my belly was bloated with

death like the cows at home. Their bellies get big and they die," she said explaining.

"You are serious? So when did you know?" Tristam asked, astonished at this admission.

"When he cried," Jayes answered, remembering.

Tristam stared at her. "I am sorry."

"I have Kealan. I am not sorry. I love him."

They heard screams coming from the river. Jayes and Tristam both jumped up searching the river for the source.

"There!" John yelled. "Over there!" He pointed to two women, they had fallen out of a log boat. The log boat was rolling in the waves from their ship.

Tristam slipped off his shoes and his shirt quickly and jumped in with Rory following not far behind him.

"Get some ropes John, now!" Jayes screamed frantically looking around for something to toss overboard. The screams were ghastly.

John and Jayes tossed the ropes over the side, it seemed like hours before Rory appeared swimming towards the boat. With one hand he climbed the short distance to the rail. On his shoulder was Frances, slumped over, her arms falling limply by her sides, her lips were purple.

Jayes helped lay her on the deck, her skin was pale and cold. "What do I do?" Jayes asked, panicked. "She is not breathing.

Rory sat over her chest. He turned her head to the side and bounced a couple times. Jayes could hear bones breaking.

"You're killing her!" She screamed and went to push Rory off her.

He stopped Jayes. "She is already dead," he said.

Tristam appeared with Bekka. She looked just as bad as Francis had. She was huge with child!

"Rory, I need a knife!" Tristam yelled. Rory handed him a

knife and told John to go to the stern and stay there.

"What are you going to do?" Jayes asked, looking at poor Bekka. Her skin was so white, her eyes huge white balls, her lips the blue of the sky.

"I am going to save the baby! Go away Jayes!" Tristam yelled at her.

"Save Bekka! Please! "Jayes cried. "I am so sorry!" She pleaded to Bekka's dead body. "I am so sorry I was mean to you!" Jayes knelt down beside her.

Tristam began ripping Bekka's clothing off.

Rory grabbed Jayes. "What are you doing?" she yelled at him, fighting Rory as he tried to pull her away.

Jayes knew it was pointless, she fell to her knees. Tristam took the knife and stabbed it into the bottom of her swollen body. A huge ball popped out of the wound. As Rory continued to cut, the ball became larger, it looked like a heart wrapped up in a clear sack. Rory grabbed the small ball protruding from her body, it was a head!

Rory pulled the baby out, clearing the thin layer of bloody slime that coated the baby.

The baby let out a whale of a cry! Everyone released their breath and celebrated, forgetting that Bekka was laying there, her body cut nearly in half, blood still oozing out from the gaping wound. She never even heard her baby cry.

"It is a girl!" Tristam smiled happily.

"Praise the Lord!" Rory released Jayes and grabbed his shirt, handing it to Tristam to wrap the baby.

"She is strong! I think she will be just fine," Tristam said looking at Jayes, she was crying with joy and sadness.

"I cannot hate you now," Jayes said and began crying even harder.

Both men and even John started laughing. They were so

overjoyed that the baby had survived.

"Can I hold her?" Jayes asked, he put the baby gently in her arms. Jayes looked into the sweetest little face. Her eyes were of the softest blue, so large and round. Her lips the perfect shape and cherry red, a tiny little pert nose.

"She is so beautiful." Jayes fell in love with this little girl staring back at her. "Abbey Kay, she is an angel and blessing sent from God." Jayes knew Abbey would become her world. She was not going to give her up.

She looked at Tristam and Rory. She did not have to tell them; she could see the concern in their faces. They knew they needed to come up with a way to keep her.

"Gin will want to see the bodies." Rory said. "It is a good thing she decided to stay in Jamestown.

"We will bring Gin one of the bodies in the morning. We will tell her they both drowned and we could not retrieve the other," Tristam said.

Jayes smiled. She looked down at the sleeping angel in her arms. "We are almost home."

"We need to keep her a secret; we cannot trust anyone to keep this quiet," Tristam said.

"You do not know my people. They are family. I trust them more than you," Jayes replied without thinking. She felt bad when she saw the hurt look on Tristam's face.

She did not hate him. She was glad he was here. She did not want him to go away again, so why was she so quick to attack him? Why was she pushing him away every chance she got? Since the day she had met Tristam James, she had no control over her emotions. Her emotions had no control over themselves!

"I am sorry, you did not deserve that," Jayes said. Tristam remained quiet. Everyone was silent until they finally arrived home.

Thankfully everyone was asleep except Gasper. Jayes thought if there was anyone to worry about it could perhaps be him.

"They sellin' babies now?" Gasper asked looking at Abbey Kay.

"No, even they would not sink that low," Jayes said. Knowing they have sold babies. Babies born on the ship, become slaves for a lifetime. At least twenty years according to the rules set in Virginia, no slave could survive that life.

"Can we talk about this in the morning?" Jayes asked.

"Yup, you have a visitor though," he said nodding towards the house.

"It's not Gin?" Jayes asked panicked.

Gasper raised an eyebrow curiously. "Nope, we will talk about that cherub in the morning," he said looking at Abbey.

Jayes entered the house alone. Rory and Tristam were carrying the boys to their beds. Jayes saw a candle lit on the table. Cuttmwa was sitting there staring into the flame.

"Cuttmwa? Is everything ok? Is Kealan alright?" she asked, startling him from his trance.

"Yes they are fine. What is that?" he asked staring at the bundle in her arms.

"This is Abbey Kay. Bekka, is dead, Francis also. They drowned. Abbey was Bekka's," Jayes said as she removed the shirt revealing Abbeys face to Cuttmwa for the first time.

"She needs milk. I can take her back with me to my village, you need to stop having white babies, my family may get concerned," he joked as he stood to leave.

"I want her here."

"Jayes, she needs milk. You cannot feed her," he said. Jayes knew he was right. She began to cry.

JAYES – 1627

Tristam walked in and saw the tears in her eyes as she turned. He reached for his revolver.

"Stop it!" Jayes whispered loudly.

"Why are you crying?" he asked her.

"She is crying because I spoke to her reason. This bodl is not a toy she can just keep. She cannot care for it or feed it. You should have told her that." Cuttmwa reprimanded Tristam.

It was obvious that Tristam took offense at being scolded by a savage. To Jayes surprise, he did not argue.

"He is right," Tristam conceded.

"No. I gave my son up. I will not miss this time with Abbey. Let the wet nurse come here," she protested.

Cuttmwa laughed. "She is not going to come here!"

Tristam instantly disapproved with a simple "No. No. That is not going to happen. No."

Now they seem to agree? Jayes rolled her eyes and sat down, squaring off with both men. "I am keeping her."

"She is not a pet!" Cuttmwa said.

"Do not be absurd Jayes, she needs a mother's milk," Tristam said, Cuttmwa agrees.

"Can you two please just go back to wanting to slit each other's throats? Please! I am going to bed, go ahead, and take her, just do it!" Jayes said as she walked to the bedroom, wishing it had a door she could slam.

Abbey cried all night. Jayes knew she was hungry. Jayes found some Eagle bones that Maybran had given the boys to make whistles. She picked out the smoothest narrowest bone, it was only a few inches long.

Jayes quietly laid Abbey Kay down in the middle of the bed and went out to the barn.

She was surprised that Tristam was not there. For a moment she wandered if they had taken her request seriously and slit each other's throats. Neither Cuttmwa nor Tristam were anywhere to be found.

Jayes milked the goat, it was a difficult task as tired as she was. Her hands had no strength in them. The poor goat kept looking at her as if to ask, 'Are you done yet?"

Jayes took the bucket to the house, lit a fire and warmed the milk.

She took the tiny eagle bone and used it to suck up some of the milk she had put in a small bowl. She used it as a dropper to feed the hungry Abbey. She was unsure at first what to do, her huge blue eyes looking at Jayes. She was quick to learn, after an hour she had drank nearly half the bowl and let out a loud burp that made Jayes laugh.

Jayes picked up Abbey Kay and held her on her shoulder, swaying gently back and forth. She began to sing.

The October winds lament
Around the castle of Dromore
Yet peace is in her lofty halls
A pháiste gheal a stóir.
Though autumn vines may droop and die
A bud of spring are you.

Sing hushabye low, lah, loo, lo lan
Sing hushabye low, lah loo

Abbey Kay stared at Jayes, cooing her little baby noises. Her eyes getting heavy as Jayes sang another tune.

There were three ravens sat on a tree,
Down a down, hey down, hey down,
They were as black as black might be,

With a down.
The one of them said to his mate,
Where shall we our breakfast take?
With a down, derry, derry, derry down, down

Down in yonder green field,
Down, a down, hey down, hey down,
There lies a knight slain 'neath his shield,
With a down.
His hounds they lie down at his feet,
So well they do their master keep,
With a down, derry, derry, derry down, down.

God send every gentleman,
Such hawks, such hounds, and such a leman.
With a down, derry, derry, derry down, down

Abbey Kay was finally sound asleep. She looked so peaceful. Jayes was smiling, it had been so long since she had sung aloud. She was happy, she laid down next to her and was quickly dreaming, one hand holding Abbey's tiny little foot.

The next morning, Persis woke Jayes with a tiny scream.

"A baby!"

Abbey awoke startled and began crying.

"Look what you did, you woke her up!"

"Where did you find a baby?" Persis asked, sitting on the bed and lifting Abbey into her arms.

"Her name is Abbey Kay, she is the lady of the lake," Jayes said sarcastically, giving Persis a look of 'do not ask.' "Where is Rory or Tristam? Where is everyone?" Jayes asked, realizing the sun was high in the sky.

"They are all gone. They should be back tonight. They took

Francis' body to Miss Gin and said they are moving the ship upriver." Persis explained.

"Of course, he is taking over all ready. That is not going to work for me. How dare he think he controls my people?"

"He is not your husband?" Persis asked.

"Yes, not that I want him to be," Jayes said as she got out of bed and started dressing.

"Is he not the owner of this plantation?" Persis asked.

"Yes. He did not have anything to do with it. I worked these fields. He cannot just show up and take over."

"Why do you believe that?" Persis asked and walked out of the room with Abbey before Jayes could say anything. Jayes stared daggers at her back. She was so angry with Tristam, even though she knew that Persis was right.

Jayes decided that she had to make Bekka a burial gown. She had given her Abbey Kay, she wanted to make her beautiful in death. She went out in search of anyone that could make a casket, no one was anywhere to be found. He took everyone with him? Everyone?

Cuttmwa came late that afternoon. With him was a young Indian girl. He walked in the house the girl stood in the doorway. Jayes was feeding Abbey Kay.

Cuttmwa watched her smiling. "Eagle bones?" he asked her.

"Yes."

"Cow milk?"

"No, goat."

"You are more Powhatan than I thought..," he laughed. "Resourceful."

"Thank you," Jayes said wondering if that was a compliment.

"Your milk," he said pointing to the girl.

"Is she staying here?" Jayes asked.

"She is," he said and walked out. He returned quickly with Kealan in his arms. The girl following him in and shutting the door.

"Kealan!" Jayes exclaimed happily. Handing Abbey to the girl who sat down and bared her breast. Abbey latched on immediately.

Jayes picked up her son and swung him around in circles. "Thank you, Cuttmwa!"

He smiled. "Where did everyone go?"

"I don't know. That man!" Jayes said upsetting her son. She sat him down and dished him up some meat pie.

"Ah, you know your son. His stomach is key to his happiness." Cuttmwa laughed.

"All men," Jayes corrected him smiling.

"I need to go. Maybran has been sick. Sacwa will bring Kealan home tonight."

"She is not staying?" Jayes asked, knowing the late night feeding would be hers if she left.

"She will return in morning," he said smiling as though reading Jayes mind.

"Thank you," Jayes said as he left.

By nightfall, no one had returned.

By morning, Jayes was in panic.

Afternoon came and went, Jayes decided something must be horribly wrong. Was this Tristam's way of getting her to send Abbey Kay away? Was he angry with her for when she told Cuttwma to slit his throat? Was Rory mad? No there was no way Rory would ever take offense to something so trivial.

When three Indians showed up to escort Sacwa home, Jayes sent Abbey Kay with them along with a note to Maybran and Cuttmwa.

She honestly did not even know if they would be able to

read it.

Jayes and Persis set out for home.

Jayes knew they were getting close; she could hear the yelling of workers in the field. Persis stopped suddenly in front of Jayes. Jayes heard a loud crackling like breaking wood and saw the tree falling. She screamed and ran towards Persis and pushed her out of the way just as the tree fell where they had been standing.

Jayes sat up as a few men came running towards them.

"What are you doing here? You could have been killed!" She heard a man screaming. The words taking her back to the day on the ship that Tristam had found her on the deck.

Jayes looked. Was it Tristam?

A tall skinny man was coming near. He looked familiar, it was not Tristam.

Jayes eyes widened as he approached. Mr. McDougal! What on earth was he doing here? Jayes tried to stand, she looked at Persis and touched her, she wanted to make sure this was not a dream. Or that she was dead and perhaps in purgatory.

Jayes faced him head-on, ready for a confrontation.

"What are you doing here?" she asked accusingly.

"My job lady! You're on Mistress Guinever's property. What are you doing here, 'sides tryin to kill yourself?"

Jayes stared at him. She was certain it was him. She would never forget him. He did not recognize her! That made Jayes happy, but also angered her at the same time.

"Where is Gin?" Jayes snapped, ignoring his remarks.

He did not even answer, he pointed and dismissed her by walking off. The man was such an ass! That had not changed. Why was he here? Jayes was shaking. He was the last man on earth she had ever wanted to see again.

JAYES – 1627

Jayes was still shaking as she sat at Gin's table.

"That tall, skinny, evil looking man, who is he?" Jayes asked her.

"I have no idea. 'Hey you?' Why?" Gin asked as she handed her a glass of water.

"No reason. So you really have not seen Tristam?"

"Not since yesterday. He brought me that girl's body and left." Gin seemed unaffected by the death. "I am shorthanded now and trying to build a fence for protection. That man you asked about is here on loan. The girls were supposed to bring fish to feed them all. I just cannot do all this alone." Gin complained.

"Why don't you marry? Then none of this will be your responsibility," Jayes asked.

"I have not found anyone worth marrying. The marrying men do not want to be here, they're too smart for that. The only men I would even consider are married. I will just have to hope their wives die."

Jayes shook her head. Was Gin really that cold of a person or was she just frustrated?

"Well, I need to go find Tristam," Jayes said standing up.

"Go home Jayes. You're wasting your time. He is going to get his ship and bring it upriver. Unless you're going to go walk the river, you're not going to find him. You are wasting your time." Gin said, picking up the glass of water and throwing it in a bucket. "And mine, I don't have any time these days," she said sighing.

"Thank you, Gin, I am sorry about your girls."

"They were servants; I do not expect them to survive long. They come, they go…"

Jayes had to leave, she wanted to remain friends with Gin. She knew deep inside Gin's heart was not as black as her outward façade. She tried to appear cold, that, Jayes would never understand.

She decided not to make the trip to Jamestown and go home to wait. Tristam did not even attempt a wedding night! Not that she wanted one, but she expected him to!

Where was he? Was he regretting marrying her? Is that why he went to get his ship? To live on it?

"He is not living on his ship!" Jayes said out loud startling Persis.

"I do not think that is his plan ma'am." She giggled.

"What is so funny and why do you think that."

"I think it is funny you always talk back to yourself." Persis giggled. "My sis used to do that too. It makes me happy to hear ya do it," she said, stepping high crushing the tall grass as she walked. "I don't think he would is all, I think he loves you, you can see it in his eyes."

It was Jayes' turn to laugh. "He does not love me, I can tell you that. Thank you, Persis, for not telling Gin about Abbey."

"Oh, I wouldn't say a word. That horrible man, the one in the woods. He murdered his wife they say, he works there, he raped those girls, I wouldn't want that poor baby livin' there."

Jayes stopped. "How do you know he murdered his wife?"

"He bragged about it. He thought it makes him tough an mean or sumthin. Bekka denied the baby was his, but I know it was." Persis looked at the ground. "If I was raped and all, I would probably not admit it either."

Jayes didn't know what to say. "If you ever feel threatened by anyone, come to me. I will take care of it. I will not let that happen."

They walked the rest of the way in silence. Jayes was numb inside. She didn't know what to think or feel. Mrs. McDougal was dead. Was she trying to save Jayes? Had she decided to tell the truth and he killed her?

That was a horrible thought but the real reality was, that horrible evil man was Abbey Kay's Da'.

She loved Abbey Kay with all of her heart. She hated that man with her all her soul.

Twenty

It was two days before Tristam returned. Two days of Abbey and Kealan not returning. Two days of obsessing over the evil McDougal, two days of madness. When Tristam returned, mad had long passed. She was infuriated.

That lasted nearly two minutes.

Jayes had heard the commotion coming from near the river. She could hear the bellowing of orders being given by Tristam. She made her way to the river, set on giving him a piece of her thoughts.

Furniture! They were carrying furniture~ amazingly beautiful carved chests, and Spanish carpets! Jayes stood in awe as she saw a beautiful writing desk, a huge oak table with the most beautiful foot rests. What brought tears to her eyes was the china and pots and pans for cooking!

Two men carried the heavy table past her, Jayes reached out and touched it, and she was in disbelief. She looked up, Tristam was standing in front of her with that annoying grin of his. It was not so much annoying at the moment.

"Where?" was all Jayes could ask.

"My ship, some was on it, some I purchased in England. I knew we would need it. I thought you may appreciate some comforts," he said.

JAYES – 1627

"We?" Jayes asked him in doubt. "You planned on a 'we' when you came here?"

"Yes I did." He smiled.

"I do not believe you," Jayes said suspiciously.

"Well," Tristam removed a bunch of flowers whose roots were wrapped up in cloth bags. "I even brought a bit of Ireland for you, to plant in the garden," he said revealing Irish wildflowers and flora.

Jayes squealed. "Really? You know every woman in Virginia is going to be green with envy!"

"Well then, my painstaking efforts to keep these things alive on the ship were worth it," Tristam said, he sounded like a little kid at the moment. He was so happy that he had made her happy. "I have never heard you squeal before, I like that sound. It is cute."

Jayes looked at him and smiled, for some reason she had such a powerful urge to kiss him. She leaned over, took his cheeks in her hands and kissed him, shocking them both.

"I love you Jayes. I do, I will spend every day showing you I am true."

"I might enjoy that," Jayes said embarrassed. Once again her emotions were jumping all over the place. She felt happy, distrust, and guilt along with several other feelings she could not even define.

Jayes spent the next few days decorating and arranging her home. It was finally becoming livable and more comfortable than she imagined.

"We are going to start working on the house, we need to do it quickly, because the barren and blistery cold months are upon us soon. Need to keep my babies warm," Tristam said, realizing for the first time, they were not there.

The look he gave her sent chills down her spine. "Where are

they?" he growled.

"Tristam," she stalled.

"Where!"

"I will get them; they will be back soon." Jayes was astonished at his reaction.

"I do not want those savages raising my son! His mother should be raising him!" He shouted at her, slamming his fist hard onto the table.

Jayes threw the pillows at him she had been taking into the bedroom and shouted back. "You would not have a son if it was not for those savages! You had made his mother a slave! He would more than likely have died by now had those savages not taken him in!"

"Jayes, I am your husband. I forbid you to talk to the Indians," he said calmly with authority.

Jayes walked up to him, within inches of his face and calmly said. "I did not choose you for a husband. I chose them as my friends. They have earned my friendship and trust." She turned to walk away.

Tristam grabbed her arm swinging her back around. "I am warning you!"

Jayes laughed, perhaps from nervousness, but she laughed. "What are you going to do? Whip me? It's not so bad. I would rather be whipped than be your slave again."

She pulled loose of his grip and ran outside. Jayes kept running past the barn, through the woods and to the river's edge. She wanted to jump in and just swim. Swim as far as she could away from Tristam James. She threw herself on the rocky beach and cried. She cried and cried. It had been so long since she had allowed herself to weep it out.

Jayes could hear Tristam shouting out her name. She stood and ran. She was going to see her children and the savages…

JAYES – 1627

Jayes stood on the small hill looking down on the village. The last time she was in this spot, she thought she was going to die. This time, she knew Tristam wanted to kill her. She was certain he would not find her here. She waited, she knew either Maybran or Cuttmwa would appear shortly, she was right.

"What are you doing here?" Maybran asked upset. "You should not come here. You put your life in danger."

"I know, I was upset. I am married," Jayes admitted, shocking Maybran.

Maybran took her in her arms. "Come," she said and led her to the village. Jayes had not realized how many of them wore no clothes, not just women and children, some of the men too! Jayes was shocked!

Maybran took her into a small mud hut on the edge of the village. Jayes heard her tummy rumble. There were small fires all about the tiny village, all with the wonderful aromas of food.

Jayes walked in and saw her babies. Kealan was toddling now. He let out a little squeal when he saw her and came towards her with surprising speed.

"My baby!" Jayes squealed back, scooping him up in her arms.

She walked towards Abbey Kay. She looked at her in a way she had not before. She could see him in her face. His chin, his nose. Abbey did not have his evil in her eyes. She was so grateful for that.

"Why are you here?" Maybran asked.

"I hate him," Jayes said.

"Your new husband? Why did you give yourself to him then?"

"I did not give myself to him. I did not have a choice!"

"You are no longer free?"

"I am free, but no I am no longer free. I am not a slave." Jayes rethought that and corrected herself. "I am his slave," she mumbled.

"So you are no longer free?" Maybran asked confused.

"I suppose not," Jayes pouted. She sat Kealan back down and picked up Abbey Kay.

"You need to go home." Maybran insisted taking Abbey from her.

"I know. Can I eat?" Jayes asked.

Maybran laughed. "I need to teach you how to cook."

Jayes was nearly home when she smelt it. She could smell burning. Not the kind of burning she was used to. She ran to an open spot in the woods and looked up. She scanned the sky, what parts she could see from beneath the trees.

Smoke, a lot of gray smoke slowly passed through the opening above her. She knew it was coming from the direction of the village. She turned, running back to the village. Tripping and falling several times. Skinning her hands and knees, ripping her dress.

The further she ran the thicker the smoke became. She could see the fire in front of her. She did not slow down. She was not concerned for her safety. She could only think of her children.

Jayes tried to cover her mouth to keep the smoke out. She screamed when she looked down towards her feet. She was shocked to see that she was running on top of several snakes and small animals were running near her feet, in the opposite direction, trying to escape the fire.

Jayes looked up, high above, the tops of the trees were burning. She looked around, there was smoke and a bright orange glow on all sides of her. She did not slow down. She had to get to her son!

Jayes tripped and landed hard on the ground, snakes and all. She sucked in her breath and tried to stand. Her foot was stuck. She couldn't release it!

She heard a loud popping, followed by a crackling and a whoosh. Jayes looked as a burning pine fell within feet of her, igniting the ground around her into flames.

The smoke was making it hard to breath, Jayes struggled trying to release her foot. Coughing. Choking. Exhausted.

Against her will she lost all energy, her eyes closed.

She heard a voice. "What are you doing?"

"You are going to get killed!" She knows he is angry. Is she dreaming, is this real?

Jayes tried so hard to open her eyes, she couldn't. Was that Tristam? Was she dreaming again?

"Kealan. Abbey Kay," she whispered with a raw throat.

"Get up!" He shouted angrily.

She opened her eyes and saw Tristam. She was not dreaming. How did he get here? How did he find her?

"I need to get my children," she moaned trying to find her strength. Tristam helped her to stand.

"It is not safe. They attacked the village. They have set fire to nearly everything. We need to get to the river!" Tristam shouted at her, trying to pull her in the wrong direction.

She broke free. "No! I would rather die than not at least try to save my children!" Jayes was crying, she did not have time to stand here and argue with this heartless man.

"You are impossible woman!" He jerked her in the direction of the village.

"Thank the Lord I am not a heartless man!"

They had not gotten far when Tristam shoved her forcibly to

the ground landing on top of her.

"Not now!" She shouted.

"Shut up!" I am not going to let you get us both killed. There are Indians coming towards us!" He said in a low voice.

Jayes tried to get up. "They know me!"

"Stay still!" He said as he put his hand over her mouth. Jayes bit it. He went to slap her but stopped.

"CAWCAWCAWCAW," Jayes yelled loudly, followed by her clicking sound.

"What are you doing?" He looked at her alarmed.

"They are my friends!" She shouted.

Suddenly Cuttmwa and four other Indians appeared. Cuttmwa looked concerned.

"Get off me now!" Jayes shouted to Tristam. He rolled off her, his hand on his pistol.

"Reach for it and you will be dead before you have the chance to raise it. Cuttmwa is quick," Jayes warned him. "I believe he likes you less than I. Actually, try it, let's see what happens."

Cuttmwa laughed aloud. Tristam gave him a malevolent look.

"Where are my children?" Jayes interrupted their exchange.

"They are safe, they have been taken to another village. You cannot go there." Cuttmwa said.

"What happened?" she asked him, knowing there was no point to argue with him. She would have to wait to see her children.

"The white skins burnt our village, they take our women and children prisoner," he said angrily looking at Tristam.

"Not?" Jayes interrupted panicked.

"No, Maybran is safe," Cuttmwa assured her again.

"Where are you going?" Tristam asked.

JAYES – 1627

Cuttmwa did not say anything for a few minutes. "How do you say? An eye for an eye?" he said and he left with the other Indians following him. Jayes heard many drums and hollering, she knew this was war. They were on their way to Jamestown.

"I need to warn the Governor," Tristam said.

"You do not need to warn him! He knew this would follow!" she said angrily. "We need to go home and make sure the boys and everyone stays inside."

"No! We are going to Jamestown!" He grabbed her arm.

Jayes slapped him hard across the face and yanked her arm away from him.

"If you want to go and get yourself killed then go! But I am not a fool that is going to follow you." She turned in the direction of the plantation.

"Do not disobey me! I am your husband!"

"Not by choice! I am responsible for those people! I do NOT care about Jamestown! I am going home!"

Home, she said it. She was never going to call this place home. Jayes shook her head angrily at Tristam and started home.

He followed her, not saying another word.

The smoke was thick, it seemed as though fire was burning all around them. They could hear gunshots in the distance, it sounded as though they were coming from the direction of Gin's place.

Tristam must have read her mind. "I hope she dies slowly."

Jayes ignored him. She did not wish death on Gin, only change.

As soon as Jayes walked through the door she realized that everyone had gathered in the house. They had tried to cover up the windows and cracks to keep the smoke out.

"What is happening out there? Corzara asked.

"There is a war happening," Tristam replied.

They all sat in silence, listening, praying.

When the sun rose, Jayes quietly left the house and walked towards the fields. The trees were gone as far as the eye could see. Smoke still rising from the burnt ground. The fields were burnt, gone.

"We were lucky that it rained," Tristam said startling Jayes, she had not known he had followed her.

"Yes we were," she said looking around. Her thoughts were on her children. She had to know they were safe. She knew they were. She honestly believed that if something had happened to them, she would feel it.

As those thoughts went through her head she heard a sound and turned to look. Maybran and three other Indians were walking towards them. With Abbey Kay and Kealan with them.

Jayes screamed with joy and took off towards them.

Governor West and Gin made an unexpected appearance that afternoon. They were checking on the wellbeing of the plantations.

The Governor had told Tristam that very few had actually died in the attack. However, thousands of acres had been burnt.

Jayes was beside herself with worry that Kealan and Abbey Kay would be discovered. She quickly sent them with Persis to hide in the barn.

"Miss Mackey, we have heard you're doing some substantial building." Governor West said as Jayes came around the corner disheveled.

Jayes tried to secure a large piece of hair that had come undone and had fallen in her face.

"Yes, we have been busy, fighting the rain storms, we have

still accomplished much," she said.

Governor West turned towards Gin. "This one is motivated. You should follow her example."

Gin looked irritated. She gave Jayes an unwarranted glare. Jayes thought quickly and tried to divert her anger.

"I have a special tea, made of sassafras, and a delicious bread that Persis invented. Shall we go into the house?" she asked.

They followed her into the house. Jayes spotted McDougal standing with a few other men that had come with the Governor and Gin. She felt shivers up her spine and quickened her pace.

Tristam, Rory and Gasper answered all the Governors questions.

"You have started a turpentine farm?" Jayes heard the Governor ask.

"Yes, and we have created a tar like substance from the pines that works as a sealer. I believe it will insulate the dwellings from the elements completely. Much better than before." Rory explained.

"You must show me," the Governor said. All three men stood. Jayes began cleaning up the table as they all left, Gin following the Governor like a puppy.

Jayes knew this was her chance. She needed to get Persis out of sight, and keep the children hidden safely.

She made her way to the barn, hoping that Rory had taken the visiting party to the turpentine cans in the woods.

She heard moaning and stifled screams. Jayes entered the barn and saw Persis laying half naked face down under McDougal. His breeches were down at his ankle. His hand was over her face, his other hand on her neck holding her down.

Jayes looked stunned at what was happening in front of her. Persis' skirt was hiked up and McDougal was brutally raping her.

Jayes saw Maybran enter from the back of the barn, Jayes reached for an ax they used to cut tobacco.

She heard Maybran's cry of rage at the same time. Jayes saw red, she screamed and ran towards McDougal.

"You are the devil!" she heard herself screaming as she swung the ax wildly in the air.

Everything went red. There were screams. She saw blood, more screaming.

It was over in an instant. Jayes stood and looked at the mutilated body of the evilest man she had ever known. His blood slowly filling the floor of the barn. Jayes looked down horrified as she saw the pool of blood slowly make its way towards her, soaking her slippers. Jayes looked at her dress, she was covered in blood.

"Oh dear Lord!" Persis cried from the corner of the room, blood covering her from head to toe, her ripped dress as she dropped the dagger she held in her hand.

"Persis, are you hurt?"

Persis did not answer, she was staring at the bloody dagger that she had dropped.

Jayes heard Abbey Kay cry. She looked at the baby sitting next to Kealan. They were safe. Had they witnessed the horrific scene? Abbey Kay kept crying.

"They are going to hear her!" Jayes cried.

"I am taking them. They are coming." Maybran said as she scooped up both children and disappeared out the back door of the barn.

Jayes turned and saw the Governor, Gin, Rory and Tristam enter the doorway of the barn. She dropped the ax that she still held in her hand.

They all stopped as soon as they realized what had

happened.

Gin screamed.

Tristam ran towards her.

Governor West shouted to his men. "Arrest them!"

Jayes turned to Tristam in horror. "I am sorry!"

"Did you kill that man?"

"I don't know….."

Virginia, 2015

The room was plunged into darkness as the last ray of sun slipped below the horizon. Kayla blinked in surprise as the awareness of how much time had gone by became obvious. She desperately wanted to know what happened next to her ancestor Jayes.

She picked herself up off of the blow up mattress and groped her way across the living room to find the light switch on the wall. After several anxious minutes, she located the switch and triumphantly flipped it up. "What?" she said out loud to herself as she remained in darkness. "No! No! No!" she cried out as she realized the power had been shut off. She was supposed to be gone from here by the end of the day and now she had no electricity.

"Now what?" she asked herself, feeling slightly foolish for talking out loud to herself. Inspiration struck as she realized she had not yet packed the camping lantern. She could continue reading by its light if only she could find it in the dark.

After barking her shins on several boxes and pieces of furniture she eventually found the lantern at the base of the ladder leading up to the attic. She had been so intrigued by the possibilities of history contained in the old documents she had forgotten where she had left the lamp. Only by accident had she even found it since the hallway was even darker than the living room. Her foot had struck the metal side and tipped the lantern over.

Kayla knelt down and managed to light the lamp after a few fumbled attempts. Feeling better about her prospects, she walked confidently to the living room and settled back down on the mattress with the lamp on the wooden floor next to her. Just as she picked up the fragile parchment to continue with the story the lamplight flickered once, twice, and then went out entirely.

"Are you kidding me?" she cried out in disbelief and had to chuckle at how ridiculous the situation had become. She picked up the lantern and shook it to discover it had run out of propane. "Great! Just great!" Kayla dropped the lamp back to the floor in disgust.

Not wanting to damage the old documents, Kayla carefully set them aside from the mattress. She punched the pillow she had been using as a backrest and decided she should try to get some sleep. Her mind kept returning to Jayes and the amazing adventures she had read about. She wondered if all of it were true or if some of it were embellishments of the truth. Either way, the story had been more amazing than she could have dreamt possible.

As Kayla lay on her back, staring up into the darkness, the house settled in creaks and groans around her. She should have been on the road back to Idaho with the moving truck. Instead she would be leaving in the morning and the historic home would be put on the market. Before, the house had simply been the dwelling of an old woman she hardly even knew; now it was more, much more. She had roots here, it was more than roots. She had family. She shared their history.

SNEAK PEEK
BOOK TWO

JAYES
JAMESTOWN 1630

AVAILABLE SOON

One

Somehow Kayla managed to fall asleep even with her mind still reeling from reading through the first of five journals left behind in the attic. She could not be certain, but she seemed to recall Jayes had been in her dreams, as if she were calling out to her. Kayla stretched out on the air mattress and yawned wide.

There was still a lot of work to do if she were going to be getting on the road back to Idaho with the moving truck. Her muscles were stiff and sore from all of the packing she had done over the past few days. She turned her head and groaned as she realized just how much work was left to be done. Boxes and small furniture littered the room and hallway leading to the front door.

Cleaning out her great-grandmother's house was turning out to be a monumental task. Kayla's mother had wanted to call an estate sale business to come out and auction everything off sight unseen until Kayla had offered to take time off of work to come and handle it herself. Up until she had found the stacks of letters in the attic, she had been thinking her mother's idea had not been half-baked after all.

Kayla got off of the mattress and began letting the air out so she could get it packed. As she rolled the plastic to get the air moving faster her eyes were drawn to where she had placed the fragile bundles of paper on the hardwood floor. Darkness had prevented her from continuing to read the night before and now it was daylight. Maybe she should take a little time while she ate breakfast to continue the journey back in time.

"No!" she said out loud. "I have got to get back to Idaho and the truck isn't going to drive itself!" She instantly recalled how much time she had lost the day before because she wanted to see what the ancient journal contained. Kayla would not make the same mistake twice.

Even as Kayla picked up several small boxes to take outside, her eyes kept fixating on the tattered old papers. Resolutely turning her head away from them, she marched to the front door and struggled to open it. Finally, she was outside on the front walkway heading toward the moving truck.

She rolled open the back door and set the boxes down on the hip-high lip. With her hands free, she unlocked the loading ramp and rolled it out for easier access. After many trips back and forth, keeping her attention focused solely on getting the house emptied, she was startled to find nothing left to be moved with the exception of the fascinating bundles of cracking paper. Wishing she had a box to put them in for protection, she gathered them up in her arm and stood back up.

One last time she looked around the dusty, empty room and wondered what kind of life the people had lived throughout the centuries inside these walls. The house was quiet, unlike how it had been the night before. Nothing remained for her here and it was time for her to go.

Outside, she shut the front door with a feeling of finality. She pocketed the old skeleton key and realized she would have to drop it off with the real estate agent before she left town. She took a final look around the large front porch before stepping down into the yard where she noticed the 'For Sale' sign for the first time. Kayla wondered if it had been there all along, or if the agent had come by only a few minutes before as she locked up the house. Either way, it seemed sort of sad and final to know the house would no longer be a part of their family's history.

Kayla opened the passenger door of the moving truck and carefully placed the fragile papers on the bench seat. She slammed the door and walked around the back where she pushed the ramp back under the cargo box and then grabbed the strap to pull down the back door. With a click of the lock, Kayla felt quite accomplished since the monumental task of packing was finally complete.

With a spring in her step, Kayla got behind the wheel, placed the key in the ignition, and started the engine. She was ready to begin her journey home until she looked down and saw the gas tank was nearly empty. With a groan of disgust she pulled out her cell phone and looked up the nearest gas station.

The GPS would guide her through the unfamiliar streets of Jamestown. She pushed the start button on the directions and began moving. Traffic was light and she quickly found the gas station. After filling up the tank, Kayla got back into the truck and remembered she still had to leave the house key with the real estate lady. With a growl at yet another delay, Kayla spent a few minutes locating and programming her phone to give her driving directions.

After going around the block several times, Kayla finally had to park several streets away from the agent's office. She got out of the moving truck and started walking. It was hard to really mind the walk since the buildings were so old and fascinating anyway. Soon she was spending more time looking than walking.

Kayla's task was interrupted when she walked in front of the Jamestown History Museum. She decided to go in and check it out since she never planned on coming back. *What can it hurt?* she thought as she opened the door and walked in. While the museum was captivating she really needed to get going. She began walking back to the entrance when her attention was caught by a small display of a brick. She stopped and read the little placard which said, "Footprint of a slave captured in time," and Kayla's breath caught in her throat. *Could this be the brick Jayes had stepped in which she had written about in her journal?*

In an instant Kayla realized something amazing: Jamestown was her family history. There was no way she could sell the house and never return. With her mind made up, Kayla left the museum and walked back to the moving truck. She retraced the roads back to the old house and parallel parked in front of it once again. She turned off the engine, opened the door, and hopped out. She marched up to the 'For Sale' sign and ripped it out of the ground.

"This house is not for sale!" Kayla announced to no one in particular as she threw the sign down in the lawn.

She got back into the truck, rolled down the window, and picked up Jayes' account of her life here in Jamestown. Before she knew it, Kayla's mind and imagination was once again moved back in time as she continued to read…

Jayes was being held within the walls of the Jamestown Fort. Her small room surrounded by guards. She looked out the small window, the fort was bustling with people selling wares, buying livestock, rolling hogsheads in and out. She took in a deep breath. It was not so long ago she had found herself in this same predicament in Ireland. Accused of stealing milk, of course she hadn't. That moment, such a trivial little thing, had sent her thousands of miles away from her home. Milk. What was she going to do now that she was accused of murder? Murder!

Jayes took another deep breath, she tried to remember. It was gone from her memory as if it had never happened. Had she really killed Mr. McDougal? There was no doubt in her mind he deserved it, he was a horrible man, and surely the world was a better place without him in it. Jayes shook her head. She just could not imagine taking a person's life no matter how awful a person they were.

She looked down at the blood soaked dress she wore. His blood, she thought as a shiver passed through her body. Was this the evidence of her guilt? Had she really taken a man's life, and if so what was going to happen to her?

Jayes panicked. Kealan and Abbey Kay, they needed her. What would happen to them if she was gone?

She heard the door open and she ran towards the larger room. The doorway to her small room inside the house was blocked with hogsheads. A guard entered, he had a chain in his hand. Jayes followed the link chain with her eyes as Persis came into view!

"Persis!" she cried.

"Quiet!" the guard shouted at her.

Persis looked up, her hair was a mess, her dress soaked in blood, her eyes red and swollen. She looked at Jayes in such a pitiful way. The guard led her towards Jayes and began rolling the hogs heads out of way, when he had cleared a small opening, he removed the chains and shoved Persis in. She landed hard and slid a half-length of the room. She began to cry.

"Persis are you hurt?" Jayes asked as she bent down on her knees next to her.

"No, bruised but I will be fine."

"What happened? I cannot remember. Do you remember?"

Persis looked up at Jayes. Tears filled her eyes. "I killed him."

Jayes stood up. She was relieved yet at the same time, now knowing what happened, the reality hit her hard. She knew she was responsible for Persis. She should have warned her about McDougal. She should have protected her. It was too much.

"Did you tell them that you killed him?"

"Yes ma'am. I did tell them, they didn't believe me. That Gov'ner West, he said he knows you did it."

Jayes took in another deep breath, she could feel a small pain in her heart and sat down on the wooden dirty floor. "I did not kill him though. Tell me the truth Persis, did I have anything to do with his death?"

"You hit him ma'am, you cut his legs I think. He rolled off me and stood up. I saw him strike you."

"I cannot remember."

To keep updated on the next book of Jayes, visit www.thestuartnovels.com for special sneak peeks.

You can also follow Kelli Klampe on Facebook at:
https://www.facebook.com/stuart.novels

About The Author

KELLI REA KLAMPE has written several historical novels in the Stuart Novel Series. She enjoys traveling to research her books. For Jayes, Kelli spent time in Virginia and Georgia. She visited Jamestown as well as Turner Farms, a Tobacco Plantation, in Georgia. This book was especially important because it was almost never written. April 29, 2015, Kelli underwent brain surgery to clip a post anterior communicating artery aneurysm (ACoA). Her recovery and determination to complete the novel which she had regretted not writing before she believed there was a chance she would never have the chance to do so.

Kelli is the mother to three wonderful children who reside in Oregon and are her inspiration in life. She is also Mommy to a four legged Pomeranian named Bear Bear: her writing and travel companion.

Made in the USA
Columbia, SC
08 February 2021